MW00332446

Seven

Jane Blythe

Copyright © 2019 Jane Blythe

All rights reserved.

No part of this publication may be reproduced, transmitted, downloaded, distributed, reverse engineered or stored in or introduced into any information storage and retrieval system, in any form or by any means, including photocopying and recording, whether electronic or mechanical, now known or hereinafter invented without permission in writing from the publisher.

All characters and events in this publication, other than those clearly in the public domain, are fictitious and any resemblance to real persons, living or dead, is purely coincidental.

Bear Spots Publications
Melbourne Australia

bearspotspublications@gmail.com

Paperback
ISBN: 0-6484033-1-9
ISBN-13: 13: 978-0-6484033-1-9

Cover designed by QDesigns

Also by Jane Blythe

Detective Parker Bell Series

A SECRET TO THE GRAVE
WINTER WONDERLAND
DEAD OR ALIVE
LITTLE GIRL LOST
FORGOTTEN

Count to Ten Series

ONE
TWO
THREE
FOUR
FIVE
SIX
SEVEN

Christmas Romantic Suspense Series

CHRISTMAS HOSTAGE
CHRISTMAS CAPTIVE

I'd like to thank everyone who played a part in bringing this story to life. Particularly my mom who is always there to share her thoughts and opinions with me. My friend Peta Fisher who shared some information about Type 1 Diabetes with me, including her personal experiences with it. My awesome cover designer, Amy, who whips up covers for me so quickly and who patiently makes every change I ask for, and there are usually lots of them! And my lovely editor Mitzi Carroll, and proofreader Marisa Nichols, for all their encouragement and for all the hard work they put into polishing my work.

JANUARY 23RD

10:30 P.M.

He couldn't take his eyes off her.

Blonde hair.

Blue eyes.

She was perfect.

Just what he'd been looking for.

Now all he had to do was find the courage to go up to her. He shouldn't be so nervous about that. He'd done it so many times before, and yet, he still got that swirling feeling of nerves in the pit of his stomach every time he approached a girl.

This one looked scared.

She kept blowing on her hands and rubbing them vigorously, and he could see from where he stood that she was shaking. She was wearing a coat that didn't look warm enough for the freezing winter night. Her hands were in a pair of fingerless gloves, and he wouldn't be surprised if she ended up with frostbite if she stayed outdoors much longer.

Such a pretty girl shouldn't be outside on her own at this time of night.

Taking a deep breath, he sidled up to her. She noticed him immediately, and he could see her weighing her options. Was he a threat? Should she run? Where would she go? Was there anyone around to help her?

In the end, she decided to do nothing.

"Hey," he said shyly when he reached her.

"Hey," she said back. Her eyes continued to dart nervously about, still unsure whether he was a threat or not.

1

"It's cold out." He stated the obvious then mentally berated himself for it. Why couldn't he be suave and sophisticated and cool? Girls turned him into such a bumbling idiot.

"It is," she agreed, a small smile creeping at the corners of her mouth. His bumbling idiocy was putting her at ease.

Eyes fixed on his feet, he said shyly, "I know a warm place where we can go."

"You do?" she asked, the last of her wariness evaporated. The lure of a warm place to spend the night was too tempting to any homeless kid to turn down.

"Yep." He chanced a look up and found that she was now beaming at him with delighted anticipation. "This way."

The girl hoisted her backpack onto her shoulders and eagerly followed him as he led her away from the well-lit diner. "Where are we going?"

"You'll see," he replied. "It's a really great place. Some of us runaways often hang out there. How long have you been on the streets?"

"Not long, only a few days."

He had suspected as much. She still had that stunned and overwhelmed look about her, like she couldn't really believe this was her life now. She was also too clean. That wouldn't last long. Soon she would find that the thought of a decent shower was akin to thoughts of heaven. He didn't think she could survive the winter night dressed as she was. "Where have you spent the last few nights?"

"The first night was on the bus. Then the last two nights I've spent them in the diner." She nodded her head behind them to the place they'd just left. "But I ran out of money and can't keep buying coffee, so they kicked me out."

Anger speared him.

Kicked her out?

How could they do that?

It was obvious she had nowhere else to go. And she didn't

look a day over sixteen. What kind of person kicked a kid out into the cold instead of trying to help them?

"Why did you offer to help me?" she asked. There was a lot of emotion in her voice, and the question felt deeper than it seemed. What had caused her to run away from her home? Had someone hurt her? She was so beautiful, but beauty sometimes hid dark and ugly scars.

"We have to look out for each other," he told her, pausing so he could turn and meet her eye. "You ran away from home, right?"

"Yes," she acknowledged. Pain flashed through her big blue eyes.

"Then you're one of us now."

"How long have you been living on the streets?" she asked, comfortable and at ease with him now.

"Almost a month."

"A month?" the girl echoed incredulously. "How have you survived a month living on the streets?"

It wasn't something he liked talking about. He had never liked talking about himself, and even less now.

"I'm sorry," she said when he didn't answer. "I didn't mean to pry. I get it. I *really* do. It's like being trapped between a rock and a hard place. You don't want to go back home, but there's nowhere else to go. Still, anywhere is better than home."

She was walking beside him now, and he saw her shudder as she said "home." Whatever she had left behind was obviously pretty horrendous if spending the winter with no warm place to sleep at night was preferable.

"I do what I have to, to survive," he replied. "Like you said, anywhere is better than where we came from."

"Have you stolen?" Her eyes were wide as she awaited his answer.

"I have." He wasn't proud of it, but he needed to eat.

"Have you hurt anyone while doing it?"

3

He felt his cheeks heat. "Not physically, although I'm sure I've traumatized a few."

"Have you ever … umm … you know … done *it* … sex … for money?" she rambled.

His cheeks flamed hotter. "Yes."

The girl finally fell silent. No doubt contemplating whether she would end up in the same place—having to sell her body for money to buy food. "There has to be something better out there," she said. Hope still filled her voice; that wouldn't last long. "One day our lives will get to that place. It can't be this bad forever."

"No?" he arched a brow. "Have you been to school since you ran away from home? Do you plan to go back? If you can't finish high school, you can't go to college. And if you can't go to college, you can't get a job—at least, not a good one. No job equals no money; no money equals no food or place to live. No food or place to live leaves you with no options but to do whatever you have to to survive. Face it, this is your life now." He didn't want to be harsh, but it was what it was, and the sooner she accepted that the easier her transition would be.

"I guess you're right," the teenager said softly, all vestiges of hope wiped from voice.

"Hey." He reached for her hand, took it and squeezed it. "I'm sorry, maybe there is a way. I don't mean to be harsh; it's just, a month is a really long time."

"I understand." She offered him a halfhearted smile—a smile that still held innocence and sweetness, and naïveté. It was a shame she would soon lose all of that.

"We're here," he announced.

She looked around, confused. "Where?"

He pointed to the house they were standing in front of. "Here."

"It's a house." She still sounded baffled.

"An *abandoned* house," he corrected.

"Ohhh," she breathed. Her smile widened, making her even

more beautiful, as she finally caught on. "A warm place to spend the night."

"There's something even better inside." He grinned.

"I can't wait." She giggled—the sound like music to his ears. It had been a long time since he had been this close to such a pretty girl.

Still clasping her hand, he tugged her after him into the house, stopping in front of a large open fireplace, beside which were a pile of sticks and broken tree branches.

"A fire," she breathed. "We can have a fire and be warm."

"We sure can." He released her and tossed a couple of the sticks into the fireplace then pulled out a lighter. A moment later, they had a modest fire roaring and heat pouring out.

The girl came and knelt before it, leaning in as close as she could and holding up her no doubt freezing hands to the fire's heat.

"You don't have a sleeping bag," he noted, already unrolling his and laying it out on the floor in front of the fireplace.

"No, I don't," she agreed, turning to look at him.

"Want to share?"

She was attracted to him; he could tell. He might be a little awkward around girls, but he knew he was good-looking. His looks combined with his awkwardness put most girls at ease, and just as he suspected, she crawled closer.

"Is there space for both of us in there?"

"Oh, there'll be enough space. We'll make sure of it." He waggled his eyebrows.

She giggled and climbed inside. He got in next to her and zipped it up. Then he gently rolled them over, so she was closer to the flames.

"Thank you ... for everything." She gave him a quick peck on the cheek.

Their eyes met. They were lying on their sides, facing each other, close enough he could feel her breath on his face. Her lips parted in a wordless invitation.

He accepted.

She tasted like coffee and raspberry muffins.

"You don't even know my name," she whispered against his lips when he ended the kiss.

"No, I don't," he agreed.

She huffed a small chuckle. "It's Colette."

"Nice to meet you, Colette." He kissed her again.

"You didn't tell me your name." She giggled.

"No, I didn't," he agreed once more then kissed her again, his tongue prodding at her lips until she opened her mouth to him. He kissed her until they were both breathless. "You're so pretty." He ran a hand through her long golden hair.

"Thank you." She blushed.

When his lips met hers this time, her mouth opened to his immediately, and his tongue hungrily pushed inside. As they kissed, his hand moved to the waistband of her jeans, trying to find its way inside

"Wait, stop!" She pushed at him. "What are you doing?"

"Making out." He shrugged. Why was she getting all shy now? A moment ago, she'd had her tongue in his mouth. He was just taking the next logical step. "Relax. You'll like it. I promise." He had no doubts he could satisfy her sexually. He was good; he'd had a lot of practice, and he knew exactly what women liked. He palmed her breast then pinched her nipple. Hard.

Colette squawked in pained surprise but didn't say anything as his hand managed to undo the button on her jeans and find its way inside, heading instinctively to the warm heat between her legs.

"Ugh," he grunted as a burning hot shaft of pain got him right in the bicep.

Something warm and sticky coated his arm.

Blood.

She'd stabbed him.

"You little witch!" he roared as he withdrew his hand.

Already, she was trying to scramble out of the sleeping bag. He obliged by undoing the zip.

The girl scrambled to her feet, but he moved quicker, lunging at her and backhanding her across the face, sending her sprawling to the floor.

"Don't do that again!" he growled as he looked down at his bloody arm. "Next time, I'll mess up that pretty little face of yours so bad even your own mother wouldn't recognize you."

Big blue eyes stared fearfully up at him as one of her hands pressed to her bleeding lip.

"What?" he sneered. "Didn't your parents ever teach you never to talk to strangers?"

It never ceased to amaze him that these girls willingly came with him then got surprised when things didn't work out the way they expected. Did she really think he was just going to bring her here to help her? If she was that stupid, she was never going to survive on the streets. If he hadn't gotten to her first, someone else would have.

"Can you tie her up while I look at my arm?" he called to his partner.

"I can't believe she stabbed you," a voice snickered as another man entered the room.

Colette's eyes darted from him to the newcomer and back again, a mixture of hurt and humiliated understanding filled them. "You planned this. The whole thing was a setup. You played me."

"Duh."

Apparently, she was smart enough not to bother trying to run. She knew there was no way she was getting out of here. She didn't stand a chance against the two men—both more than twice her size. Just because she was resigned to her fate didn't mean she wasn't afraid. Fear, terror, and apprehension rolled off her in waves. Her eyes were watery, and she was shaking even more now than she had been when he'd first seen her out in the cold earlier tonight.

She was like a scared rabbit in the shadow of two wolves. She was his prey and the knowledge that he could play with her as he pleased turned him on.

"What are you going to do to me?" she asked. Her voice trembled, and a lone tear rolled down her cheek.

"You don't want to know," he answered, the first truthful thing he'd said all night.

JANUARY 24ᵀᴴ

6:53 A.M.

Caden Gervase was tired.

It was only seven in the morning, and he felt like he'd already worked an entire day.

He hadn't told anyone yet. Not that there was really anyone to tell. He wasn't married—never had been—and he had no children. He had grown up an only child raised by a single parent. His mother had died in childbirth, and his father had passed away over fifteen years ago, so he didn't have any family.

He was pretty much all alone in the world.

Except for *her*.

And their relationship was complicated.

Most of the time, it didn't bother him. He was used to being alone and enjoyed his own company. But at times like this, it would be nice to have someone else around.

Some days he was tempted to tell her, to ask for her support, to let her know what was going on. He knew if she knew, she would be there for him, no questions asked. She would do whatever she could to help.

But that wouldn't be fair. She had enough going on in her own life without having to worry about what was going on in his.

So, he kept his mouth shut.

Not that he could do that indefinitely. Soon he wouldn't be able to keep it a secret. The symptoms of his brain tumor were already getting worse. Some days it was all he could do to keep upright while pain sliced relentlessly back and forth through his skull from the headaches. And the memory problems—he used to

9

be able to recall the name of every student—as well as their parents—in the middle school where he worked as a principal. Now he frequently attempted to search the recesses of his mind for a name but still came up empty. He had given up riding his bike to work due to balance problems and had started taking the bus instead. He had become grateful that his office had its own private bathroom that he could enter without having to leave his room when he was overcome with nausea. And the fatigue had left him so drained, he often left shortly after the end of the school day instead of staying well into the evening like he'd always done before.

His tumor was inoperable, he wasn't going to get better. He wasn't going to survive this; it was going to kill him. The only question was when. His doctors had told him he likely had six months left, maybe a year. But how much of that was going to be quality time, and how much of it he was going to spend confined to a bed was anybody's guess.

For now, though, he was just going to enjoy his job for as long as he could.

He might not have any children of his own, but in a way every child that he had taught over his nearly three-decade career was a part of him. He loved his job. He loved working with kids; he loved seeing them grow, and he loved watching them learn new things. He had determined that he was going to see out this school year, then he would retire. And once he retired, he'd have nothing left in his life, so cancer may as well take him.

The halls were empty as he walked toward his office. School always felt a little odd when it wasn't filled with kids. Caden had been working with children most of his life. As a teenager he'd worked with his church's youth group, then he'd been a summer camp counselor. Once he'd gotten his teaching degree, he'd begun teaching math in the local middle school. He'd worked his way up the ladder until he'd become a principal six years ago. He loved his job. It gave his life meaning. He could make a difference in these kids' lives, and that meant a lot to him.

Caden knew something was wrong as soon as he opened his office door.

Nothing appeared to be out of place, but he felt it in his gut.

He was just turning around when the blow came.

Strong and well placed, it connected firmly with the back of his head.

His world exploded into a mess of stars.

He crumpled.

He tried to move, but he seemed to have lost the ability to control his arms and legs.

Instead, he sort of just flopped about like a fish out of water.

His brain was trying to make sense of what was happening. It took it longer to connect the dots than his body had, which knew instinctively it needed to flee. If the strike to his head hadn't stunned him, he would have been out the door already.

Fight or flight.

It seemed neither was an option right now.

A large figure hovered above him, grabbing hold of him and dragging him farther away from the door. He was dropped unceremoniously by his desk while his assailant closed and locked the office door.

Caden tried his best to get his legs beneath him. He had to do something, or he wasn't walking out of this room alive.

He'd been fighting death's grip on him ever since his brain tumor diagnosis. He had known it was coming. That his time on earth was going to end earlier than he had anticipated. That he was never going to enjoy retirement. That he was never going to worry about ending up stuck in some dark, depressing nursing home.

But he thought he still had time.

Time to finish out this school year, maybe do a little traveling, enjoy a little more with her.

Now it seemed he wouldn't even get that.

He would scream for help, but there was no one to hear him.

No one was here but this man who wanted to attack him.

Why?

It made no sense.

He was a fifty-year-old man with no family and few friends. His whole life was his job. Could this be about one of the kids at the school? They were all good kids; he couldn't see any of them doing something like this. Besides, they were too small. This was middle school—grades six through eight. The man who'd hit him was adult size.

His vision was still blurry, but he looked up at the man towering above him. Definitely *not* a kid.

Again, the man grabbed his arm, this time to drag him up and prop him in a chair.

What was he going to do?

Caden assumed the man was here to kill him, but why? This couldn't be random. The man had been waiting here at his work in his office. Maybe a case of mistaken identity?

But who would they be mistaking him for?

There had been a time when he might not have been surprised if he was ambushed and murdered, but that was a quarter of a century ago. Those people were long gone. Now there was no one who would want to hurt him.

It didn't make any sense.

He needed it to make sense.

If he was going to die, then it should make sense.

Something cold pressed against his skin, and he blinked his eyes trying to clear his vision.

A sharp little prick on his cheek had his mind processing what the object was, even if he couldn't see it.

A knife.

If there had been any doubt about his attacker's intentions, it had just been wiped away.

The tip of the knife dug deeper into his cheek, and he let out a strangled scream. Did this man intend to torture him first?

This had to be some deranged psychopath. Caden really couldn't think of any other explanation.

Until he looked up.

Slowly, as though a fog were clearing, the face of the man came into view.

His heart sank.

He knew who it was, and he knew why the man was here.

A slow smile spread over his attacker's face when he saw recognition dawning.

With one hand, he dug the knife deeper still, twisting it from side to side and piercing through his flesh. With his other hand, he harshly grasped Caden's chin. The man leaned in close. "Remember me?"

The knife had worked its way completely though his cheek; the tip now poked at his gums. The pain was excruciating, worse than even the most severe headache he'd had. Blood was pouring down his throat, choking him. He couldn't speak. The best he could do was gurgle and nod.

"Then you know why I'm here." The man removed the knife and held the tip above his eye.

Caden couldn't speak. All he could do was stare at the knife. Any second now it was going to pierce his eyeball. His heart was hammering so hard inside his chest that if it were possible, it would have left bruises. The blood streaming down his throat activated his gag reflex, and he threw up all over himself.

How could this be happening?

It all felt so surreal.

"I said, then you know why I'm here." The man pried his eye open so he couldn't blink as the knife moved closer still.

Caleb managed a nod.

"Then you also know you deserve it."

That, he didn't know. In fact, he knew the opposite was true. He'd done the right thing. The only thing he could have done in that situation. He didn't regret it. Even if twenty-five years later he was going to be killed because of it. He had made the right choice. He knew it. Knew it deep down inside his soul.

He screamed as the blade pierced his eye. He was shaking all over, his limbs trying to move—to fight his assailant off—but doing little more than twitching uselessly.

The knife moved to his ear and ripped more screams from his blood clogged throat.

Pain swam inside him, filled him up till it was overflowing into every atom of his being.

If the man kept this up much longer, then the school would start to fill with people, and he'd be caught.

Everywhere the knife went, it found new ways to torture him.

He looked death in the face and realized he wasn't afraid.

It was his time.

Caden accepted that.

It gave him an odd sort of peace.

All he wanted now was to be out of pain.

The knife sliced through his flesh and he fixed his gaze on the bright white light that encompassed him.

* * * * *

7:29 A.M.

She wasn't coming.

Ten-year-old Tony Xander kicked his foot into the concrete sidewalk and fiddled with his backpack.

She was supposed to pick him up at seven; she was almost thirty minutes late. His mom never used to be late for anything, but these days she was so different. *Everything* was so different.

It had been almost six months since she moved out of their home. His dad said he didn't know if she was ever going to come back. Tony wasn't sure if he even wanted her to come back.

14

His sixteen-year-old brother Brian said he thought their mother was having an affair.

He didn't like to think of that. He didn't think it could be true. His mom belonged with his dad, not with anyone else. A lot of his friends' parents were divorced, but he'd never thought it would happen to *his* parents. *His* family was supposed to stay together. It was weird not having his mom there when he went to bed each night and not in the kitchen cooking breakfast when he got up each morning. His dad tried to cook breakfast, but his eggs never came out quite right. It wasn't the same.

Nothing was the same anymore.

It had happened so quickly.

There hadn't been lots of loud screaming fights like Jarod's parents had before they got divorced. And his dad hadn't lost his job like what happened before Harry's parents split up.

Everything had just been normal.

The same.

And then one day he had come home from school, and his dad had announced that mom was moving out for a while and wasn't going to be living with them anymore. When he'd asked if they were still going to see her, his dad had been vague and said that maybe once mom found a place of her own they might, but that he wasn't sure.

Why would they split up now?

It didn't make sense.

Before he was born, his brother had been really sick. Brian had had cancer, and for a while, they thought that he might even die. But he hadn't. He had gotten better, and now he'd been in remission ten years.

If that didn't break them up, then nothing should.

Mom wasn't going to come. He may as well go inside and call someone to come and pick him up. Eve and Elise were already at the pool with their swim team, and Dad was probably already at the hospital by now. Maybe he could call one of his aunts to come and get him.

Tony headed inside, making his way to the principal's office so he could ask to use the phone. His parents wouldn't let him have his own cell phone—not until he reached middle school, which was still more than six months away.

Dad was going to be mad when he found out that Mom had never turned up and just left him standing outside on his own on a cold winter's morning.

He was mad.

Next time she wanted to see him or make plans to see him, he was going to say no. If she didn't care about him, then he didn't see why he had to care about her.

She'd hurt all of them by walking away.

Especially Dad.

When he thought about it, it made Tony angry. His dad was always so nice to his mom. He kissed her good morning and goodbye when he went off to work. He always put his arm around her shoulders when they sat together on the sofa. He ate all the dinner she cooked and always told her how delicious it was. Why would his mom walk out away from that?

Why would she walk away from him?

Didn't she love him anymore?

This wasn't the first time she'd forgotten to pick him up. Once a month she was supposed to collect him from Eve and Elise's school and take him to breakfast before dropping him off at his school. She'd forgotten to come and get him last month, and she'd forgotten again today.

She was so different now.

Ever since she moved out, she wasn't the same mother he had known his whole life.

His thirteen-year-old sisters thought that she was having a midlife crisis. They said that was why she was acting weird, why she wasn't acting like herself, and why she wasn't interested in them anymore. They said she didn't want to get old, and when she was around them she felt old, so she wanted to stay away from them, pretend they didn't exist, so she could pretend she was still young. They said when you had a midlife crisis you got depressed and you bought weird stuff and got a shiny car and dyed your hair to feel better about yourself.

They also said it was usually men who had midlife crises. They said it was lucky Dad wasn't having one, too, so there was still someone to look after them.

Tony didn't quite get the whole midlife crisis thing. How was buying a new car supposed to make you think you weren't getting old?

Whatever.

He didn't really care why Mom had changed; all he cared about was—

"Ooff," he grunted as he walked headlong into something.

Some*one*.

Large hands gripped his shoulders.

"Watch where you're going, kid," an annoyed voice spoke.

Tony blinked and looked up. Way up. The man was tall—so tall he would even tower over his dad. Remembering his manners, he said, "Sorry."

The man scowled. "You should pay more attention so you don't walk into people."

Because he was only ten and he'd always been taught to be respectful of his elders, he didn't add that the man hadn't been looking where he was going, either. If he had been, they wouldn't have crashed into each other.

Instead, he just nodded.

With a last angry frown, the man shook his head, released his grip on Tony's shoulders, and stalked off down the corridor, muttering about being in a hurry.

He shrugged and rounded the corner, reaching the school office. It was empty. He'd thought that someone might be here. Even the principal's office door was closed, and Mr. Gervase was usually here early. He must be running late today.

What should he do?

Should he just use the phone anyway?

Should he go and try to find his sisters and use one of their phones?

Should he go back outside and see if Mom had finally turned up?

He didn't really want to do any of those things. He just wanted to get to school with minimum fuss. If he went to his sisters, Eve and Elise would just complain about Mom letting them all down. If he used the school phone without permission, he might get in trouble. And he knew that Mom wasn't going to be outside waiting for him.

Tony sniffed.

Something smelled weird.

Kind of bad and disgusting.

What was it?

His curiosity got the better of him, and he headed for the closed door of Mr. Gervase's office—the smell seemed to be coming from inside.

At the door he paused, his hand on the knob. Should he open it or go?

He should go.

He knew it.

He released the handle and took two steps in the opposite direction.

Then he stopped and came back.

There was no one here; he wasn't going to get into trouble. He'd just take one quick little look in the office to see why it smelled, then he'd go find his sisters. As much as he didn't want to hear their complaining, he had to get to school. If he didn't, Dad was going to be just as angry with him as he was going to be with Mom.

One quick little look couldn't hurt. No one would even know

he'd been in there … he wouldn't touch a thing.

Slowly, he turned the doorknob and inched the door open. A feeling in his stomach told him he shouldn't be doing this, but he ignored it. What harm could it do?

Pushing the door the rest of the way open, Tony froze.

Blood.

There was blood everywhere.

Everywhere.

Mr. Gervase was there.

At least, Tony thought it was him, but it was hard to be sure because of all the blood.

It was all over him.

It was his blood.

Someone had hurt him.

Someone had *killed* him.

Mr. Gervase was dead.

Dead.

He'd never seen a dead body before.

Before he even realized it, he had thrown up all over himself.

Mr. Gervase was dead, and someone had killed him.

What if that someone was still here?

Tony turned and ran.

He heard someone screaming.

He didn't realize it was himself.

Then someone grabbed him. Strong arms wrapped around him. Pinning him against a strong, hard chest.

He fought as hard as he could and screamed at the top of his lungs.

* * * * *

8:46 A.M.

His partner was quiet as they walked through the school halls.

Detective Ryan Xander suspected he knew the reason, but he asked anyway. "You all right?"

"Yes," Paige replied, but her voice was hollow.

"Thinking about the kids?" he asked. He knew he was thinking of his ten-year-old daughter and seven-year-old son.

"School is supposed to be a safe place," Paige said. "Hayley and your Sophie are the same age as Tony. They're all going to be coming to this school in the fall, and now ..."

Paige let her sentence trail off, but she didn't need to finish it. Ryan knew what she was saying. A murder at the middle school made you want to homeschool your kids and never let them go out into the world. Which was ridiculous. Danger could lurk anywhere; both he and Paige knew that better than most.

"I'll have to try to keep Hayley off the computer and away from the news for the next few days," Paige said.

His partner's daughter was an extremely sensitive and emotional child. Before Paige and her husband had adopted her, the little girl had spent the first five years of her life in the hands of a demented madman. Although Hayley had made great strides living with Paige and Elias, she still tended to become very upset over things most ten-year-olds barely noticed.

"I'll tell Sophie to keep her mouth shut around Hayley," Ryan told his partner. His daughter was the complete opposite of Paige's. She was like a whirlwind of peppy energy and often spoke without thinking. On more than one occasion she had upset Hayley by telling her things she'd seen or heard. Sophie had a fascination with his job; she was definitely a little cop in the making.

"Thanks. They really make an interesting, if unusual, pair." Paige smiled.

That they did. The girls were the best of friends and had been ever since Hayley first came into their lives, and Sophie had taken her under her wing.

"Where's Tony?" she asked as they entered the school offices.

Ryan had almost had a heart attack when he'd heard what had happened to his nephew. Making that call to his younger brother had been one of the worst moments of his life. Mark had been through enough—his oldest son's battle with leukemia, a health scare with one of his daughters a couple of years ago, and then, most recently, the separation from his wife. He didn't need anything else to deal with.

"He was found just outside the school office," he replied.

"He's not here now," Paige said, looking around.

"Maybe they moved him somewhere else." Ryan both needed to and dreaded seeing his nephew.

"Over there." His partner suddenly pointed to a small room; they could see Tony through the open door.

"Tony." He hurried forward.

At the sound of his name, the child's head bobbed up, and he launched himself off the chair he'd been perched on and quickly closed the space between them, then flung himself into Ryan's arms. He held the little boy tightly, so thankful that he hadn't turned up at the principal's office just a little earlier. If he had, whoever had killed Caden Gervase might have killed *him* too.

"Are you okay, buddy?" he asked, resisting the urge to pick the child up. Tony was ten and didn't like to be treated like a baby anymore.

"I'm okay," Tony said, calmer than Ryan thought he would have been able to muster if he'd stumbled upon a murdered and mutilated body when he was ten. "Is my dad coming?"

"He should be here soon. We called him. He was just waiting for someone to arrive to cover his shift," Ryan told him, noting the boy hadn't mentioned his mother. "I want you to go wait in there with the officer, and Paige and I will come and ask you a few questions when we finish up in the office."

"Okay." Tony nodded. Despite how well he was holding it together, his eyes were haunted. He could never unsee what he'd seen this morning, and it would stay with him for the rest of his life.

It was time to go into the office.

Ryan admitted to himself that he was a little nervous. He was forty, and he'd been a cop for close to half his life. He'd been to hundreds of crime scenes, many of which had been horrifically violent. But this one was different. His nephew had witnessed this scene.

Aiming for clinical detachment, he snapped on a pair of gloves, put some booties over his shoes, and entered the office.

The first thing that hit him was the smell.

Blood mixed with vomit.

There was a small puddle of vomit by the door. That was from Tony. The poor kid had lost his breakfast at the horrific sight he'd walked in on. It might mess with their forensics, but given that it was over by the door, away from the majority of the action, Ryan hoped it wouldn't.

"Doesn't seem like a crime of opportunity," Paige noted.

"I agree." He nodded. "The killer was already here waiting for him."

It seemed unlikely that this was random. Someone had come here to Caden Gervase's workplace and hidden in his office, ready to strike when he came through the door. That wasn't typically the way you killed someone if you just picked a random stranger. Chances were the victim knew his murderer.

"Looks like he knew the man's work schedule, too. He was here early, so he must have known that Caden came in early to get some work done in the quiet. He knew he would have time to do whatever he wanted without having to worry about anyone walking in on them and interrupting," Paige said.

Again, he agreed with his partner. And from the looks of the body, their killer had obviously wanted some time alone with his victim.

"Was he dead before or after the killer did all of that?" Ryan directed the question toward the medical examiner. He was sure he already knew the answer, but part of him was hoping that he was wrong.

Billy Newton looked up from where he was hunched over Caden Gervase's body. Billy was in his mid-fifties, and between his long hours with the medical examiner's office and being a father of seven, including three sets of twins, the man looked perpetually tired. Today his dark eyes had dark circles underneath them, and his thinning black hair was a little mussed.

Still, his gaze was sharp and focused when he answered. "Vomit mixed with blood all down his front says he was alive, as does the amount of blood around the wounds."

That's what he'd thought.

"Cause of death … what it looks like?" Paige asked.

His partner's question drew his gaze to Caden's neck—or what was left of it. It had been sliced so deeply, it practically severed his head from his body, and he could actually see a glimmer of white which he guessed was bone from the man's spine.

"Exsanguination from the cut to the neck. From the looks of it, he severed both carotid arteries," Billy replied.

"Whoever did this obviously doesn't like Caden Gervase very much," Paige said quietly.

"From the way he tortured him before he killed him, I'd say that's a given." From what he could see, one of Caden's eyes had been pierced with what he assumed was a knife, and one of his ears had been cut off, then just dropped casually right beside the chair where he assumed the man had been sitting. "Can you see if he has any other injuries, Billy?"

The ME leaned over the body, careful not to move Caden until he'd finished photographing him. "From what I can see, there's what looks like a deep wound in his cheek, probably the cause of the blood he vomited up. He's missing a finger." Billy paused and looked closer. "No, make that seven. Seven missing fingers. They must be under the body; he probably fell on them when the killer slit his throat, and he slumped out of the chair."

The killer obviously hadn't been interested in staging the scene. He'd just let body parts—and the body itself—fall wherever they fell and left them there.

"He clearly wanted Caden to suffer … but why?" Paige looked thoughtful.

"They knew each other. Hopefully, when we look into Caden we'll find someone in his life who hates him enough to do this." Ryan waved a hand at the bloody scene before them.

"Defensive wounds, Billy?" his partner asked.

"None that I can see."

"Why didn't he fight back?" Ryan wondered aloud. Caden Gervase was fifty years old. He didn't look like he was in the best shape, but surely, he would have done his best to fight off his attacker.

"I see a wound to the back of his head," Billy supplied.

"So, he got him as he came through the door. Delivered a blow that stunned him enough that he wasn't capable of fighting back."

"But not hard enough to knock him unconscious," Paige added. "He wouldn't have gone to all the trouble of torturing him if he wasn't conscious to suffer."

This was personal.

Very personal.

Someone hated Caden Gervase enough to torture and kill him. Ryan couldn't see how that person wouldn't stand out when they started looking into Caden's life.

Forensics would go through the room with a fine-tooth comb and find anything that the killer had left behind. Hopefully, something that would get them a hit in a database and lead them straight to him. They knew that he'd planned the attack ahead of time, and it seemed like he'd brought his own weapon with him, but they didn't know how meticulous he had been about not leaving any of himself behind.

Plus, they had a potential eyewitness.

Tony had bumped into a man when he was on his way to the office to use the phone. Chances are, it was the killer. While it terrified him to think of his ten-year-old nephew being so close to a vicious murderer, it also put them one step closer to finding and apprehending this man.

* * * * *

9:01 A.M.

Anger and fear battled inside him.

It was taking every single bit of his willpower to wait for another doctor to arrive at the hospital so he could go running out of here.

Mark Xander was desperate to get to his son.

So desperate that if it wasn't for the fact that he knew his brother was at the school, he would have left without any regard for leaving the hospital understaffed and down one trauma surgeon.

But Ryan was there, and Paige, and he knew that Tony would be safe until he could arrive.

He was trying to hold on to that.

Tony was okay.

No doubt terrified about what he had walked in on, but he was safe.

Safe.

Maybe if he kept repeating the word, it would finally sink in.

His fear about what Tony had seen and what it would do to him was rivaled only by his anger at Daisy.

That anger had been burning for the last six months. Ever since she announced that she was moving out. It had come as a complete shock. Only, at the same time, it hadn't.

Mark had known that something was going on with Daisy. She'd been different, quieter, more withdrawn—even with the kids.

But moving out? That was such a big step. And one that she had taken on her own. They hadn't discussed it. She hadn't given him an opportunity to ask her to stay. She hadn't cared what he thought or what he wanted. She hadn't even offered any explanation. She had simply packed a bag, informed him she was leaving and didn't know if she was coming back, and walked out the door.

That was it.

If she wanted to leave, that was one thing, but to abandon their kids was quite another.

Daisy hadn't asked to take the kids with her when she left, and she hadn't asked for them to come and stay with her since—not even for the weekend. A few months ago, she had asked to take them out to breakfast. Brian had refused to go. Eve and Elise had as well under the cover of not wanting to miss their swim training. But Tony had seemed excited to spend some time with his mom, who he'd seen only a handful of times since she left.

They'd made arrangements for him to drop Tony off with the girls and for her to pick him up at the middle school, take him to breakfast, then drop him off at the elementary school.

She had never turned up.

When he'd phoned her to find out why, she'd been vague but apologetic and promised it wouldn't happen again.

But it had.

This morning she had forgotten about Tony again, and this time their son could have been killed because of it.

Snatching up his phone from the table on one of his frantic pacing circles of his office, he dialed her number again. He'd been trying without success to get ahold of her ever since he'd gotten Ryan's call.

Once again, the call rang out.

Where was she?

What was she doing?

What could be more important than their son?

He punched redial a little more firmly than was necessary.

It was driving him crazy. He couldn't understand it. What on earth could make her forget about their ten-year-old son that she would leave him standing alone outside the school at seven in the morning in the middle of winter?

"Mark," her voice floated from the phone. With it came the accompanying stab to his heart he got every time he heard her voice. He might he angry with her, but he still loved her.

"Daisy."

"I'm so sorry I forgot to pick up Tony for breakfast. Did he get to school okay?"

"You forgot?" he echoed. "I don't understand. How could you forget him?"

"I was busy," she replied vaguely.

"Busy?" he repeated. "Doing what?"

"Something came up."

"Something came up?" He was going to have to stop repeating everything she said, but it all sounded so ridiculous that he was having a hard time believing it. "Something more important than Tony?"

"No, of course not."

"Well, it had to have been, wasn't it," he snarled. "Since it took priority over our child. Our ten-year-old child. Who you just left standing alone at the school."

"I'm sorry. I'll make it up to him."

Daisy sounded repentant and truly distressed, but more than that she sounded tired. Really tired. Exhausted. The kind of exhausted that seeped into your bones and your soul and filled you up until you could barely function because the weight of it was crushing you.

The part of him that still loved her wanted to go to her. To find out what was wrong. To find out why she'd left. To find out what was hurting her and help her make it better. But she hadn't wanted his help. She had left. She could have come to him. They could have talked through whatever was going on and found a way to face and fix it together, but she had chosen not to do that. She had chosen to leave and to deal with things on her own.

That decision had affected not just the two of them but their four kids as well.

And while Daisy may be prepared to disregard not only their children's feelings but their safety as well, he was not. There would be no more chances. From now on, if she wanted to see the kids, she could come to the house on time when he was there. He didn't trust her with them anymore, and he couldn't risk one of them being hurt again because Daisy was too wrapped up in herself.

"Mark? Are you still there?"

"I'm still here," he said quietly, trying his best to set the anger aside. Anger wasn't going to help him or his kids right now. "*You* were the one who made plans to see Tony this morning. To say that something came up is ridiculous, and I won't let it happen again. I think, for the time being, it's best if you don't take the kids anywhere. If you feel like seeing them, you can call me, and we can make a time for you to come around to the house."

He expected her to fight him, to argue, to refuse his terms, but instead, she said softly, "That's probably best."

His anger was gone now. In its place was sadness. What had happened to the woman he'd fallen in love with? The woman who would sit at their children's bedsides all night when they were sick or had nightmares. The woman who loved to spend hours in the kitchen cooking a dinner that was going to be devoured in minutes, who somehow managed to juggle a full-time job, four kids, and his unpredictable work hours. Where had she gone?

Mark didn't want to tell her about Tony and what had happened this morning, but she was still his mother, and she had a right to know. Perhaps it might even be the wake-up call she needed to sort herself out. Even if she no longer wanted to be his wife, she still had four kids who needed a mother.

"There was a murder at the school this morning."

He could practically hear the color drain from her face. "Which school?"

"Middle school."

"The kids?" Her voice trembled.

"They're all safe." He paused and drew in a long, deep breath. "But Tony was the one who found the body."

Silence.

It lasted for so long that he started to worry that she might have fainted. "Daisy?"

"Is he all right?"

"Scared, but all right," he assured her. "I'm just waiting for someone to show up here so I can go to him."

"I'm on my way." He could hear her rustling about.

"I don't think that's a good idea."

Anger heated her voice. "He's my son, Mark. You can't keep me away from him. I'm going. I'm his mother. He needs me."

Emotion had finally come back into her voice. She finally sounded alive again. But he didn't understand her. *She* was the one who had walked away from her family. *She* was the one who acted like she didn't care about them anymore, and yet, now she didn't like the idea of being told to stay away.

It made no sense.

Mark didn't offer any more arguments against her going to the school. Maybe this really *was* the wake-up call she'd needed. Maybe there was hope for her. For them. For their family.

"Who was killed?"

That question extinguished the hope that had just ignited inside him. How could there be hope for his family when his wife refused to be honest with him? "It was Caden Gervase."

Daisy gasped.

A horrified sound full of heartfelt anguish, and his suspicions were confirmed.

His wife had left because she was interested in someone else.

The principal at their daughters' school.

Mark had seen them together. Their heads bent over cups of coffee at a local café, so deep in conversation, they hadn't seen him enter.

His marriage was over.

He hadn't wanted to admit it, but he had to face facts.

He hung up without another word.

* * * * *

9:28 A.M.

No one better try to stop her.

She needed to get to Tony.

Needed to.

Daisy couldn't believe this was happening. Caden was dead, and her own son had found the body.

How could that happen?

She had really messed up.

She should have been there this morning like she'd said she'd be. How could she have been so stupid and so selfish? She didn't even have a good reason for not turning up. She'd been up late, not falling asleep until the early hours of the morning, and although she had set the alarm, she must have slept right through it, not waking up until her ringing phone had finally ripped her from sleep.

When she'd seen all the missed calls, she'd known that something was wrong, but nothing could have prepared her for what Mark had told her.

Her poor baby.

She just wanted to pick Tony up and hold him and kiss him and try to make it all better.

Unfortunately, Daisy could imagine all too well what he was

feeling right now. She had only been a little older than Tony when she saw her first dead body.

It hadn't sunk in yet that Caden was dead.

She couldn't believe that she was never going to see him again, never going to speak to him again. That she couldn't just pick up her phone and call him when she needed to talk.

He was gone.

He was really gone.

It felt so surreal.

Tears were building up. She wanted to curl up in a ball and sob, but she would have to cry for Caden later. Right now, she had to keep her focus on her son. Tony needed her.

Tonight, in her motel room, she would let herself cry. She would let all those memories come tumbling out. She would think of all the good times with Caden, of the day they met, and the first time he held her in his arms, and everything they had shared together.

Tonight she would mourn the man who had played such an important role in her life.

Now she would be the mother her son needed. The mother she should have been earlier today. She would never forgive herself for putting her ten-year-old boy in this position. Was he angry with her? Mark was, and Tony had every right to be as well; she couldn't blame him if he was.

As she opened the door to the classroom where Tony was sitting with Ryan and Paige, she let out a sigh of relief.

He was there. He was whole. He was alive. He so easily couldn't have been.

"Baby," she said as she hurried toward him.

Tony looked over at her, his gaze cold. It wasn't just the haunted look in his eyes; he clearly wasn't happy to see her. Daisy faltered for a moment. She deserved his anger; it was her fault that he'd been put in danger. But whether he was angry with her or not, she needed to hold him.

She dropped to her knees in front of the chair he was sitting in and wrapped her arms tightly around him, burying her face in his messy blond hair. She breathed in his scent, felt his warm body against hers, felt his heart beating against her chest. He didn't hold her back, but right now she didn't care. All she cared about was that her baby was alive and in one piece.

"Have you interviewed him yet?" Daisy asked when she finally released Tony.

"We were waiting for you or Mark to arrive," her brother-in-law replied.

She was thankful for that. This was traumatic enough for a ten-year-old child. If he had to relive everything he'd been through, he needed to have a parent there. "Is Mark on his way?" He'd hung up on her earlier, but she assumed he was coming.

"He should be here soon," Paige replied. "But we're going to start now. You okay with that, Tony?"

Her son shrugged. He looked so small, so young, so vulnerable. She wanted to pick him up and hold him but didn't think that would be well received, so instead, she stood and pulled up a chair. She didn't think Tony would appreciate her holding his hand, so she clenched her hands together and set them in her lap.

Tony's eyes were glued to his shoes. They cost almost a hundred dollars—much more than she liked to spend on shoes for the kids. He'd begged for that pair of sneakers for months before she and Mark had given them to him for his birthday. He'd been so excited, put them on immediately even though the day had been hot, well over one hundred degrees. She missed her family so much. So much it physically hurt.

"Your dad dropped you off a little before seven?" Ryan asked.

Tony nodded.

Daisy was swamped by guilt. This was all her fault.

"The girls hang around with you or go straight off to the pool?"

"They left right away," Tony mumbled.

They weren't supposed to. Eve and Elise were supposed to wait with Tony until she arrived to pick him up. She understood why they hadn't wanted to. They were thirteen; they didn't want to hang around with their little brother. They wanted to be with their friends.

She didn't blame her girls.

This was all on her.

"Did you see anyone while you were waiting for your mom?" Paige asked.

"A couple of kids," he replied.

"Was there anyone—?"

"I'm sorry," Tony interrupted Paige.

"Sorry about what?" Ryan asked.

"I messed up." Tony looked more miserable than scared now.

"Messed up how?" Paige asked.

"I got sick." Tony dropped his gaze back to his shoes.

"That's okay." Ryan patted his shoulder comfortingly.

"No, it's not." Tony's sad blue eyes finally lifted. "I ruined the scene. You're not supposed to get sick or touch anything, right? That messes things up. I'm sorry," he said again, fighting back tears.

"Hey, look at me." Ryan waited until his nephew's gaze was fixed firmly on his. "I don't want you to worry about it. Okay? Where you were sick, it was over by the door, away from everything else. It'll be fine. Okay, bud?"

Tony looked a little less worried. "Okay."

"Did you touch anything in the office?" Paige asked.

"No." Tony seemed more confident now that his fears about ruining the crime scene had been assuaged. "Just the door handle. When I saw the blood, I threw up, then turned and ran. I crashed into someone. I thought it was the killer, but it was Mrs. Clayton, the school secretary."

Thankfully, it wasn't the killer Tony had run in to. Daisy's blood turned to ice as she once more realized just how close her baby had come to being hurt or killed.

"Let's talk about the man you saw," Paige said.

Tony nodded. All serious now. Her little boy never ceased to amaze her. Even though he'd been through something so traumatic, all he cared about was doing his part in finding who had killed Caden. Daisy wouldn't be surprised if he followed in his grandfather's and uncles' footsteps and became a cop when he grew up.

"What do you remember about him?" Paige asked.

"He was tall," Tony said immediately.

"How tall?" Ryan asked.

"Really tall ... taller than my dad."

Mark was over six feet tall so this man must have been huge. If he had tried to hurt Tony, her son wouldn't have stood a chance at getting away from him.

"How old was he?" Ryan asked. "My age? Older? Younger?"

Tony thought about that for a moment. "Younger than you. Maybe twenty something? Or thirty something?" He didn't sound altogether sure of that.

"Do you remember what color hair he had?" Ryan asked.

"Blond."

"Eyes?"

"Blue."

"Do you remember any distinguishing features? Scars or tattoos or birthmarks?"

"He didn't have any," Tony said confidently. She was so proud of him and how grown up he was being.

"What was his demeanor like?" Paige asked. "Was he angry or scared or nervous?"

"He was angry. He said it was my fault we crashed into each other, but he wasn't looking where he was going either," Tony said a little indignantly. "If he had been, we wouldn't have walked into each other."

"What else do you remember about him?"

"When he left he was muttering something about being in a hurry. And his hands were wet," Tony said.

The killer had obviously cleaned up before leaving. Tony was wearing a sweater that was several sizes too big and a pair of sweatpants that were also too big. CSU must have collected his clothes to search them for evidence. The man who had killed Caden had touched her son. *Touched* him. She shivered at the knowledge.

"We're going to get you to work with a sketch—"

"Tony."

Tony's gaze darted to the door, and he launched off his chair. "Dad."

He flew across the room and into Mark's arms.

Daisy knew it was stupid to be jealous. She had brought all of this on herself. She had chosen to leave; she had to suck it up and deal with the consequences, but it still hurt to know that although their son didn't want anything to do with her, he wanted his father's comfort.

Mark's eyes met hers. His were cold and distant and nothing like the husband she knew. She shivered again. He was so angry with her, she understood and knew she deserved it, but it didn't make it any easier to take.

"We'll find who did this," Ryan assured his older brother.

Then her husband said the last thing she'd expected.

"Maybe you should be looking into Daisy since she and Caden Gervase seem to have a *special* relationship."

She froze.

How did he know about her and Caden?

It took all her strength not to faint dead away in shock.

* * * * *

12:17 P.M.

Her head felt like it had been filled with concrete.

Not just her head; her entire body felt heavy.

So heavy it almost pulled her back under the black cloud that hovered above her.

Colette fought with every fiber of her being to stop that from happening.

Her last conscious memories shimmered at the back of her mind. She could see them, although not quite clearly, but enough to remember the cold ... the boy ... the fireplace ... the sleeping bag ... the strike to her face that was still throbbing ... the other man ... and the realization that she had been tricked. It was all still there.

For now, though, anger at herself took the place that fear should rightly hold.

What was wrong with her?

How could she be so stupid?

She knew better than to talk to strangers.

She knew better than to trust anyone.

She would rather be back out in the freezing winter night than here in this claustrophobically, warm place.

She was warm.

The thought was enough to prompt Colette to pry open her concrete laden eyes. A dull gray ceiling came into view. It spurred her into clambering into a sitting position so she could properly survey her surroundings and find a way out of here.

Colette made into a half sitting, half prone position, propped up on her elbows.

She was in a cage.

An actual *cage*.

Indignation flushed through her, warming her further and loosening up her stiff muscles enough that she was able to heave herself to her feet.

A cage.

How dare that boy kidnap her and put her in a cage. She wasn't an animal. She was a person—a living, breathing human being. She had been treated pretty badly in her sixteen years, but no one had ever humiliated her quite like this.

Long metal bars surrounded her on all four sides, stretching from the floor to the ceiling. Her cage was about ten feet square. There was a mattress on the floor, a wooden chair and small round table, two buckets, one empty and one full of water with a washcloth folded over the side, and a hose dangled down from the ceiling.

It looked like someone expected to keep her in here for a long time.

That was not going to happen.

The floor was cold and scratched at her bare feet. Which drew her attention to the fact that she wasn't wearing the clothes she'd been wearing when that boy approached her on the street.

Her jeans and sweater were gone—as well as her coat. She was now in an oversized, green T-shirt.

And she wasn't wearing any underwear.

She froze.

Her whole body went cold.

Sweat broke out on her forehead.

Had he raped her?

She focused all of her energy down there. Did she feel different? She wasn't sore. Her legs didn't feel sticky. Maybe he hadn't touched her.

Quickly, she sat back down, bringing her knees up and bending over to try to look between them, examining her inner thighs for any bruises or signs that she'd been violated.

"I don't think they would have raped you."

Colette screamed and jumped up at the sound of the voice.

"Sorry, I didn't mean to startle you."

The voice was female.

And young.

She whipped her head in its direction and saw a girl probably only a few years older than herself, standing at the bars of her cage. She had been so busy looking around her little prison that she hadn't even taken in the rest of the room. There was another cage beside hers, then across the other side of the windowless room there was what appeared to be medical equipment. There was a hospital bed and an exam table with stirrups.

What exactly did they have planned for her?

"They probably just took some blood," the girl continued.

Took blood?

Why would they take her blood?

Her gaze fell to the inside of her left elbow where a small white bandage had been taped. She hadn't noticed it, but now her fingers picked at the edges of it.

"Who are you?" she asked the girl. Fear was starting to sink in. This was too weird. It made no sense. She wanted answers. She *needed* them. Now. Before she lost her mind.

"Heather."

Colette turned and examined this girl. She had smooth black skin, large dark eyes that seemed even darker in the stark fluorescent light of the basement, and ebony hair that hung around her shoulders in a frizzy mess. Heather was beautiful. Except for her eyes. They were haunted, broken, devoid of hope, and they sucked out any vestiges of hope left inside herself.

Then her eyes fell on the girl's neck.

There was some sort of weird collar around it.

Did she have one too?

Her hands touched her neck and found that indeed there was a collar on her neck.

Why hadn't she noticed it?

Why did she keep not noticing things?

That was going to have to change. She was going to need to pay attention to every single little detail if she was going to find a way to get herself out of here.

"What is this?" she asked, tugging on it. It was a thin metal band, but not too thin.

"You'll find out soon," Heather answered vaguely.

She didn't like the sound of that. "What is this place?" she asked, no longer sure she wanted to know.

"Hell," came the soft reply.

"How long have you been here?"

Heather shrugged. "It's hard to tell. You kind of lose track of time in here without being able to see the outside. Two years, maybe closer to three."

Three years?

This girl had survived three years in this place?

Colette wasn't sure she could survive three minutes.

"Why did he take my blood?"

"To run tests. Make sure you're healthy and not on drugs."

"Why would he care?"

This place made no sense. She didn't understand what they wanted from her. She didn't understand why they'd brought her here. This seemed so elaborate. She knew they were going to do something …

Her train of thought was disrupted by a cry.

"What was that?"

Heather walked over to the mattress in her cage and picked up a pile of blankets.

Colette knew the answer, and suddenly everything began falling into place, but she asked anyway. "What is that?"

"That is my son." Heather held out the tiny baby so she could see him, then sat down and lifted the baggy T-shirt she wore, exposing her breasts. She held the infant to them and he immediately began to suckle.

The world was tunneling.

She had thought she'd fled hell when she left home, but instead, she'd come running right to it.

"That's why I'm here," she said in a small voice. "Babies."

"Yes," Heather agreed, her gaze focused on her child. "You're here to have babies. Babies that are going to be ripped from your arms. Black market babies."

She was breathing too fast, panting.

She was too young to have babies.

She didn't want to have babies.

She wanted to leave.

She wanted to flee, to be far away from here, to be anywhere but here, and she didn't care where.

Heather said she'd been here for almost three years. Her baby was so little. He wasn't very old. Was this her first or had there been others?

"How old is he?"

"Four days old. They'll be taking him soon. When he's one week old. They probably already have a buyer for him." Heather's grip on the baby tightened.

Obviously, this wasn't her first. "How many?" Colette asked, her heart brimming with pain for this girl. She didn't think she could take being impregnated, carrying the child inside her for nine months, giving birth, having to care for the baby for a week then having it ripped from her arms.

"This is my third. My first boy."

Colette couldn't take this.

It was insanity.

Black market babies. She knew they existed; she'd just never really thought about where they came from. She thought people probably just abducted infants. She didn't really think they abducted girls and forced them to provide babies.

"Someone will find us," she said confidently. It had to be true. Surely, it did.

"No one's come for me," Heather said softly.

Colette couldn't accept that.

For the first time since she'd run away from home, she prayed that someone had reported her missing. That someone was looking for her. That someone knew—and cared—that she existed and that she needed help.

"You're awake."

Her head snapped toward the voice.

It was him.

The man who had tricked her, who had brought her here.

She met his gaze squarely.

In this harsh light she could see he was a little older than she'd thought when they'd first met. He wasn't a teenager, but he wasn't more than twenty-two, maybe twenty-three.

He had a bandage wrapped around his left bicep. At least she'd stabbed him. Always carrying a knife had worked out in her favor more than once. She just wished she'd realized earlier that this man was a threat to her and used her knife to get away from him before he ever got her to the house.

Still, she was pleased she'd inflicted the small wound and shot him a smug smile.

He smiled back, a twinkle in his green eyes. "I like you." He beamed. "Well, stabbing tendencies aside. You're going to be a great asset to our business. I take it Heather clued you in."

She was afraid.

Terrified.

Even more now that she saw the way he looked at her. To him she was just an object through which he could make money. Nothing more and nothing less. That scared her more than anything else because it meant she couldn't talk her way out of this. There was no way he was giving up his new little bundle of money.

She had met a lot of bad men in her life, but no one had looked at her with such utter cool, calm detachment as he did. It scared her, but it also made her so furious. He had no right to do this to her. He couldn't just take girls and use them at his whim to make cash from them. Tears burned the backs of her eyes but she wasn't going to cry. She was too angry for tears.

How could he just snatch her and act like it was no big deal?

He had no right to take her and bring her here.

"It's meal time." He produced a tray.

Apparently, Heather knew what that meant because she picked up the baby and moved to the back of her cage.

"Move," her abductor jerked his head at her. "Down the back, like Heather."

She stood her ground. This seemed like a potential opportunity to escape. The man held trays in his hand. It seemed like he was going to open the cage's door to put one inside. As soon as he did, she was going to make a run for it. There was no way he could force her to the back of the cage. He couldn't even reach her. That definitely gave her a little bit of an upper hand.

At least, that's what she'd thought.

But a jolt of lightning in her neck had her crumpling to the ground.

* * * * *

2:09 P.M.

Paige wanted this case wrapped up as soon as possible.

Since becoming a mother, she felt uneasy working any cases related to children. She still did her job, but it felt different now than it had before Hayley and Arianna had come into her life.

After an assault that had robbed her of her chance to have children of her own, she'd given up on the idea of her and her husband having a family of their own. And then those two little girls had walked into their lives. She couldn't love either of them more if they had grown inside her body, and she couldn't wait to get home tonight to hug them.

Although this case wasn't technically a child case, the fact that it had happened at a school—a school her daughter would be attending in less than a year—made it much too close for comfort. She hoped that she and Ryan found the answers they needed here.

"It's just up there." She pointed up the block.

"Okeydoke," Ryan said as he pulled the car to the curb in front of the house she indicated.

"Okeydoke?" She smirked at Ryan; she hadn't heard him say that before.

"It's Ned's new favorite word," he said in way of explanation.

She laughed. Her partner's seven-year-old son was such a funny kid. Sometimes when she looked at him, she thought about adopting a son. She and Elias had room in their home and their lives for another child, and their girls would adore having a baby brother to shower attention on.

"Nice house for a principal," Ryan said as they climbed out of the car.

"Really nice." School principals earned a pretty good salary— more than she earned—but this house looked like it was worth millions.

"Maybe he's into something he shouldn't be and that's what got him killed," Ryan suggested as they headed for the front door.

"Could be. It's hard to figure him out. He doesn't have any family, not a lot of friends from what his colleagues said, and although everyone at the school seemed to like him, no one seemed to know him all that well."

"There's Daisy," he said quietly.

She had been thinking about that, too. "Do you think what Mark said is true?"

"Judging by the look on Daisy's face when he said it, I think there's something to it. She completely drained of color. For a moment, I thought she was going to pass out. You don't get that upset if there's nothing to it."

"You think they were having an affair?"

"I want to say no because I don't want to think that my sister-in-law would break my brother's heart by having an affair, but she did move out, and there's clearly something between her and

Caden Gervase."

"We'll have to talk with her and find out what it is."

"We will," her partner said, although he didn't sound pleased about it. "For now, let's just see if we can find out anything about Caden that will help us find his killer. He and Daisy might have something going on between them, but we don't think she killed him."

"At least, not directly."

Ryan's blue eyes grew round. "You think she hired someone to do it?"

"No," she answered honestly. "But we can't discount it just because it's Daisy."

Although Paige didn't think that Daisy was involved, she did believe that her friend knew something. Maybe something important. They *would* find out what she knew. Paige just hoped it didn't end up further destroying Daisy and Mark's family.

"House is just as nice inside as it is on the outside," Ryan said as they entered.

"It's kind of big for just one guy. There has to be at least six or seven bedrooms. I wonder what he did here."

As they wandered around, it soon became clear that the house may be big, but Caden didn't use much of it. Although it was fully furnished, most of the doors were closed, and the rooms didn't look like they'd been entered in months.

Since Caden didn't use much of his home, it was hard to get a feel for him from it. It didn't seem to represent him; the man was a bit of an enigma, and it was hard to get a read on him. If they couldn't get a read on him, they wouldn't be able to find who had killed him.

"Maybe, instead of being here, we should be interviewing Daisy," she said to Ryan as they headed upstairs. "She might be our only inroad into learning about who Caden was and who might want to hurt him."

"There has to be something here," Ryan said, beginning to

sound frustrated. This case was personal to him—to her, too, as she was close with her partner's entire family—since his nephew had been the one to discover the body.

They checked the entire upstairs. There were six en suite bedrooms, and just like the downstairs, all of them looked like they hadn't been used in years, except for one. Caden's bedroom revealed as little about him as the rest of the house. There were a few old photographs of him as a boy with his father. There were his clothes, and a TV beside which a pile of animal documentary DVDs were piled, and that was it.

"He seems to like animals," she said a little halfheartedly. She had hoped to come here and find something definitive; instead, it looked like they were going to walk away empty-handed. "Could he be involved in some sort of animal smuggling ring?"

"I guess," her partner agreed with as little enthusiasm for the idea as she had been able to muster.

Surely there had to be something here.

Caden was dead.

Murdered.

Viciously murdered.

And tortured.

The crime looked personal. It wasn't someone who had randomly picked a house, broken in, and killed whomever lived there. Someone wanted him dead. There had to be a reason, and somewhere there was evidence of what that reason was.

"Basement or attic." She turned to Ryan. "We can assume whatever got him killed wasn't something he would want anyone stumbling upon. The attic or the basement would provide a much safer place to keep anything he wanted kept away from potentially prying eyes."

"There wasn't an office anywhere in the house, so it does make sense that he'd keep things out of sight."

"Which do you want to try first?"

"May as well go with the attic since we're already on the

second floor."

They located the door to the attic and headed up. This was the only room in the entire house that was one big mess. There was stuff everywhere. Boxes and cases were stacked over most of the space, and there were several filing cabinets off to one side.

"Start with the filing cabinets?"

"May as well," Ryan agreed and they headed over there.

Paige drew up a couple of boxes and sat on them as she pulled open the first drawer and began to sift through the mountain of papers inside.

Time blurred as she flicked through page after page of old bank statements, old gas and electric bills, and old pay slips.

She didn't really notice it at the time, but something began to irritate her throat. She started coughing as she continued to go through the papers but put it down to the dust. The room was covered in it, and with her and Ryan rifling through things, they were disturbing it and it was rising in little clouds everywhere.

"I found out how he can afford this house," Ryan announced.

"Oh yeah?" she arched a brow.

"Belonged to his parents. Apparently, his mother was fairly wealthy, and when she died, she left it to her husband; when he died, he left it to his only son."

"Caden."

"Yep."

"So I guess the house didn't come from doing anything illegal. He really doesn't seem like the kind of guy who would be into anything criminal. I mean, I know looks can be deceiving, but ..." She broke off as a coughing fit grabbed hold of her lungs.

Then she smelled it.

"Ryan—"

"Smoke," he finished.

They both darted for the attic door. She reached for the metal handle but yelped and snatched her hand back when she touched it.

"What?" Ryan demanded.

"It's hot!" She clutched her burned hand to her chest.

"The fire must be right outside," Ryan growled. He pulled the sleeve of his sweater down to cover his hand and then tried the knob. "It's locked."

Locked.

They were trapped.

Someone wanted to kill them.

This fire couldn't be an accident.

It was arson.

A fire at a murder victim's house hours after he was killed couldn't be anything but.

The killer knew they were here. He'd either been here when they arrived or had arrived shortly after and decided to take them out while presumably destroying any evidence that could lead to his identity.

Her heart began to hammer in her chest.

She'd been claustrophobic ever since her car had been run off the road into a river and she'd been trapped inside as it slowly filled with water.

They were going to die.

The windows were boarded up. They could never get them open and climb outside in time. Smoke was already filling the attic, which a few minutes ago had seemed quite large but now seemed impossibly small.

Air was wheezing in and out of her chest, which felt like it was tightening with each passing second.

"Paige." Ryan's face appeared before her, inches away. "I know you hate small spaces, but you're breathing way too fast. Hyperventilating is going to fill your lungs with smoke too quickly; you have to try to slow your breathing down."

She tried to do as he asked, but she couldn't.

The room was getting so smoky, and as it squeezed oxygen from the air, she was starting to feel sluggish.

Panic was clawing at her.

She wanted to get out of here.

The walls were closing in on her.

The space continued to grow smaller.

Her body continued to grow fuzzier.

Ryan must have noticed because he snatched her up and carried her to the far side of the attic where the smoke was a little thinner.

But that wouldn't last.

The smoke was coming for them.

The fire wouldn't be far behind.

She was going to die in this horrible little room.

She'd been there, done that. She didn't want to do it again.

Paige thought Ryan was talking to her but she couldn't hear him. All she could hear was her pulse thundering in her eyes.

Her vision grayed.

Then faded to black as she slipped into unconsciousness.

* * * * *

2:59 P.M.

Smoke was filling the attic.

Smothering them.

Ryan had moved himself and his partner to the far side of the attic, trying to keep as far away from the thicker smoke as was possible.

Paige had passed out and lay slumped at his side. Her claustrophobia had gotten the best of her. Those hysterical short breaths had sucked the oxygen from her lungs too quickly, and now he was concerned that the panic attack was going to cost her her life. This wasn't the first time he'd seen it push her to the point of fainting, but this was the worst time for her to hyperventilate and then pass out.

He'd called in the fire, and he'd tried to get through the door, but as well as locking it, it looked like whomever had started the fire had also barricaded their way out.

That meant that the intention was for him and Paige to perish.

Obviously, whoever had killed Caden Gervase wanted to make sure that there were no loose ends left behind so had come here to burn the house down. Taking out the two cops investigating the case was probably just a bonus.

He didn't want to die, but he was helpless to do anything about it.

Pressing his fingertips to Paige's neck to make sure she was still alive, Ryan was relived to feel her pulse fluttering weakly. He carefully lifted her upper body and propped her against his knee while he slipped her arms out of her coat then lay her back down, draping the coat over her face. It probably wouldn't do much but it might filter out a little of the smoke.

Then he headed to the boarded-up windows.

Ryan didn't think he could really dislodge them, but he wasn't going to just sit back and wait to die. He couldn't do that to his family.

Quickly, he shoved thoughts of Sofia, Sophie, and Ned from his mind.

He couldn't think about them right now.

If he did, he wouldn't be able to function, and if he couldn't function, then he couldn't get Paige and himself out of here.

After yanking at the wooden planks of wood that blocked their exit for several minutes, he realized it was never going to happen.

They were trapped.

He wanted to keep trying to get out, but the smoke was getting to him.

He felt sluggish. Every movement required effort.

As much as he didn't want to admit it, it was hopeless.

His eyes and his lungs burned from the smoke.

Each breath was a struggle.

They weren't getting out of here alive.

Ryan dragged himself back to Paige, practically falling down at her side. Again, he touched his fingers to her throat and felt her pulse thumping slowly. She didn't have long left.

Neither of them did.

Shrugging off his own coat, he covered his head and pulled Paige closer. At least they didn't have to die alone.

As he rested his head back against the wall, his family flashed before his eyes.

He loved them so much.

They were his world. His heart. His reason for living.

He didn't want to leave them and hated that he had no choice in the matter.

He was getting sleepy.

His eyes wanted to close.

But he knew he couldn't let them.

Once he passed out, death was just around the corner.

Ryan was fighting against it.

He couldn't leave his family without knowing he'd fought death as hard as he could.

Sofia was strong. The strongest woman he'd ever met, but she'd lost so much. How was she going to cope without him?

And his kids were only ten and seven. He was going to miss out on so much.

His eyelids were starting to flutter.

They felt so heavy.

Keeping them open required more strength than he had left.

He mentally apologized to his wife and children for letting them down.

He pictured Sofia's golden-red hair shimmering in the sunshine, her silvery-gray eyes sparkling, the way her hands felt when she traced her fingertips over his body, the way her mouth tasted when he kissed her. She was the most amazing wife, better than he could ever have wished for.

He heard his children's laughs.

His eyes finally fell closed.

Then he heard a loud splintering crash and footsteps pounding toward him.

Firefighters appeared before him, and for a moment, he feared it might be a mirage.

But then one of them crouched down, ripped off his mask, and grabbed Paige.

It was Elias.

His partner's husband.

Elias held his cheek above Paige's mouth, his fingers on her neck.

"Is she still alive?" Ryan asked. It came out like a harsh, barely recognizable croak, but Elias obviously understood him because he gave one hard nod, then put his mask on Paige. "I don't think you're supposed to do that," he said. A firefighter wasn't supposed to remove their mask in the middle of a fire.

Elias just glared and scooped Paige's unresponsive form into his arms.

Ryan wasn't sure how he was going to walk out of here; just keeping his eyes open was almost more than he could manage.

His problem was solved when an arm hooked around his shoulders and he was dragged to his feet.

Then they were moving.

Flames leapt and danced about them, the house was an inferno. If Elias and his team hadn't found them when they had, then he and Paige would have died in here.

His lungs twitched as they finally burst out into the fresh air.

Elias was swaying; he'd breathed in too much smoke.

People swarmed toward them, and Ryan spotted his brother Jack, and Jack's partner, Xavier Montague, among them. Xavier took Paige from Elias and headed for the closest ambulance.

Ryan dropped to his knees as fit after fit of wracking coughs gripped him in an unrelenting vice.

Jack and the firefighter who had pulled him out of the burning building yanked him back up onto his feet and farther away from the fire.

The world around him was as fuzzy as it had been up in the smoke-filled attic, and it grew distant, as though he wasn't really a part of it anymore.

The next thing he knew, he was sitting in the back of an ambulance wearing an oxygen mask.

Already, his breathing felt easier, although his throat still felt like he'd swallowed a pot of boiling water. He turned. Paige lay on a gurney, her skin ashen, eyes closed, also wearing an oxygen mask. Elias sat at her side, clutching her hand.

Tugging away his mask, Ryan asked, "Is she all right?"

"Her pulse is stronger," Elias replied, voice rough from both the smoke and emotion.

"Put the mask back on," Jack ordered. The glare of the paramedic beside him echoed that sentiment.

Ryan complied, then rested his head back against the side of the ambulance and just concentrated on filling his lungs with clear, fresh oxygen.

When he felt better, he tugged the mask away again, earning him glares from the paramedics, his brother, and Xavier. He didn't care. The better he felt, the angrier he felt.

Someone had just tried to kill him.

Very nearly succeeded.

Almost ripped him away from his wife and kids.

That was unacceptable.

He *would* make sure this killer was found.

"This wasn't a coincidence," he rasped.

"There were two dressers in front of the attic door," Elias supplied.

"He wanted us dead," Ryan growled, ignoring the way the words tore at his throat.

"Did you see anyone?" Jack asked.

"No, and Paige and I walked the whole house before we went up to the attic."

"So he came once you were already there. Or he was here and saw you go in and waited for you to be distracted before striking," Xavier said.

"It has to be the same person who killed Caden." Ryan twisted so he could see the burning house.

"Did you find anything?" Jack asked.

"No. At least, not before we noticed the smoke. And now whatever secrets the house held are gone." He felt helpless. He wanted to find the person who had killed Caden Gervase, who had traumatized his nephew, who had almost left his wife a widow and his children without a father, but right now they didn't know what direction to turn in. They didn't have any leads, except possibly Daisy, and depending on what her relationship was with Caden, she might not even know anything useful.

"He won't get away with this," his brother said quietly, darkly. They were a close family, and when someone messed with one of them, they messed with all of them. "But first, you and Paige go to the hospital to get checked out."

"Paige needs to go, but I'm fine," he insisted. He didn't want to be stuck in a hospital bed while everyone else worked this case.

"You know better than that, Ryan," his bossy older brother rebuked. "Smoke inhalation is serious, and there can be complications. Go. Get checked out, then go and see Sofia and the kids. Xavier and I will stay here, see what the arson investigators find, then tomorrow we'll work on finding answers."

There was no point in arguing. He knew his brother was right. And he *was* aching to see his family. They would find this killer. He just hoped it didn't end up destroying Mark's family in the process.

* * * * *

53

8:44 P.M.

Walking into his house felt weird ever since Daisy had moved out.

It no longer felt like home.

Now it just felt like the building he lived in.

Mark was working hard to try to make the changes as seamless as possible for the kids' sake, but it was hard. His job was time-consuming with unpredictable hours, but his family was helping out, and Brian had been really stepping it up, helping out with his younger siblings whenever he could.

And yet, without his wife there, things just felt wrong.

He was going to have to get used to it.

Daisy had made it abundantly clear that she had no interest in returning home, and if he was right and she had been having an affair with Caden Gervase, then he wasn't sure he wanted her back anyway.

It was going to take a lot of adjusting for all of them to get used to, but it was what it was. They were just going to have to make the best of things.

Mark set his keys down on the small table by the front door, then locked up and set the alarm. He hadn't wanted to leave Tony alone after what his son had experienced this morning, but Ryan and Paige had almost been killed in a fire, and he couldn't not go and check on his brother and one of his closest friends. Ryan had been treated and discharged and gone home with his family. Paige had been admitted and would be kept overnight, but she'd been conscious, lucid, and trying to talk despite the obvious pain it caused.

They were alive and mostly unharmed, but this case was hitting far too close to home. His wife's boyfriend murdered, his son finding the body, his brother and friend almost killed by the same man. It was too much.

Despite what he'd said earlier at the school, he didn't really think Daisy was involved in any of this.

At least, he *hoped* she wasn't.

He would never have suspected the "old Daisy," but this new one—well, he had to admit he didn't know his wife as well as he'd thought he did.

Bypassing the kitchen, he couldn't stomach the thought of eating right now. Mark headed upstairs to check on the kids.

The girls' room was first. Although there were enough bedrooms in the house that Eve and Elise didn't have to share one, they had always insisted on it. He wondered how much longer that would last. His girls were growing up; sooner or later, they would want their own space.

That was a scary thought.

He knocked on their door.

"Come in," Eve called out.

Mark opened the door and saw his daughters lying together on Eve's bed, pouring over something on one of their iPads. They were teenagers now. Gone were the pink walls and princess décor. In its place were mint green walls and posters of teen heartthrobs. Already his sweet little babies were into makeup and boys and asking about going on dates.

He wasn't ready for this.

How was he going to do this?

How was he going to raise two teenage daughters on his own without their mother?

"Dad."

He blinked and realized he'd zoned out. "What, honey?" He faked a smile.

"Are Uncle Ryan and Paige okay?" Elise asked.

"They will be," he assured them and came to sit on the edge of the bed. "How are you two doing after today?"

The girls exchanged glances. "We're really sorry we didn't stay with Tony like we were supposed to," Eve said, her big blue eyes watery with unshed tears.

He wasn't angry with the girls. They should have done what he'd told them to, but really, Tony wouldn't have been put in this position if it weren't for Daisy.

"Next time you do as you're asked," he told them.

Eve looked surprised they weren't getting in trouble. "You're letting us off easy—"

"Because of Mom," Elise finished. "You're mad at her."

Despite what Daisy had done, he wouldn't badmouth her in front of their children.

"Is she going to come back now?" Eve asked, hope replacing the unshed tears in her eyes.

"I don't think so, honey."

"Oh." She dropped her gaze to the bedspread.

"We thought maybe after what happened, after what Tony saw, that maybe she would realize she missed us and come back," Elise explained.

His heart broke for his kids. If Daisy had decided she didn't love him anymore and wanted to end their relationship, then she could at least have done it in a way that gave closure to all of them. She should have filed for divorce and worked out a custody arrangement with him so their children didn't feel like they'd been abandoned.

"I don't think she's coming back, girls," he said honestly. As much as he didn't want to hurt his kids, he also didn't want to give them false hope. And it seemed like the girls were still holding out hope that their mother would return and things would go back to the way they'd been before, but he didn't think that was going to happen.

"Maybe she will once she gets over her midlife crisis," Elise persisted.

Midlife crisis. He wished that was all that was going on with Daisy, but he had a feeling that it ran much deeper than that. "I don't think that's going to happen. I know it's hard, but we have to respect Mom's choices. I don't want you two staying up too late tonight, okay?"

"Okay," both girls said simultaneously.

"Eve, you want help checking your blood sugars before bed?" Eve had been diagnosed with type one diabetes almost eighteen months ago. So far they'd managed to keep things fairly well under control, and Eve was very independent checking her blood sugars and administering insulin as required. He was proud his little girl was able to handle something so big with such a mature and positive attitude, but it was just another reminder that she was growing up whether he liked it or not.

"No, I'll be fine," she replied.

"Okay, then, sweet dreams." He kissed both girls on the forehead. "I love you."

"Love you, too, Dad," they said, their attention already reverting to whatever they'd been doing before he entered the room.

"Mom should be here for Tony." Brian's angry face met him as he closed the girls' bedroom door behind him.

"She should," he agreed.

"I guess she cares more about her dead boyfriend than her own son." Brian looked disgusted. "Or maybe it's guilt because she had something to do with the murder."

"Brian," he rebuked, although he wondered again just how tied up in Caden and what had happened Daisy might be.

"What? I think it's like eighty percent of murder victims are killed by someone they know. Most of those by a partner. Based on the statistics, Mom could very easily have been involved."

Mark wasn't surprised that his oldest had looked up the statistics, but he didn't like his children thinking of their mother as a murderer. Even if he had some doubts about Daisy's innocence.

He was also a little interested to find out why Brian thought Daisy and Caden were a couple. "What do you know?"

Brian arched a blond brow. "I saw them together. In the park. They weren't doing anything—I mean, kissing or making out or anything—but what other possible reason would they have to be together in the park? If they wanted to talk about school stuff, Eve and Elise, then they'd do it at the school in his office. There was no other reason for them to be together at the park except they wanted to spend time together without anyone seeing them."

Unfortunately, Mark agreed with his son's assessment. Out of the corner of his eye, he noticed Tony's bedroom door ease closed. His youngest had overheard their conversation.

"Brian, try to give your mom a break, okay?"

"Why?" Defiance gleamed in his son's eyes.

"Because I'm asking you to." He and Daisy might be over, but she was still the mother of his children, and despite everything, he still loved her and felt protective of her.

"Whatever," Brian mumbled, turning away.

"Don't stay up too late," he said as Brian went into the bathroom. His son had a bad habit of studying well into the early hours of the morning. He knew Brian took his studies seriously and wanted to do well so he could be accepted into a pre-med program with a full scholarship, but he still needed sleep.

Brian just grunted and closed the bathroom door. Mark let out a breath and headed for Tony's room. Inside he found his ten-year-old standing in the middle of the room looking lost.

"Is it true?" Tony fidgeted with the hem of his T-shirt. "Was Mom dating Principal Gervase?"

"I don't know," he answered honestly. He always preferred to be honest with his children unless there was no other option.

"Why would she do that?" Tony looked up at him, looking so small and young tonight.

"I don't know," he replied again. It hurt. A lot. Most of the time he tried to keep his own feelings about Daisy leaving well buried so he could keep his focus on the kids, but every now and then that pain stabbed brutally at his heart making sure he knew it hadn't gone anywhere. "How are you doing, bud?"

Tony shrugged.

"Would you like me to sleep in here tonight? On the floor beside your bed?" He was asking for his own benefit as much as his son's. He wanted his kids close to him tonight.

"You don't have to," Tony said, looking decidedly undecided.

"It doesn't make you a baby to be scared, bud. *Everyone* gets scared sometimes, grown-ups too. If I'd seen what you saw today, I'd want to have someone there with me."

"But you don't anymore. You're alone now that Mom's gone."

There would always be a hole in his heart left by Daisy, but he was never alone so long as he had his family. "I've got you and your sisters and brother," he reminded Tony, who looked thoughtful now, and much more grown up than he had a couple of minutes ago.

"Then you can sleep in here tonight, and that way we'll both have someone."

He ruffled his son's hair. "Sounds like a plan. I'll go grab a pillow and some blankets."

Before he could turn around, the door to Tony's room swung open and Eve and Elise stood there in their pajamas, pillows in their hands. "Dad, can we sleep in your room tonight?" Eve asked.

He couldn't help but smile. His kids might be growing up, but they hadn't grown up all the way yet. They still needed him, and he would be there for them, whatever they needed. Always.

* * * * *

10:11 P.M.

They thought she was involved.

Daisy had seen it in their eyes.

Not just her husband, but her brother-in-law and friend, too.

It hurt.

A lot.

But she couldn't blame them. She had been acting so out of character lately.

It wasn't what she wanted.

None of this was what she wanted.

She just didn't know how to change it.

Despite what her husband and the others thought, she was *not* having an affair with Caden Gervase or anyone else. She didn't want to have an affair. She wasn't interested in anyone else. She loved her husband.

That wasn't what this was about.

She hadn't walked away from her family because she didn't love them anymore or because she didn't want to be with them anymore. She had walked away because she had no other choice. For now, this was how things had to be, no matter how much she hated it.

And she did hate it.

It felt weird living in a hotel. It wasn't a home. It wasn't *her* home. She missed her home. She missed that feeling she got when she walked in the door, that feeling of peace and belonging, of safety and warmth. She missed cooking dinner and then sitting down with her family to eat. She missed checking on the kids' homework and driving them to and from their activities. She missed going to bed at night with her husband's warm body at her side, knowing her kids were all asleep in their rooms just down the hall.

She missed everything about her home.

She hated it here.

She felt so lonely.

Lonelier than she had felt in a very long time.

Mark was right about one thing. She and Caden did have a relationship, just not the kind he thought. She loved him very deeply. He was an important part of her life, and he'd played a big role in it. She missed him terribly already.

Her heart was breaking.

Caden was dead because of her.

She had brought him into this.

His death was her fault.

Daisy moved from the window and dropped down onto the bed, curling up into a little ball as the tears came.

They came like a hurricane.

Ripping through her entire being.

It tore her up inside.

He was a good man. He hadn't deserved to be murdered.

Had he known what was happening? Was he awake? Had he been killed quickly? Had he suffered? Did he know his killer?

She had to assume he did.

Who else could it be?

Her tears didn't let up. Her chest ached from the heaving sobs, and her eyes burned from the never-ending flow of tears.

Time faded into nothingness as she lay on the bed crying.

The pain was too much.

She couldn't bear it.

She couldn't survive this.

Grief and guilt were going to rip her to shreds.

And there was no one to help her.

She was alone.

Completely alone.

There was no one to support her. No one to lift her up. No one to hold her. No one to comfort her.

She was broken.

She shouldn't have brought Caden into her mess. If she hadn't, he would still be alive.

She may as well have held a gun to his head and killed him herself.

Daisy wasn't sure how her friend had been murdered, but she could guess that it was bad.

She didn't know what to do.

What was the right choice?

She wasn't even sure she was capable of making choices right now. She hurt so much. She just wanted to lie here in this hotel room in this bed and cry for the rest of her life. It was what she deserved. Someone had to pay for what had happened, and it should be her. Not Caden and not anyone else. Just her.

Wave after relentless wave of tears kept coming. Every time she thought they were easing, she would picture Caden's face or hear his voice, and a fresh barrage of tears would assault her.

It wasn't fair.

Life wasn't fair.

She'd known that for a very long time, and yet, sometimes the reality of it really hit close to home.

Home.

She couldn't let this darkness touch her sanctuary and the people she loved who lived inside it.

But how could she stop it?

She honestly didn't know.

She had kept her secrets for so many years, she didn't know how to let anyone in.

And what would they think of her if they knew? Would they still love her? Would they see her differently? Would they see her for the dirty, disgusting creature she felt like?

Daisy wasn't sure she could take it if they turned their backs on her.

She had to keep her secrets. There was no other choice. But like it or not, soon they were going to find out who she really was. It was inevitable. There was no way to stop it from happening.

She felt so helpless.

Another violent fit of tears grabbed hold of her, and for the next few minutes conscious thought left her, and all she did was cry.

In a way, the tears felt good. They felt freeing. They were an outlet for her pain—a way to let it out before it grew so big inside her that it killed her.

Eventually, her cries dwindled and her tears dried up.

Exhausted, Daisy just lay there, trying to recover from the emotional and physical toll weeping had taken on her.

She felt so drained.

Drained and yet as tired as her body was her brain just couldn't switch off. This was why she hadn't been sleeping much lately. Every time she lay down in bed, all she did was think. And the more she thought, the more agitated she became. And the more agitated she became, the more awake she was.

Sleeping right now was a luxury she couldn't afford.

Dragging herself out of bed, Daisy stumbled to the bathroom. She missed the light switch three times before her hand finally contacted it and stark white light filled the room.

She stared at herself in the mirror. She almost didn't recognize herself. She looked so much older, and she'd lost weight. Her cheekbones were too prominent, and her cheeks were starting to hollow out.

Maybe the changes in her physical appearance would help her. She could dye her blonde hair brown, maybe get some contacts to make her eyes brown as well. She could even get a fake tan, add some color to her porcelain doll like appearance. She'd already moved out of her house. If she made herself look different enough, then maybe he wouldn't be able to find her.

No.

No matter what she did—no matter how much she changed her appearance—he would find her.

It was inevitable.

He would come.

Unless she found him first.

Turning on the cold tap, Daisy splashed some water on her face, washing away the tears and refocusing herself.

She didn't have time for a pity party.

A pity party was only going to get her killed.

She had to keep working. There was still a chance that she

could end this before he came for her.

How? She didn't know that yet. But she couldn't give up. Giving up spelled certain death. As long as she was breathing, she still stood a chance.

She and Caden had gone through every potential scenario they could think of. Trying to figure out everything he would try and everything they could do to stop him, attempting to decide on a course of action.

In the end, they hadn't been able to decide.

And now she was on her own.

It was all up to her.

She had to figure out what her next best move was.

She shut off the water and didn't bother drying off. She kind of liked the feel of the cold water on her hot skin; it was refreshing. Grabbing her laptop, she sat down at the table and turned it on.

It would help if she knew for sure just who she was looking for. Daisy was pretty positive she knew, but there was no way to be certain. Who else could it be? As far as she knew, he was the only one left and the only who would want to hurt her. Everyone else was dead.

She would find him.

She would search every corner of the internet until it led her to him.

What scared her most was what was she going to do when she found him?

Go to the police? That might get her family killed.

Confront him herself? That was likely to get herself killed, and she wasn't sure she had what it took to kill him.

That didn't really leave her many options.

She would just have to worry about that when the time came. For now, she needed to focus on finding where he was hiding out.

Doing what she had every single night since she'd moved out of her home, Daisy scoured the internet in search of her own personal boogeyman.

JANUARY 25TH

2:14 A.M.

He was in a pretty good mood.

A *very* good mood.

Life was good.

He had waited so many years for this. Patiently biding his time until he was ready to make a move. And now was that time. Now he was ready to strike, and he was going to strike every single person who was responsible for destroying his life. He was going to get his revenge.

Now he was going to revel in every delicious second of making his enemies suffer.

It was going to be perfect.

He had a plan, and he was going to stick to it. He'd have to if he wanted to finish off everyone on his list before the cops figured out who he was and came for him. He was going to have to be careful and work smart.

He had picked the order very carefully. Starting off with some of the easier targets. There should be plenty to keep the cops busy. Yesterday's victim should have them in a tizzy trying to figure out who would kill a nice middle school principal and coming up empty. While tonight's victim would leave them trying to figure out who of the many potential suspects was the killer.

There was a connection between the victims, but the cops would have to dig to figure it out. Hopefully, they wouldn't find that connection until he was finished and had slunk back into the obscurity he had been hiding in for most of his life.

He thought of himself as a shadow, a ghost, an apparition.

In fact, *The Apparition* was his nickname.

He flitted around the edges of society. There but not really there. Seen but not really seen. Heard but not really heard. He existed, and yet, at the same time, he didn't.

The man he was visiting tonight was certainly going to wish he didn't exist.

But, unfortunately for Devon Paddy, he was all too real.

By the end of the night, it was Devon who would cease to exist.

He was a little excited. He'd never thought of himself as a killer before. Yes, he'd taken lives, but that was just business, tying up loose ends, doing what had to be done. This was personal.

Yesterday had been fun. He'd enjoyed the fear, the resignation, the realization in Caden Gervase's eyes.

It had been exhilarating.

He'd never felt that way before.

He had never gotten a rush from killing; it had always been a bit mundane. A cleaning up task that needed to be done that he neither hated nor loved. But now, it felt different. Now, it felt right. He had waited so long, and now he was finally doing what he'd dreamed about. He was getting his revenge. He was getting his justice. He was getting exactly what he deserved.

Carefully, he crept out of his hiding place. His muscles were cramped from being crammed into the too small space for so long.

He'd arrived here several hours ago. After watching Devon for weeks, he'd gotten a feel for the man's routine and decided that breaking in while he was at work would be best. He'd wanted to be prepared, but he wasn't sure that this kill would go as easy as the other one. Caden was a man in his fifties, and according to his research, he was dying of a brain tumor. He hadn't expected Caden to put up a fight, and he hadn't.

Tonight's target, Devon Paddy, was forty-five and a cop. Cops were tricky because they tended to be more safety conscious and careful than the average person.

But he had no intention of walking out of this house without having achieved his goal.

He *would* kill Devon Paddy.

And he *would* kill everyone else on his list.

Every single person who had played a part in ruining his life was going to pay. It only seemed fair. They had hurt him, and he was hurting them back. An eye for an eye and all that.

While he'd felt safe and comfortable killing Caden in a more public environment and at a riskier time of day, he didn't feel comfortable taking those risks with Devon.

Killing Caden at the school had added to the excitement, knowing that someone could potentially stumble upon them.

That kid almost *had.*

He'd changed his sweater, scrubbed his face and hands, and then hurried away, only to walk headlong into some kid. He'd been annoyed; although it was kind of fun to think that someone might walk in on him teaching Caden a lesson, he didn't really want it to happen. He didn't want to go to prison. He wanted to finish what he'd started. After waiting so long, it would be devastating to be forced to stop this close to getting retribution.

The kid could ID him. That could become a problem. And yet, the thought of killing the boy had never occurred to him. He killed only when it was necessary. And killing the kid wasn't necessary, so he'd let him walk away. He prayed that wasn't going to wind up being a mistake.

He wasn't going to worry about that right now.

Now he was just going to have fun and enjoy his evening.

Devon Paddy was single, divorced, and his only kid lived with her mother on the other side of the city so there would be no one to get in the way. He didn't want to kill anyone who hadn't been involved in the plot to destroy him. He would if he had to; he just didn't want to. But, thankfully, tonight it wouldn't be an issue.

Tiptoeing up the stairs and down the hall, he paused at the

bedroom door. He could hardly believe he was really here. It was so exciting.

Before proceeding, he scanned the room thoroughly. Devon was in bed, his breathing heavy and even. He sounded like he was asleep. He waited for a moment to make sure that the man wasn't faking, then when he was sure the man was indeed sleeping, he stepped closer.

He wasn't afraid.

He was doing what was right, and nothing was going to stop him. Justice was on his side.

Striding toward the bed, knife in his hand, he didn't pause, just swung the knife toward the man in the bed.

Devon woke midswing, but he didn't have a chance to react before the blade sliced through his flesh and buried itself deep in his shoulder. He wasn't a doctor, and he didn't have any medical training, so he hoped the stab wound was well placed and wasn't going to make the man bleed out too quickly. After what Devon had done to him, he didn't deserve a quick, painless death.

The man's eyes grew wide. In the dark, they looked like two bottomless pits. The cop in Devon spurred into action, and he fumbled for the nightstand.

He couldn't allow the man to arm himself or to start screaming, which was self-defense 101. Yanking out the knife, he plunged it up, through the man's lower jaw and up into his upper jaw and nose.

Devon tried to claw at the knife protruding from his head. With the man distracted, he pulled out another knife and grabbed one of the cop's hands. Immediately, Devon tried to fight him. That was tedious. The man had caused him enough trouble; he wasn't having any more.

Digging his fingers into Devon's bloody shoulder wound, not because it really achieved anything but because he just wanted to, he shoved one of Devon's hands up against the wall behind the bed and rammed the knife through it, pinning him in place.

While the man—now groggy from blood loss and pain—tried to reach for the knife, he took hold of his other hand and similarly attached it to the wall.

Then he stood back and admired his handiwork.

There was a lot of blood. He hadn't quite realized just how much people bled when you stabbed them until yesterday. Usually, he just went with a snap of the neck—clean, quick, efficient. It got the job done, and that was all he needed. But this was so much more fun.

"Do you know who I am?" he asked.

Devon's eyes had glazed over a little. He couldn't have that, not yet at least. He wanted this man to suffer. He wanted him to feel every single stab of pain that was inflicted on him, just like he had.

He jabbed the man and repeated, "Do you know who I am?"

The movement jarred Devon, and no doubt jostled all of his wounds, but his eyes cleared, and he shook his head.

"No? Well, that's okay. I know who you are, and I remember what you did to me. By the end of tonight, it's all going to come back to you." Reaching into the bag he'd brought with him, he pulled out a pair of scissors. He'd bought them, especially for tonight. He positioned them around one of Devon's fingers, then paused and grinned. "It's time to take a little trip down memory lane."

The gargled scream when he snapped the scissors closed was music to his ears.

* * * * *

8:48 A.M.

"You two taking over the case?" crime scene tech Diane Jolly asked as they stepped into the house.

"We're working *this* case," Detective Xavier Montague replied.

"Right now we don't know that the two cases are related."

A fifty-year-old middle school principal and a forty-five-year-old cop didn't appear to have a lot in common. At least, on the surface. But someone had almost killed Paige and Ryan in an attempt to burn down Caden Gervase's house. A successful attempt it was; the house was completely destroyed. Whatever evidence might have been there was now gone. That someone had bothered to go to all the trouble and risk of setting fire to the house suggested that there had, in fact, been something there that the killer hadn't wanted the cops to get their hands on.

Which hinted that perhaps Caden might have been mixed up in something he shouldn't have been. Something bad. Something that got him tortured and killed.

So, maybe there was a connection after all.

Although what that could be, Xavier had no idea.

"So you two are working this case. Who's working the Gervase case?" Diane asked.

"Ryan and Paige," Jack replied.

His partner didn't sound pleased about that. No doubt he didn't like the idea of his brother and friend returning to work so soon after nearly dying in a fire. But Ryan was already cleared to return to work, and Paige would be back tomorrow.

He echoed Jack's concerns, but if they'd been medically cleared, then he didn't see any way to stop them from working, and voicing their concerns was only going to irritate both Ryan and Paige. They'd been friends for a decade now, and they'd been through a lot together. He was closer with them than he was with most of his own family.

Jack and his wife, Laura; Ryan and his wife, Sofia; Paige and her husband, Elias—they had supported him through the ups and downs in his relationship with Annabelle. They'd stood up for him at his wedding, and they'd been there every step of the way through the last six months of Annabelle's pregnancy as she suffered from violent morning sickness. They were the friends of a lifetime, and friends he would lay down his life for. That someone had tried to kill them got his blood boiling.

They *would* find who'd done it. Anything less was unacceptable.

"You think this case is related to the principal?" Jack asked.

Diane nodded as she pulled her shoulder-length gray hair into a ponytail. The crime scene tech had recently celebrated her sixtieth birthday and was retiring in a month, but she'd had gray hair as long as he'd known her.

"Any particular reason?" Xavier asked. To him, the settings of both crimes were sufficiently different that they indicated a different perpetrator. From the relatively high-risk location of the first murder to the relatively low-risk location of this one. It seemed like going backward. The killer had struck at Caden's workplace at a time when he'd known that colleagues and students would soon be arriving. Why would he go backward to kill someone in their home in the middle of the night?

"Yep," Diane replied but didn't elaborate.

"Care to elaborate?"

"Nope, but you'll see when you get to the bedroom."

"That where the killer struck?" he asked.

"Yes."

If this was the same killer, he had really played things safe this time. Striking when his victim was asleep and vulnerable was completely different than striking when the victim was able to fight back. Whatever they were going to find when they saw the body must be pretty compelling if it had led Diane to believe that the two cases were related.

"You found anything yet?" Jack asked.

"I think so. Over here." Diane led them through the house and into a den near the back. "It looks like this is where he came in." She stopped next to one of the windows. "See here?" She pointed to the sill where there were a few wood shavings.

"He pried open the window," he said.

"That would be my guess," Diane confirmed. "Looks like he

gouged away enough wood that he could get something underneath the window and force it up."

So whoever had killed Devon Paddy had been determined. He'd also been careful to make sure that the cop didn't know he was here. This room didn't look like it was used very often. Did the killer know that or was it just a coincidence? The window was hidden around the side of the house where he wouldn't have been seen by anyone as he worked away at getting inside.

A thought occurred to him. "Can you and your team check to see if you think he was hiding out someplace in the house?"

"You think he broke in earlier and laid in wait?" Jack asked.

"I think it makes sense. If he knew the guy was a cop, then breaking a window and coming in in the middle of the night would have been riskier. But if he broke in and hid, waited until he was sure Devon was asleep before striking, it would be much safer."

"Will do," Diane said.

"Thanks. Want to go up to the bedroom?" he asked his partner.

"Sure, call us if you find anything, Di," Jack said as they left the den to head upstairs to Devon Paddy's bedroom.

When Xavier walked into the room, the amount of blood splattered across the walls, the bed, the floor, was scarily reminiscent of the crimes that had first led him to Annabelle. For a moment, the sense of déjà vu was disconcerting, and he had to remind himself that that killer was long since dead and buried.

Whoever had committed this crime seemed to have an affinity for blood that almost rivaled that of the man who had ripped Annabelle's family from her.

There was a lot of anger in this room.

Especially when you looked at the body.

"How bad is it?" he asked the medical examiner.

"Pretty bad," Billy replied. "Evidence of torture."

That was in line with the Gervase body.

"There are several stab wounds. One to his shoulder, one to each of his hands, and one that goes up from under his jaw and through the roof of his mouth with the tip stopping just into his nose." Billy shuddered. Xavier had known the medical examiner for approaching two decades, and he'd never seen him this emotional at a crime scene.

The body was slumped over on the bed. It was hard to see what else the killer had done to him. "What else?"

"At least a couple dozen cuts of varying depths all over his arms and upper body."

"He wanted the man to suffer," Xavier said quietly. This was just like Caden Gervase's killer. Both crime scenes virtually screamed a deep seeded rage aimed directly at the victims. Both men knew their killer—he was sure of it.

"Cause of death exsanguination?" Jack asked.

It seemed logical given the gaping wound to Devon's neck, and Billy nodded.

"Defensive wounds?" Jack asked.

"None that I can see," the medical examiner replied. "I'll know more when I do a full autopsy, but for now, I'm going to say no."

"So he most likely caught Devon still asleep, managed to get in at least one wound before the man was awake and able to fight back," he observed.

"Looks like he brought multiple weapons with him," Billy added. "I don't see signs of restraints around his wrists or ankles, so I'd guess he stabbed a knife through Devon's hands and into the wall here ..." He gestured at one bloody spot on the wall, and then another. "... and here. Also guessing he used one of the knives as a gag. With the knife through his mouth as it was, Devon wouldn't have been able to speak or yell for help."

Sadistic and yet it seemed to fit perfectly with the picture that was building in his mind of the man they were looking for.

"Diane said that there was something here that implied a connection between Devon Paddy and Caden Gervase," Jack said.

73

"There is." Billy carefully lifted one of Devon's hands. "He's missing fingers, just like Caden Gervase was. The killer took off seven of Caden's fingers, and six of Devon's."

The significance of that struck him immediately.

It was a countdown.

The killer had started out with seven specific victims in mind. Two were now dead. That left five more.

Five innocent people going about their lives unaware that their days were numbered.

Or maybe not.

If these murders were personal, then maybe these five people knew what was coming. Maybe they knew that the things they'd done were going to catch up with them sooner or later. Maybe they'd been looking over their shoulders waiting for this day to come.

Devon Paddy was a cop, and yet the killer had taken him out without a fuss. This guy was organized; he planned things out. He knew what he was doing, and he did it with ease.

It had been a long time since he and Jack had worked a case with Ryan and Paige, but it looked like that was about to change. He was now convinced that their two cases were, in fact, one, and if this killer was counting down to something, then they could expect at least five more victims to fall before he was done.

* * * * *

11:32 A.M.

The jolt from the shock collar had not only knocked her to the ground, but it had also knocked the wind out of her sails.

Colette hadn't done anything since then.

She hadn't been knocked unconscious from the zap, just momentarily lost control of her body. It had been pure agony like someone had set her blood on fire—it burned up and down her entire body. By the time it had faded enough that she could move, her abductor had opened the cage, deposited her meal, relocked the door, and left the basement.

She hadn't touched the food.

Or the other two meals that had been delivered since.

She had no appetite.

She was perfectly happy starving to death.

She had no will to live left.

She had crawled into a corner of her cage, the one farthest from the door, pressed her back up against the bars, pulled her knees to her chest, buried her head in them, and sat there.

That was it.

She wasn't angry anymore. What was the point of being angry? Yes, she had been tricked; yes, she had been drugged and kidnapped; yes, she had been locked up in a cage like an animal, but being angry wasn't going to change any of that. It wouldn't solve her problems.

She was stuck here indefinitely.

She accepted that.

She just wished she would hurry up and die already.

Colette knew that death was the only way she was walking out of this room.

She was a little disappointed in herself.

She would never have thought she would give up this quickly. She thought she was a fighter. She had survived so much. She had started sleeping with a knife under her pillow at the age of nine when her father's drinking buddies began to come knocking on her door. She had fought them off several times before the first one managed to get out of her what he'd come for.

It had been the worst night of her life.

Made infinitely more horrific by the fact that her father had stood in the doorway and watched without lifting a finger to help her.

Instead of saving her, watching one of his friends rape her had given him an idea. She was young, only twelve by then, and his friends were drunken losers who liked little girls. He took advantage of that. Soon, he was making good money off pimping her out.

But she'd fought back.

She'd packed her bags and run.

Only it seemed she had run straight from the fire and into the frying pan.

And now the fight seemed to have drained out of her.

She was tired.

Tired of fighting, tired of hurting, tired of living.

"Hey."

It was Heather.

The other girl had been sporadically attempting to talk to her, but Colette was ignoring her.

She didn't want to talk.

She wanted to wallow in the hopelessness of it all.

"Please don't give up," Heather continued. "We can't. We have to believe that someone will find us, rescue us."

How could Heather still believe that? She had been here for almost three years. She had given birth to two children who'd been snatched away, and she was soon to lose her third. No one had come for Heather, and no one was going to come for her, either. Who would? Her father could just move on to her younger sister to make money. Her mother was rarely sober enough to know what was going on around her. She didn't have friends. There was no one to notice she was gone or care about what happened to her.

"You can't just sit there and give up. If you do, he'll just kill you," Heather pleaded.

That caught her attention.

How did Heather know that?

Had she seen it happen before?

How many other girls like her and Heather had these men

kidnapped?

Her curiosity got the better of her, and she lifted her head to find Heather sitting at the bars between their cages.

"What's your name?"

"Colette," she whispered. "How many others?"

"Have been here?"

"Yes."

"Two others while I've been here—Joanna and Cara. A girl called Skylar was here for just a short time. Joanna had been here for almost four years, and she knew of another three girls—Lillie, Freya, and Tasha. I don't how many there have been before that."

"What happened to them? The others?" Colette was sure she knew the answer, but she needed to hear it said out loud.

"They were killed. At least, I assume they were. One day they were just taken away and never came back. I can't imagine that they'd let us go. They know we'd go straight to the police, so they were probably murdered, their bodies dumped where no one would ever find them."

"Who are *they*?" She was feeling so out of control. Maybe having answers would help her. Knowledge was power, and perhaps, if she and Heather worked together, they could find a way to escape.

"I don't know their names," Heather replied. "The younger guy ... he's the one who brings us our meals."

"Did he trick you too?"

"Yes. I was a runaway. He offered to help me ... I thought he was just a kid like me who'd run away from a home he couldn't stand to live in for another second. As soon as he got me alone, he tried to make out with me. I didn't want to, but it distracted me long enough that I didn't notice the other man until it was too late."

Heather may as well be repeating her own story. "Who is the other man?"

"I'm not sure, but we call him the Scar Man."

"I don't remember seeing any scars on his face," Colette said.

"Not on his face—on his chest, a huge ragged scar that runs from his left shoulder down across his chest and abdomen. It disappears down below his waist."

"How do you know about the scar?" she scooted closer toward Heather, suddenly needing the comforting presence of another human being.

"I've seen it."

"Did he …?" She couldn't even make herself say the word. "Is that how you got pregnant?"

"No, he never raped me. No one has. Other than shocking me a few times with the collar when I first got here and still wanted to rebel and not follow the rules, no one has physically hurt me."

Colette might have believed that if Heather hadn't averted her gaze. Maybe these men hadn't beaten her or hit her or kicked her, but they had certainly done something to her. She'd had three babies against her will; she hadn't gotten pregnant by immaculate conception.

"If they didn't rape you, then how …" She trailed off as the door to the basement clunked open. Was it mealtime again?

Her stomach growled loudly; maybe she *should* eat something. If she let herself waste away, she'd stand no chance at getting out of here. She couldn't give up. No matter how much she wanted to. Someone would come. One of her teachers would notice she hadn't turned up to school in a while and report her missing. The police would find her; she just had to make sure she was alive when it happened.

"I didn't think we'd be able to get to work with you so quickly, Colette, but you're actually ovulating right now." Her abductor spoke so matter-of-factly, like impregnating her while she was his prisoner was no big deal.

She was *not* letting this man get her pregnant.

She was not providing him with any babies to sell on the black market.

A thought occurred to her.

If she didn't provide them with a baby, would they kill her? How many chances would she get?

Her gaze fell on the exam table in the middle of the room, and she realized how they intended to try and get her pregnant.

Artificial insemination.

It was all so clinical. So well thought out. So business like.

This was crazy.

She backed farther away from the man, then realized he wasn't alone.

A woman was standing behind him.

She looked about his age—early twenties. She was pretty, with large brown eyes, and long, chocolate-colored hair that reached all the way down her back.

How could a woman be involved in this sick plan?

How could she let other women be abducted and forced to provide babies for them to sell?

Women were supposed to stick together against all the sick, perverted men in the world, not help them hurt other women.

Apparently, they anticipated she wasn't going to be very cooperative because a jolt of pain started in her neck and shot out along every inch of her body.

She heard her cage being opened, and she heard them coming toward her. She wanted to fight or run or do something, but all she could do was whimper and jerk in pain. She was scooped off the floor and carried to the exam table where she was deposited. Straps secured her stomach, chest, arms, thighs, and ankles in place and prevented her from moving.

With her legs spread wide in stirrups, her private parts were exposed for all to see, and she felt her cheeks flush with humiliation as the woman pulled up a stool between her open legs.

"Don't, please," she whispered. "Just let me go. I won't tell anyone, I promise."

Both the man and the woman ignored her.

The woman picked up something with long metal arms. Colette couldn't remember what it was called, but she remembered learning about it in health class and knew what it did. Her bottom began to wiggle in protest, trying to prevent that thing from breaching her body. But with her legs in stirrups and her thighs, ankles, and abdomen bound with leather straps, she couldn't do more than squiggle a couple of inches from side to side.

"Stay still; this won't hurt," the woman ordered as she rubbed lubricant all over the thing.

She fought against the intrusion, her internal muscles clenching to try to prevent the foreign object from entering her body, but the woman pressed it inside her anyway. It was cold and uncomfortable. It didn't hurt exactly, but it felt weird.

The man watched intently as the woman took a long, thin catheter and threaded it inside her. Against her will, Colette also found her eyes glued to the woman's actions.

A syringe was prepared, and the woman inserted the sperm inside her.

Was it going to find its way to an egg and make a baby?

Colette was torn between being repulsed by what she was being subjected to and hoping the procedure worked. She was terrified of what they would do to her if she didn't provide them with the baby they wanted.

"All finished," the woman announced as she removed the catheter and cold metal implement, and put a sponge just inside her vagina.

"We'll leave you to lie there for a while, then you can go back to your room, and you and Heather can have lunch," the man said, already heading for the stairs that led to freedom.

This couldn't really be happening.

It felt to surreal.

They had just put someone's sperm inside her.

She didn't even know whose.

Was it the man who tricked her? His friend with the scar? A complete stranger? Maybe they had men in cages they could steal sperm from somewhere around here too.

Colette couldn't stop the tears from coming.

It wasn't fair.

She had run away from home expecting to find something better, something safer. Instead, she had found something more horrible than she could have dreamed up even in her worst nightmares.

* * * * *

2:21 P.M.

"Someone just set Devon Paddy's house on fire," Ryan announced as he entered the room.

"Was CSU still there?" his brother Jack asked.

"They were just packing up when all of a sudden someone noticed a fire near the back door."

"Anyone hurt?" Xavier asked.

"No—thankfully, everyone got out. The fire spread quickly but didn't do as much damage as at the Gervase house. Still, between the flames and the water, it wiped out anything that was left behind," he explained.

His throat still hurt from all the smoke he'd inhaled yesterday, but other than that, he felt fine—completely back to normal. Seeing his wife and kids, hugging them, kissing them, holding them, then going to sleep in his bed with his wife in his arms had made all the difference. Now, he was ready to work.

He missed his partner when she wasn't here, but Ryan was glad that Paige hadn't argued against taking the extra day to recover from the fire. There was a time when she would have shown up to work today just to prove that she could, but since she had become a mother, she looked at things differently.

"Why would he set fire to the house?" Jack looked confused.

"It makes no sense. He knew that we'd found the body; he knew that the crime scene techs would have gone through the place. Whatever was there to be found, we would have found already," Xavier added.

"Did you guys go through the house while you were there?" he asked.

"Yes, we went through the place before we left," Xavier replied. "There was nothing of interest in the office, and the rest of the house was fairly bare. Pretty much what you'd expect of a single man living alone."

"So why set it on fire at all?" Ryan wondered aloud. It didn't seem to make sense. They'd been going on the theory that Caden Gervase's killer was the same person who had nearly killed him and Paige yesterday when he'd tried to burn down the house. It made sense given that the fire was just hours after the murder. They had assumed it was because the killer was covering his tracks and wanting to make sure that any evidence that might lead them to him was eliminated.

But maybe it wasn't about that.

Maybe the fires weren't just cleaning up. Maybe they meant something to the killer. Maybe he was setting them, not because he had to, but simply because he wanted to. Maybe it even had something to do with why he was killing these particular people. Maybe it was what connected them all together.

"Did anyone see anything?" Xavier asked.

"No."

"There had to be at least a dozen people there," Xavier protested. "How could no one see anything?"

"I don't know. I guess he blended in, and then, once they noticed the fire, everything got kind of crazy, and they were more concerned with making sure everyone was out," he said.

"Tell me the body was at least out," Jack said.

"It was," he confirmed. "And whatever else CSU had found was already bagged and in the trucks."

"That was a risky move," Xavier noted. "Someone could have seen him, realized he didn't fit in and brought him in for questioning. Why risk it? Especially since we'd already gone through the house. So you would assume that anything that might lead us to him we'd already found. He could have set the house on fire after he killed Devon, then any evidence would have been destroyed before we ever even knew it existed."

"He couldn't," Jack said. "He couldn't destroy the body until he was sure we saw it."

"I agree," Ryan nodded. "He wanted us to see the body. He wouldn't have killed Caden in such a public place if he didn't want it found. He set the fire at Devon Paddy's house either because he just wanted to, or because he knew something we didn't and destroyed something hidden away in there, or because he just wanted to play it safe."

"Killing a cop isn't really playing things safe," Xavier said.

"Billy said no defensive wounds, right?" Ryan confirmed. Jack nodded, and he continued. "Caden didn't have any either, maybe he drugged them or something to incapacitate them. He could have used something short acting. He knocks them out, restrains them, then once they're awake again he tortures and kills them."

"Drugs do make sense," Xavier agreed. "Devon is a big guy, approaching seven feet tall and nearly three hundred pounds. He's a cop, and he knows how to defend himself, and yet this killer overpowered him with no problem. It would explain things if he'd drugged him ..."

"No drugs," Billy said as he swung the door open and joined them. "Tox screens on both victims were clean."

"He's good. Really good." Which was a terrifying prospect, especially in light of what Jack and Xavier had learned. It seemed like their killer had other victims in mind. Five to be exact.

"I might be able to explain why Caden didn't fight back. He

had a brain tumor; based on the size, I'd estimate he had maybe twelve months max."

"So, Caden maybe wasn't capable of defending himself. And the killer probably struck while Devon was still asleep. Probably delivered the blow to his shoulder first to incapacitate him. Then went with the hands and face to secure him in place so he could torture him without having to worry."

"I noticed something with the fingers," Billy told them. "The knife he used to cut off Caden's fingers didn't cut smoothly. He struggled. But what he used to remove Devon's fingers worked much better."

"He didn't plan on doing it at first," Ryan said. "It was spur of the moment. It appealed to him for some reason."

"He was leaving us a message," Jack added. "That part was for us. Everything else he did just to hurt them, but to cut off the seven fingers, and then six with his next victims, that's to tell us that he's not finished. He's taunting us, letting us know that he intends to finish what he started and we're not going to stop him."

"If we can't figure out how he connects to his victims, then he might well finish what he's started," he said. "Caden doesn't have a criminal record. Nothing at all. Not even any DUIs or speeding tickets. So he and Devon Paddy don't know each other because Devon arrested him."

"Maybe he's a victim," Xavier suggested.

"Nothing so far that I've found."

"Devon has a clean record; nothing in his file to indicate that he's been involved in anything untoward," Jack added.

"Then how are they connected?" Ryan was getting frustrated. How could they stop this man before five more people died if they couldn't find out how he was choosing his victims? The simple answer was, they couldn't. They needed something. Anything. A direction to move in. They needed something to give them a break.

"If Caden Gervase doesn't have a criminal record, and he's not a victim, then maybe he's a witness," Billy suggested.

That was a possibility.

"That could be the link. The killer could be a victim of a crime who's angry that he didn't get the justice he feels he deserved and he wants to take his anger out on those he deems responsible for that. A cop who didn't catch a bad guy, a witness who didn't give a good enough testimony—that could be Devon and Caden. Next, we could be looking for a lawyer, a judge, a crime scene tech or medical examiner, maybe a psychologist, anyone involved in the legal process could be the next victim."

"It would help if there was someone who knew Caden well that we could talk to who would know if he had ever been a witness to a crime," Jack said.

His brother was right. It would be much quicker to find out if an old case was the connection between the victims and their killer through Caden than it would be through Devon. "There's Daisy," he said tentatively. He didn't want to make the situation between his younger brother and his wife worse than it already was, but right now solving this case was more important.

"We don't know that Daisy and Caden were having an affair." Jack looked as unenthused about the possibility of talking to Daisy as he felt.

"But we know that they knew each other. And right now, she's all we have," he said.

"Since we don't know the nature of their relationship, we can't count on anything Daisy might or might not know," Xavier said. "We'll have to work through every single one of Devon Paddy's cases to see if Caden pops up in any of them."

Devon had been a cop for a quarter of a century. Going through every single one of his cases would take hours, probably days.

Days they didn't have.

Caden and Devon had been killed roughly twenty-four hours

apart.

If the killer stuck with his pattern, then another person would be dead in about twelve hours.

* * * * *

6:03 P.M.

"What's for dinner, Dad?"

Mark kicked the door closed behind him and carried the armful of grocery bags toward the kitchen. "Whatever you and your sister make," he called over his shoulder to Eve.

"Why do we have to make dinner?" Eve whined, following him.

"Because we all take turns to cook dinner. Those are the rules," he replied, setting the bags down on the counter and beginning to unload the groceries. Having been flung unprepared into the role of a single parent with a full-time job, he needed his kids to start helping out more around the house. His parents, brothers and sisters-in-laws were always only a phone call away, but he didn't want to have to rely on them all the time. It wasn't their fault that Daisy had left, and he didn't want to visit his marital problems on them.

"They never used to be the rules." Eve dropped into a chair at the table.

"Well, they are now." He was tired. It had been a long day on top of a night without much sleep, and he wasn't in the mood for an argument with his thirteen-year-old daughter.

"When Mom was here, we never had to cook dinner or do our own laundry or help with chores around the house," Eve complained, a pout on her pretty face.

"Mom isn't here anymore, is she?" he snapped, more grumpily than he had intended, but it hurt to think of Daisy. Her moving out had been bad enough, and at the back of his mind, he had always suspected that the reason for her leaving might be another man, but now that the other man had a face, he was so much more real.

His daughter's face crumpled and tears welled up in her blue eyes. "Is Mom ever coming back?"

Mark set down the bottle of milk he'd been holding and went to Eve, wrapping his arms around her. "I don't know, honey."

Eve entwined her arms around his neck and clung to him in a way she hadn't since she was a little girl. So far, the girls had held up better than the boys with Daisy leaving. Brian had been so angry, and Tony was so confused, always asking questions, but the girls hadn't spoken about it much, and he had assumed they were handling things fine. That had obviously been a mistake.

"I don't want you and Mom to get divorced," Eve cried into his neck. "I want her to come home."

While he would do whatever he could to make his kids happy, Mark wasn't sure that he could ever take Daisy back, even if she wanted to come home. She had walked out on him, and more importantly, she had walked out on their kids, for some other man. How could he look past that? Every time he looked at her now he would be picturing her with Caden Gervase.

"Brian says that Mom was having an affair and that's why she left. But she wouldn't do that to us, would she, Dad?" Eve's tearstained face lifted, and her watery eyes begged him to tell her what she wanted to hear.

Tenderly, he kissed her forehead and wiped away her tears. He didn't know what the future held for their family. All he knew was that nothing would ever stop him from being there for his kids. Whatever they needed. He might be the only parent they had going forward, which meant he had to learn a way to be both mother and father figure.

"I don't want to lie to you, honey. I don't know what's going to happen. All I know is that we'll get through it together, okay?"

Eve sniffed and nodded.

She needed some fun, relaxed family time.

They all did.

They all needed a night just to hang out together, have some fun. Forget about Daisy leaving. Forget about the murder at the school. Forget about everything except that they were a family who loved each other.

"Hey." He tugged on Eve's braid. "Why don't you go round up your sister and brothers and we make something fun for dinner. What about homemade pizzas?" His mom had given the girls her pizza recipe a few months back, and ever since, it had been a firm favorite in their house.

"Yeah, okay." Eve nodded.

"Then we'll make popcorn and watch movies together," he added.

"Can we make our own cookie dough ice cream?" Eve asked.

"Sure." Whatever it took to help the kids unwind. It had been a rough few months for all of them, and the events of the last two days had made things so much worse.

"Okay." Eve ventured a small smile.

"Love you." He pulled her in for another hug.

"Love you, too, Dad." She gave him a quick peck on the cheek, and his heart melted a little bit. He knew his kids were getting older, that his girls were teenagers, which automatically placed him in the embarrassing dad basket, but he still had a few years left before he had to let them grow all the way up. He still relished giving them hugs and hearing them say that they loved him.

While Eve went to round up her siblings, he returned to unloading the groceries, quickly realizing some were missing. He'd thought he'd brought in all the bags from the car. Mark hoped he hadn't forgotten anything. He didn't feel like making a return trip to the grocery store tonight. Now that they'd planned on having family time, he was really looking forward to it. He needed the time to just chill and enjoy his kids as much as they did.

Hoping he'd merely overlooked it, and it was still sitting in the trunk of his car, Mark hurried outside. It was cold, and he shivered as he crossed the porch and walked down the path to the driveway.

Snow was fluttering in the air, and there was a thick covering on the ground. Maybe the kids would be up for building snowmen tomorrow after school. It was his day off, and it would be fun to spend a bit of time hanging with the kids. When they'd been little, the kids had adored building a snow family in their front yard each year. They would work out a theme, and everyone would make their own. He and Daisy had started doing it the first winter they'd moved into this house. Brian had been two, Daisy was pregnant with the girls, and it had soon grown into a tradition that they'd all loved.

With Daisy gone now, he wanted to keep things as normal as he could for the kids. He hoped it would help them adjust to the changes in their lives.

At his car, he unlocked it and opened the back where the missing bag of groceries sat patiently waiting for him to find it. Mark snatched it up and relocked the car, then headed back for the house.

A couple was going past, walking their dog. The kids had been talking about getting a dog for years, but Daisy wasn't really a pet person. Maybe now was the time to look into it. Well, perhaps once the warmer weather came. He wasn't sure he wanted to be standing outside in the freezing cold trying to teach a puppy to relieve itself in the backyard and not on the floor indoors. He'd talk with the kids about it, find out what breed of dog they were interested in and what kind would best suit their family.

His gaze fell on a car parked right in front of his house.

It had been here earlier, too.

He looked closer. There was someone inside. Why would someone be sitting in their car in the snow? Maybe it had broken down, and they were waiting for help to arrive.

Mark headed closer, but just as he was approaching it, the car suddenly roared to life and drove off down the street.

Maybe it had just been someone pulled over to the side of the road to make a phone call.

Freezing without a coat on, he quickly crossed the front lawn and was immediately cocooned in warmth as soon as he stepped back inside. Voices sounded from the kitchen where the kids were busy getting started on the meal.

He paused for a moment to watch them. They were laughing and chatting away. Tony was working on the cookie dough, Eve and Elise were kneading pizza dough, and Brian was setting the table.

They were such great kids. Sometimes his heart felt like it was going to burst with all the love for them it held.

How could Daisy walk away from this?

A family of his own was what he'd wanted since he was a kid and he'd seen how much his parents loved each other and him and his brothers. He'd thought Daisy was on the same page, that they wanted the same things, but it seemed he had been wrong.

Eve laughed as Tony turned on the mixer without remembering to put the lid on and chunks of butter and puffs of flour sprayed the kitchen. It seemed like she was feeling better.

Sulking one minute, tears the next, then laughter, teenage girl hormones were going to be a roller coaster ride he wished he wasn't riding alone.

* * * * *

8:44 P.M.

She couldn't go on like this.

Physically or psychologically.

Daisy felt like she was falling apart.

Caden was dead, and now Devon was dead, too. Just because

she'd always known their deaths might be coming didn't make it any easier to deal with.

She had worked so hard to keep her past in the past, but now it was trying to shove its way into her present.

It didn't seem fair.

She hadn't done anything wrong.

In fact, the opposite.

She had tried to do the right thing, no matter how hard it had been or how risky it was. All the others had done was try to help her.

She didn't deserve what was happening now.

None of them did.

Least of all, her family.

He was still watching them.

He had sent her a picture.

Although looking at it was the last thing she wanted to do right now, her hands apparently had minds of their own. They reached for the envelope on the table and slid out the photo inside.

It was Mark, in their front yard with a grocery bag in his arms.

The photo was date stamped just a few hours ago.

To know that he was watching her family was terrifying.

He was obviously ready to follow through on his threat.

The other note sat beside the envelope the photo had been in.

It had arrived six months ago. It had been in the mailbox with the rest of the mail one day after she'd picked the kids up from school.

When she'd opened it, her world had come crashing down around her.

She had finally moved on, found some measure of peace, found a way to let go of her past and have a future. She was finally happy. She finally had what she'd always wanted. And in one moment, it was all gone.

The note he'd sent her said that if she went to the cops, he would kill her kids and her husband. The threat was real; Daisy knew that he would follow through. So, the next morning, she had packed up her stuff and told Mark she was leaving. It had been the only thing she could do. How could she let him hurt the people she loved?

She couldn't.

It broke her heart, but she had left and she'd kept her mouth shut.

Now she just had to decide if she should keep it shut.

She had brought Caden and Devon and all the others into this, and now they were *all* going to wind up dead. If she had kept her mouth shut all those years ago, then they wouldn't be.

What if she went to the cops with what she knew and they couldn't keep Mark and the kids safe? What if he got to them? He wouldn't kill them quickly. He would make sure they suffered because he believed that she deserved to suffer.

Maybe she should just stay here and hope the cops were able to catch him before he came for her.

Gone was any hope that he didn't know where she was hiding out. The photo had been delivered to her hotel and had been waiting for her when she returned this afternoon after work. He knew she was here. He could come for her any time he wanted. There was nothing to stop him.

Caden and Devon were dead, but there were five others. She would be the last, which meant there were four people he had to work through before he came for her. Had he already moved on to victim number three? She didn't know how quickly he planned to work through his list, but he'd killed two of them in just two days, so she didn't think he was going to wait long before moving on to the next.

Daisy was surprised that Ryan and Paige hadn't come to see her already. They knew that she had a connection to Caden, so she thought they would have contacted her to make a time to interview her. But they hadn't.

At least, not yet.

She knew that wouldn't last.

She knew that sooner or later, they would turn up at her door, and she had to decide what she was going to tell them.

She could play things safe. She could follow the orders she'd been given and not talk to the cops to ensure her family's safety. She could lie. She could claim that she didn't know anything, that she and Caden were just friends, that she didn't know who would want to kill him.

Or she could take what might be the second biggest risk of her life.

She could tell them everything. She could trust the cops to keep her family alive. She could tell them about her past. She could give them every single detail of the horror her life had turned into. She could tell them who she thought the killer was. She could tell them everything and hope that they could find him before he tried to kill her. Or before he killed her family to punish her.

And that was basically what it all boiled down to.

Whether or not she could trust the cops to protect the people she loved more than life itself.

She loved Ryan and Paige, and she trusted them with her life, and with her husband and children's lives, but she knew who they were up against. He was ruthless. He would never stop. He had nothing to lose, and those were the most dangerous people.

Her brain hurt.

How was she supposed to decide something like this?

If she got it wrong, her family would be the ones to pay the price.

She needed someone to help her decide, but who? Who could she turn to? She was alone. Caden was gone, and there wasn't anyone else she could reach out to. If she brought someone else into this, she was endangering them. If he found out that someone else knew about him, then he was likely to want to kill them, too.

She was stuck between a rock and a hard place.

There was no good option.

Either way, someone died.

If she told what she knew, he would kill Mark and the kids.

If she didn't tell what she knew, then he would kill her.

She wasn't ready to die. She was only thirty-eight. Her kids were still kids, and she wanted to see them grow up, graduate high school, move on to college, get jobs, fall in love, get married, have kids of their own.

She didn't want to leave them. She didn't want them to have to grow up without a mother. She didn't want Mark to grow old alone. And even worse, she didn't want him to move on and fall in love with someone else. That might be selfish of her, but it was how she felt.

She wanted her family back, but the only way to make it happen was to risk their lives.

Exhausted, she shoved the photo of her husband away and staggered to her feet. Stumbling to the bed, she practically collapsed onto it. The second her head touched the pillow, her eyes wanted to close. She was so tired.

A couple hours of sleep a night for six months was killing her. If he waited too long to come for her, she might be dead already.

Maybe that was best.

Maybe if she just went to sleep and never woke up it would solve everything. Her family would no longer be at risk, and she wouldn't have to suffer a horrible, painful death.

It would be so nice not to have to worry anymore.

Most of her life she'd worried about people finding out who she really was. She kept her secrets close to her heart. She didn't talk about her past with anyone, not even Mark. It was tiring. She always had to be careful about what she said and how she answered questions.

Daisy couldn't imagine being free.

Her past was always going to be a chain around her neck

pulling her down and holding her back.

She wanted to give up.

She wanted to just lie here and wait for him to come for her.

It was so tempting.

And yet something in her just couldn't do it.

She had to keep fighting.

Even if it was futile.

Giving up wasn't in her nature. No matter how much she might want to, she couldn't. She had to keep trying. Even if she pushed herself to the point of collapse, she would keep spending her days at work and her nights on her laptop doing whatever she could to try to find him.

There had to be a way where they all walked out of this alive.

Something would come to her.

She would figure something out.

She still had time. How much, she didn't know, but until he came knocking on her door, she still had a chance.

She just couldn't give up. She had to keep hope alive; otherwise, she was already dead.

She would get back to her searches, but first, she'd just close her eyes for a few minutes and get a little rest.

Daisy was asleep in less than a minute.

JANUARY 26TH

4:59 A.M.

Maddie Pickle stepped out into the snowy morning and closed her front door behind her.

She loved jogging—had ever since she was a teenager. Cross country running was her thing. She could go for hours, keeping a steady pace, letting her mind wander.

Throughout her fifty-three years, jogging had been the one constant. Her mother had died when she was eight, her father had remarried within a year. That relationship produced two more kids in addition to her and her little brother. He'd married another four times, had another seven kids. Maddie wasn't close with any of her half-siblings, but she and her brother maintained a good relationship.

As she put in her earphones and set out for the park, she was thankful that her marriage was rock solid. Of course, she and her husband had had their shares of ups and downs. There'd been financial troubles when she was pregnant with their youngest. There'd been the problems that came with raising a disabled child. Plus all the normal issues of being married and living with someone day after day.

But through it all, her daily run had kept her centered.

Healthy body, healthy mind, healthy life, had always been her motto, and so far it seemed to have worked.

Her job was draining. She was a social worker, and most of the cases she worked tore at her heart. Her home life was draining too. Every time she looked at her daughter, she was filled with guilt and pain. Tabitha had fallen into the family pool when she

97

was two. Distracted by their crying colicky newborn, neither she nor her husband had noticed right away.

By the time they did, Tabitha had stopped breathing.

They had performed CPR, and she had survived, but not without suffering brain damage from being deprived of oxygen.

Maddie would never forgive herself for what had happened to her daughter. Watching her two sons grow up was a daily reminder of everything her daughter would never do.

Although there were things she would obviously change if she had the power to do so, she was happy with her life. A husband she loved, three kids who were her heart, a job she enjoyed and could make a difference doing. It was a pretty nice life.

Rounding the corner, Maddie paused, looked both ways, then crossed the street. She was lucky; her favorite place to run was the park, and there was a beautiful one just two blocks from her house.

There was just something about the park that made her feel good. The trees, the grass, the flowers, the stream, the lake, the birds—everything about it was so relaxing. It made her feel like she was in the middle of nowhere, right out in the countryside where it was quiet and peaceful. Some days she half expected to see a bear or a deer come wandering out from behind the bushes. The park was her little piece of paradise in the middle of the city.

It was quiet this early on a winter morning. Maddie liked it that way. She always ran early, so she didn't have to see anyone. This was her time, and she liked to enjoy it alone.

As she entered the park, she started on her usual route, down through the wooded area, then around the lake, up the hill and back to the road. Her husband always insisted that if she was going to run while it was still dark, then he wanted to know where she was going to be—just in case.

She picked up her pace as she headed past the playground and into the woods, she wanted to get her heart racing. She loved that feeling. Where you ran so hard it felt like your heart was going to burst right out of your chest, but if you pushed through and kept going you reached this almost Zen-like place.

Maddie was lost in thought, the rhythmic pounding of her shoes on the track had lulled her into distraction.

The next thing she knew, she had tripped over something and landed with a thud.

Her hands took the brunt of the fall, and pain shot up from her wrists through her elbows and up to her shoulders. She hoped she hadn't broken something. The pain in her left arm began to dwindle, but her right wrist burned like it was on fire. As she sat up on her knees and looked down at her arm she saw it was crooked, her wrist jutting out at an odd angle.

It was broken.

How could she be so stupid to get distracted and not pay attention to where she was going?

Cradling her injured arm, she staggered to her feet.

A blow from behind sent her sprawling back down.

She landed on her broken limb and white-hot agony engulfed her.

Her stomach heaved and she vomited.

The pain made her dizzy. She couldn't think, couldn't move; all she could do was lie there and dry heave over and over again until her stomach cramped.

Finally, the pain ebbed, and coherent thought returned.

This time she hadn't tripped.

This time someone had knocked her down.

Still groggy, Maddie rolled over onto her back. Someone stood above her. In the half light of the lampposts, she could just make out that it was a tall, blond man. With the coldest blue eyes she had ever seen.

Rape was the first thing that flew into her mind.

That's what these kinds of men did, right? They waited until a woman was alone and vulnerable and then they struck.

Is this what he was going to do to her?

She was alone. The park was empty, so there was no one to hear her if she called for help. And she was injured. How could she fight back with a broken arm?

The man just stood there, staring down at her. Why was he doing that? Maybe he wasn't going to rape her. Did he just want to rob her? All she had on her was her cell phone.

Slowly, he reached toward her and Maddie tried to scoot backward on her bottom. She didn't get far before his hand clamped around her broken wrist, and she screamed in pain.

He didn't seem to mind. He knew just like she did that no one was going to come running to her rescue.

He began to drag her off the trail and deeper into the woods. Being pulled along by her injured arm sent shafts of pure agony arrowing all over her body. She had never felt such pain in all her life. He jerked her sideways, and the pain spiraled and then tossed her down into the deep, dark pit of unconsciousness.

When she came to, she was sitting propped up against a tree. Rope encircled her middle, securing her tightly to the trunk, her arms pinned uselessly at her side.

She looked at the man who was sitting cross-legged in front of her. He had tied her up, so it didn't look like he wanted to rape her. Her cell phone was sitting on the ground beside him, so it didn't look like he wanted to rob her either. That only left one other possibility, and that was making her head swim with terror.

"Wh-what do you w-want with m-me?" she stammered.

He smiled. It wasn't pretty. "You don't remember me?"

Maddie squinted, studying the face. She couldn't recall ever having seen this man before in her life. Was he the parent of a child she had removed from the home? No, she knew all the children in her cases and the adults in their lives.

So, who was he?

If he thought he knew her, then this was personal.

He had been lying in wait for her. This wasn't some random thing. He wanted her. He wanted to *kill* her.

"P-please, I don't kn-know who you are," she cried.

That didn't seem to faze him; his creepy smile remained in place. "Don't worry about it, you'll soon remember." He picked up a knife and began to twirl it in his fingers.

Her eyes fixated on it.

Watching it twirl.

Following its every move.

"Open wide," the man said as the knife moved toward her face.

Maddie didn't know what he intended to do with it, but her mouth clamped closed in protest. She didn't want this man or his knife anywhere near her.

He didn't ask again.

He didn't order her to do as he'd asked.

His fist just came swinging.

It connected with a crunch that reverberated through her head.

She felt her lips split, her teeth splinter and break off.

As she gagged on the sudden influx of blood in her mouth and throat, she swallowed several of her broken teeth.

Then more pain came.

It felt like someone had set off an explosion in her mouth.

Before she could process everything, the man's fingers were forcing their way inside her mouth, prying it open. They curled around her tongue, holding it in place as the cold, smooth blade of the knife pushed between her bloody gums.

She knew what he was going to do a second before he did it.

The sharp knife sliced smoothly through her tongue.

Maddie screamed.

Well, screamed as best as she could with no tongue and a mouth full of blood.

"Hey," a voice yelled, and light danced across them.

Help.

Someone was coming.

She was saved.

Her mouth was a mangled wreck, but she was alive. Maddie had never been so happy, or so relieved, in her entire life.

Her tormentor disappeared, and she relaxed.

It was over.

She had survived.

"Ma'am?" her savior approached slowly, seemingly unsure what he was going to find.

She tried to speak, but all she could do was gurgle helplessly. It felt like she was drowning in her own blood.

His face grew horrified as he looked at her, and she saw him shudder, but he leaned over her and patted her shoulder then pulled out a phone. "Just hold on, ma'am, I'm going to call for help."

Maddie saw a blur of movement.

Then a snap.

The phone fell from her savior's hand and landed with a thump.

A moment later, his body joined it on the ground.

The man she knew was going to kill her stood before her. There was no way he would keep her alive; after all, she had seen his face and could successfully ID him.

"Sorry for that interruption," he said apologetically. "Now, where were we?"

The man picked up something and crouched before her.

Her world became nothing but pain.

She prayed for death.

* * * * *

7:35 A.M.

She needed answers.

Daisy had decided that in order to decide whether talking to the cops was worth the risk, she needed to know more about the case and what was going on. Maybe if she knew what Ryan and Paige knew, that would help her to know what the right thing to do was. For all she knew, they were already close to making an arrest.

Putting her family in danger was not something she took lightly. She would rather he come for her and kill her than hurt a hair on her husband or children's heads.

She wasn't comfortable going to Ryan to pump him for information. He was family, and since she'd walked out on his brother, she felt awkward around him. So, she had decided Paige was the safer option. Just. She'd known Paige pretty much as long as she'd known Mark and his family. They were very close friends, and Daisy practically considered her a sister, but talking to her was still a little easier than talking to her brother-in-law.

So, she was standing at Paige's front door, here under the pretense of wanting to see how her friend was doing after the fire, and hoping to get enough information on Caden's case to help her decide what her next step should be.

She had been terrified when she'd heard about the fire that had almost killed Ryan and Paige. And not just because she loved them both, but because it was further confirmation that she was right.

He had set a fire that day, too.

To cover his tracks, to make sure there was nothing left that could lead anyone to him. Was that why he'd set the fire at Caden's house? Daisy didn't think there would have been anything there that would have incriminated him. Maybe he'd done it just because he wanted to send her a message, let her know that he hadn't forgotten what she'd done that day and that he was coming.

She took a deep breath and knocked on the door.

"Daisy." Paige looked surprised to see her when she threw open the door a minute later. "Is everything okay?"

Other than a hoarse voice, Paige looked like she was all right.

"I heard about the fire, I just wanted to come and check on you, make sure you were doing okay. Can I come in?"

Paige raised an eyebrow, her brown eyes clearly said she wasn't buying that, but she held the door open farther. "Sure. We're just getting ready for school."

She followed her friend to the kitchen where Paige's five-year-old daughter Arianna sat at the table, she was half in her clothes and half in her pajamas. The little girl's sweater had a unicorn on the front. Her pajama pants also had unicorns. Daisy remembered when her own girls had been obsessed with the mythical creatures.

One half of Arianna's hair was braided; the other half hung loosely around her shoulders, and Paige went to resume what she'd obviously been doing when Daisy knocked on the door.

"Ari, would you please sit still," Paige said in a tone that said she's already asked this several times.

"I'm busy," the five-year-old replied. She was eating cereal and sticking stickers in a book.

"As soon as you're done eating breakfast, you need to go and finish getting dressed. Daddy is leaving to take you and your sister to school in ten minutes. Ten minutes, Ari," Paige repeated. "You can do stickers later."

"Okay, okay," Ari said, eating a last mouthful of cereal. As soon as Paige finished with her hair, the child jumped up and hurried out of the room.

"Where's Hayley?" Daisy asked. She missed this—the hustle and bustle of getting ready in the morning. Even when she'd been at home, her kids were older now, more independent, but she still missed the busyness of family life.

"In her room, reading or on the phone with Sophie," Paige replied, clearing up the table.

"Want some help?" she asked.

"Sure, thanks." Paige was still looking at her like she knew there was more to this sudden visit than just checking up on a friend.

Daisy collected dishes and loaded the dishwasher while Paige wrangled her mass of brown curls into a ponytail, then walked to the bottom of the stairs. "Five minutes, girls," she yelled up. "Ari, do you need help with your shoelaces?"

"No, I can do it," Arianna yelled back down.

"Hayley ..."

"Yeah, I'll help her," the ten-year-old answered her mother's unasked question.

"How's Ari liking kindergarten?" Daisy asked as Paige tossed some fruit in the two lunchboxes on the counter.

"She loves it. She gets sad on Friday nights because she has to wait till Monday to go back."

Daisy smiled. She remembered how much her kids had loved school when they were that age. The older they got, it became more about their friends and less about the school itself. She loved her children so much it physically hurt to think of them getting hurt because of her.

So many people had been hurt because of her.

If Ryan and Paige had been killed in that fire, she never would have forgiven herself.

"Are you really okay?" she asked.

"I'm fine, Daisy, really," Paige promised. "I'm even going back to work today."

That made her feel better. She knew Mark would have checked on both Paige and Ryan. The doctor in him just couldn't help himself, and if he was okay with her going back to work, then she must really be okay.

"Oh, Daisy, hi." Elias came down the stairs, giving her a quick hug before going to Paige and kissing her cheek. Then he reached for her arm and pressed his fingers to her wrist.

"You're really doing that?" Paige glared and tried to snatch her arm back. "And in front of people."

Elias just shrugged and continued to check Paige's pulse. "If you're really going to go back to work not even forty-eight hours after almost dying, then yes, I am going to check your pulse."

Paige rolled her eyes, but gave Elias a kiss before she went to the bottom of the stairs. "Girls, time for school!"

"Stay safe today, please." Elias slipped his arms around Paige's waist and pulled her back against his chest.

"I will." She twisted her head and kissed his jaw.

Daisy couldn't help but feel a little jealous watching them. They were so happy together. They loved each other so much. They'd been through a lot, and yet it had brought them closer together. She missed Mark. Right about now she wanted nothing more than to be wrapped up in her husband's arms, feeling the safety and security she felt there that she couldn't feel anyplace else.

"Are you all right, Mom?" Hayley asked as she and her sister came downstairs. The little girl had the most serious blue eyes Daisy had ever seen in a child.

"Fine, honey," Paige told her.

"*Really* all right?" Hayley persisted.

"*Really* all right."

"Dad?" Hayley turned her attention to her father.

Paige shot him a look, and Elias sighed. "Mom will be fine."

"And a doctor said it was okay to go back to work?" Hayley checked.

"Yes. And Mark," Paige added.

That seemed to assuage Hayley's fears, and she took her lunchbox and Arianna's off the counter and handed one to her little sister.

"Have a great day." Paige picked Arianna up and kissed her.

"I will, Mommy."

"You, too." Paige set her younger daughter down and kissed her older one.

"Be safe," Hayley said as she hugged her mother tightly.

"I will. Try not to worry, okay?"

"I love you." Hayley held on for a moment longer.

"I love you, too. And you," Paige kissed her husband.

"School bus is leaving," Elias said.

"Last one in is a rotten egg." Arianna squealed with delight and ran for the front door.

"Coats!" Paige yelled after them.

"I got them, Mom," Hayley said as she followed her father and little sister out of the house.

"Okay, now that they're gone, you want to tell me why you're really here?" Paige pinned her with a serious stare.

"I just wanted to make sure you were okay," Daisy said lamely.

"Nice try, but you could have texted or called to do that. Why are you here?"

"Do you have any leads? On who killed Caden?"

"No, I'm sorry." Paige looked sympathetic.

She fought to keep the disappointment off her face. Of course, they didn't know who it was. They didn't know where to look.

"If you know something, Daisy, then you have to tell us." Paige was studying her closely.

She wanted to.

She really did.

But she was scared.

If she talked, then she was putting her family in danger.

Daisy wasn't sure she could do that.

"Daisy, if you're scared of someone, we can help you. You can trust us."

She did.

She trusted Ryan and Paige implicitly, but that didn't mean they could catch him before he hurt her family.

"Daisy, we know that you know Caden. We don't have anyone else who knew him well enough to help us figure out who killed him. His death has been linked to the murder of a cop." Paige paused to gauge her reactions, and Daisy fought to keep her face neutral. "Was Caden ever involved in a crime in any way? Maybe as a witness?"

That was freakishly close to the truth.

"We believe Caden's killer isn't finished. That he has more victims in mind. If you know something, you have to tell us. It might be the only way we can stop him."

Maybe Paige was right.

She was the one who'd started this, so maybe she was the only one who could end it.

She'd get them to put her family in a safe house until this killer was caught.

Daisy was just opening her mouth when Paige's phone rung.

"Hold on." Paige picked it up off the counter and hit answer. "Hey, Ryan, I'm about to leave. What?"

She watched as Paige's face grew pale.

Whatever news Ryan had, obviously wasn't good.

"What is it?" she asked the second Paige hung up.

"Another victim. I have to go; we'll talk later, okay? We need you, Daisy. Whatever you know, we need to know. Please. Think about it."

She wouldn't think about anything else.

She couldn't.

Another victim.

No one was safe.

He was relentless.

He wouldn't stop until she was dead, and he would kill whoever he had to in the process.

How could she risk Mark and their children's lives?

She couldn't.

She had to keep her mouth shut.

* * * * *

11:56 A.M.

"Three days, three victims," Ryan said. "This guy is on a mission, and he's not pausing to give us time to figure out why or where he's going to strike next."

"The newest victim adds a new dimension," Paige said. She'd been thinking about it ever since they'd left the crime scene.

"You got a theory?" Xavier asked, setting a bottle of water down on the table in front of her.

She smiled at him gratefully. Her throat still felt raw from all the smoke she'd inhaled in the fire. She didn't remember much of it after she'd freaked out and had a panic attack and passed out in Ryan's arms.

Paige knew that it had been her husband's team who had entered the burning building to rescue them. And that Elias putting his mask on her had probably saved her life. She had a few fuzzy memories of fresh air hitting her, of being carried, the movement making her nauseous, of the flashing lights and whirling sirens of the ambulance.

Her first clear memory was waking up in the hospital with her husband sitting beside her bed holding her hand.

She was so thankful that she and Ryan had survived.

Downing half the bottle, the cold water felt like heaven gliding down her sore throat. Feeling refreshed, she voiced her theory to the guys. "What if this is all about a kid?"

"A kid in the system?" Jack asked.

"It would make sense. It could be what ties all three victims together," she said. "What if Caden Gervase found out that one of the kids at his school was being abused. He gets social services involved, and the social worker assigned to the case is Maddie Pickle. Maybe Devon Paddy was the cop who arrested the parents."

Ryan nodded enthusiastically. "That's the first direction we've had to move in."

"All three have been working for years. We could be looking at a case maybe two or even three decades old," Jack said.

"Maybe we're even looking at the child in question as the killer," Xavier suggested. "Sometimes bad stuff happens in foster care. Or maybe he's angry that his family was destroyed. Just because someone hurts us doesn't mean we no longer love them."

"Could be." Paige nodded. "Tony said that the guy was younger than us, he could be the child grown up. Or he could be the parent of a child at the middle school. He lost his kid, and now he wants to punish the people he feels are responsible."

"We'll have to cross reference Maddie's files with Devon's. Maybe the school can let us know of any of the kids enrolled who are in the system," Ryan said.

"I think Daisy knows something," she announced.

All three pairs of eyes zeroed in on her.

"So you think Mark's right? You think she was having an affair with Caden Gervase?" Jack asked.

She considered this and went with her gut. "No. I don't think they were involved romantically."

"But you do think they were involved?" Ryan asked.

"I think they knew each other. What if Daisy is connected to this case? What if she was the one who went to Caden with her suspicions that a kid was being abused? Mark said he's seen them in a café together, but no one has ever seen them acting romantically. Maybe this was why. Maybe they were simply discussing this case."

"That could make her a potential victim," Xavier said slowly.

Nobody liked that idea.

Although, nobody could deny it was a possibility.

"This guy has four people left to kill," Jack said. "He's killed a school principal, a cop, and a social worker. If this is about revenge for a child being removed from a home, then we need to think about who he might go after next."

"Doctors, maybe," Ryan suggested.

"Friends, either friends of the kid or family friends, who might have played a part in revealing the abuse," Paige said.

"Other teachers, maybe, or sports coaches, pastors," Xavier rattled off. "Until we figure out who the kid was, there's no way to know for sure."

"Paige, you said you thought Daisy knew something—why?" Jack asked.

"She came by this morning. She said she wanted to see how I was doing after the fire, but I think that was just an excuse." Daisy had watched with a sense of longing as she'd interacted with her daughters and her husband. Paige didn't think she was enjoying being separated from her family.

"Did she say that?" Ryan asked.

"Not exactly. But when I suggested that to her, she didn't deny it. I think she was getting ready to tell me something when Ryan rang to tell me about Maddie Pickle's murder."

"If she knows something, then why not tell us?" Ryan looked confused, and a little angry.

"Maybe she's afraid," she suggested. Daisy had seemed scared.

"This guy we're looking for is big. Huge. And obviously well trained. If she knows who he is, it makes sense she would be afraid of him," Xavier agreed.

"He snapped that man's neck like it was nothing." Paige could still see Davy James' body lying beside the tree, his neck at a ninety-degree angle.

"He's dead because he tried to save Maddie Pickle's life. Wrong place, wrong time." Jack looked sad.

"But the killer didn't make him suffer," Xavier said. "He killed him quickly out of necessity. He did it like it was nothing more than a task that had to be done for his own protection. The complete opposite of what he did to Caden Gervase, Devon Paddy, and Maddie Pickle."

"He has so much anger toward them. He wants to destroy them. He wants to see them suffer; that's important to him. Then once he's done playing with them, he kills them efficiently by slicing right through their carotid arteries. There's no way they can survive that." She was both intrigued by and confused by the two different sides of the killer's personality. He was able to be both organized and frenzied in the same attack.

"He's certainly not bothered by killing," Ryan said. "These murders may be related to a possible social services removal of a child from the home, but he's killed before."

"Agreed," she said, and Jack and Xavier also nodded.

"He's comfortable with the torture, as well," Jack said. "He cut off Maddie's tongue and gouged out her eyes like it was nothing. Then cut off her fingers like he did with the others."

"Public location again," Xavier said. "She had a broken arm. I'm guessing he tripped her while she was running—used that to get to her. He's comfortable taking care of any threats that present themselves, and he's not worried about anyone finding the bodies."

"We wouldn't have found her so quickly if it wasn't for the husband." Apparently Maddie's husband was concerned with her running alone so early in the morning and knew her route. When she hadn't returned around the time she usually did, he waited another fifteen minutes then headed out to search for her.

"I can't imagine finding your partner like that." Ryan shuddered, no doubt picturing Sofia finding his dead and mutilated body, or him finding hers.

"He's working through his list quickly," Xavier said. "He knows if he gives us time, then we're going to figure out who he is. Which means there is a connection there. We just have to find it."

"And preferably before tomorrow morning when he kills victim number four," she said. Paige had no doubt that if they didn't figure out who he was, then the next person on his list would be dead within twenty-four hours.

"Maybe we'll get lucky and he'll follow his pattern and try to burn the Pickle house down. We have officers there in case he shows up," Jack said.

"What about Daisy? I still think she knows something that can help us." She'd been able to feel it when they were together this morning. She and Daisy had been friends for a long time, and she knew her well enough to read her body language, which had been all but screaming that she wanted to talk but was afraid.

"We'll make a time to talk with her," Ryan said. "But right now, we don't know if she's involved and a potential victim, or if she and Caden were just friends who hung out, or if they were a couple and she's just scared to admit it. All we know is that she's been acting out of character for the last six months."

"If she's involved, it still doesn't explain why she walked out on Mark," Jack said.

"Maybe its related," she said.

"How? Why?"

"Maybe this started months ago, before she moved out. Maybe once she realized that this guy was a threat to her, she was worried he might try to go after her family. Especially if she was part of the reason that his family was destroyed. Maybe she thought that if she made it look like her family wasn't important to her, he would leave them alone." Paige really hoped Daisy wasn't involved in this case. She didn't want to be investigating her friend's murder. For the first time since Mark and Daisy split up, she actually hoped that Daisy was having an affair. This time, that was definitely the lesser of two evils.

* * * * *

4:29 P.M.

This wasn't a good idea, but she couldn't stop herself.

She had to see them.

Daisy missed her husband and their kids so much. The longer she stayed away from them, the more distant and disconnected she felt from their lives.

Even though it was risky, she just wanted an hour or so to spend with her family. He already knew where they lived, and he had made sure she knew he was watching them. But, so far, he hadn't made any move to hurt them, and hopefully, if she continued to keep her mouth shut, he would keep it that way.

She turned onto her street, and immediately she spotted them.

They were in the front yard building snowmen.

Their family tradition.

They were doing it without her.

Daisy pulled her car over to the side of the road and dropped her forehead to rest on the steering wheel.

They were moving on.

They were laughing.

They all looked so happy.

Even sixteen-year-old Brian looked like he was having fun.

It was like they didn't even care that she wasn't there.

She scrunched her eyes closed, and a couple of tears seeped out the corners. She felt like her heart was breaking. It wasn't as though she had thought that the world would stop spinning because she had moved out, but seeing Mark and the kids doing things they had always done together as a family hurt. Hurt more than she could put into words.

What if there was no going back from this?

What if she somehow made it out of this alive, and she tried to come back home, but they didn't want her?

What if the choices she had made had ruined beyond repair her relationships with her husband and children?

Her tears began to flow faster.

They would understand, wouldn't they?

They would get why she had had to do this, that it was the only way she could ensure that they stayed safe.

She couldn't begrudge them trying to move on with their lives. They didn't understand because she hadn't told them anything. They thought that she had left because she didn't want to be with them anymore, and she hadn't corrected them.

They were hurting, too.

Because of her.

It seemed no matter how hard she tried to do the right thing, she always seemed to end up making people sad and angry.

She didn't have long left. He'd killed three of the seven of them in as many days. If he stuck with that pattern, she had four days left, for Daisy had no doubt that he was saving her for last. She would spend every second of time she had left trying to find him, and if she couldn't, then at least she would die knowing she had done everything she could to live.

If she was going to die, then she wanted to give her kids one last happy memory of her. The idea that she would die with her family hating her was almost more than she could bear, but at least they would be alive to hate her.

That had to remain her number one priority.

Brushing away her tears, Daisy opened her car door. She had chosen this path, and she had to accept everything that came with it. Her family was doing the best they could with the information that they had. She had to accept that.

Pasting a smile that she certainly didn't feel on her face, she strode up to her husband and kids. "Hey, guys." She forced her voice to sound chirpy.

"Daisy." Mark's blue eyes grew wide in surprise, and he adjusted his stance, so he was in between her and the kids.

That hurt.

Did her husband think she was a threat to her own children?

She would never, ever do anything to hurt Brian, Eve, Elise, or Tony. They were her heart. Her life. She was sacrificing them so she could keep them alive.

"What are you doing here?" he asked, sounding suspicious.

"You said if I wanted to see the kids, I should come by the house," she reminded him. She hated having to follow someone else's rules to see her own kids, but this distance was for the best.

She just had to keep reminding herself of that.

Mark frowned. "I thought we agreed you would call first."

It was an effort to keep her attitude upbeat. "I was in the area ... I just thought I'd pop in for a few minutes. I won't stay long ... I thought it would be okay." She looked up at him anxiously. Was he going to tell her no?

With a scrutinizing look, he finally nodded and took a step back so she could see the kids.

None of them had come to say hello to her.

Tony was staring at his shoes, refusing to look up at her. The girls both looked teary. And Brian was glaring at her with open hostility. Daisy wasn't used to seeing her kids this way. Or to feeling so awkward around them.

"You guys building snowmen?" She took a step closer, noting that all four kids took one back. Were they afraid of her? Bluffing a confidence she didn't feel, she asked, "What theme did you choose?"

No one answered.

Daisy swallowed back a giant lump in her throat.

She had known coming here was a mistake, but she'd thought that was because he might realize that using her family to get to her would work, and she'd be putting them in danger. She hadn't realized it would show her just how angry her family was with her.

They hated her.

At least that would make her impending death easier for all of them to handle.

"Safari," Mark said quietly from behind her.

She spun around and shot him a grateful smile. "That's a great idea." She beamed at the kids. "Who thought it up?"

Again, the kids remained stonily silent.

And again, Mark came to her rescue. "It was Tony's idea."

"Great one, Tony." She ached to reach out and touch him, ruffle his hair, pat his shoulder, kiss his cheek, anything. She just wanted to feel close to him. But she knew it wouldn't be well received right now, so instead, she stepped closer to the collection of snow creatures. "This one is yours, Tony? The elephant?"

Her son glanced up at her and gave a cautious nod.

"And Eve made the giraffe. Elise's is the hippopotamus, Brian's the lion, and, Mark, yours is the crocodile," she said.

"You're right." Mark offered her a tight smile. At least he was trying.

"Dad, we have to get started on dinner," Brian announced. His scowl had only grown over the two minutes or so she'd been here.

"Okay." Mark nodded.

"Let's go." Brian began to usher his younger siblings back toward the house.

This had gone even worse than she'd been expecting.

Daisy felt crushed.

"Call next time, okay?" Mark said quietly. He didn't look angry—just sad. That was almost worse. "I'm not trying to be mean, or bossy, Dais, I just have to put them first. This has been hard on them. Especially because you won't give us any answers. They need time to adjust. Once they do, if you want to, we can work out something, but until then, I don't think you should just turn up here unannounced."

She wanted to tell him not to worry about it, that in a few days he wouldn't have to worry about her at all.

She'd lost them.

Maybe forever.

She had to do something.

If she didn't make a move now, it could be too late.

She had come here to convince herself that keeping her mouth shut was the best option, but in fact, the opposite had happened. She had moved out to protect her family, but all of them were miserable. This wasn't helping any of them.

Unable to talk, she merely nodded at her husband and turned away.

"Talk to me, Daisy. Tell me why you left. Was it because of

Caden Gervase?" Mark followed her.

"No," she murmured.

"No, you won't tell me, or no, it wasn't because of the girls' principal?"

"I didn't leave you because of Caden." She stopped walking but didn't turn around.

"Then why?" Mark sounded desperate.

She wanted to tell him, but not yet. First, she needed to get all her ducks in a row. "I'm sorry, Mark. I never wanted to hurt you." With that, she hurried toward the car.

Footsteps pounded on the sidewalk behind her, and a moment later, a pair of arms wrapped around her waist.

"Eve."

"I love you, Mom," her daughter cried.

"I love you, too, baby." Tears were trickling down her cheeks.

"I miss you."

"I miss you, too."

"Are you going to come home?"

How much she longed to tell her daughter she would, but she couldn't make promises she might not be able to keep. "Go back inside; its cold out," she said.

With a disappointed sigh, Eve released her and walked away. Because she apparently enjoyed torturing herself, Daisy turned and watched her go. Mark was waiting for her in the driveway, and he wrapped an arm around their daughter's shoulders, and together they walked into the house.

Unlocking her car, she dropped down into the driver's seat and burst into tears.

It was a long time before she was calm enough to drive.

At least she had a plan. She knew who she had to talk to. Someone who could hopefully help her figure out how to do what she should have done all along, and how her family was going to be kept safe when she spilled all the secrets she had worked so hard to bury.

* * * * *

6:41 P.M.

Heather couldn't take her eyes off her tiny baby boy.

He was about to be ripped from her arms.

Any minute now, they would come in and take him. He was one week old now, the same age as her daughters when they'd been taken. She could keep track of the days by the meals that they were delivered. Breakfast was cereal, lunch a sandwich, and dinner was usually some vegetables and occasionally some pasta or rice. The meals were small but nutritionally balanced. They didn't want her or any of the other girls becoming malnourished; that would mess with the whole reason for them being here.

Some days Heather still couldn't believe this was her life.

Had it really been almost three years since she'd been plucked off the streets and brought here?

Before Colette had asked, she hadn't thought about it in so long. Time became nothing here. At first, she'd kept track of the days, pulling out her earring to scratch a line into the concrete under her mattress to mark off each day she'd spent here, but that had quickly become depressing, doing more harm than good, so she'd stopped.

It was weird. She still had hope that she'd be found and rescued, and yet, at the same time, she'd long ago given up hope of ever seeing the sky again or feeling the wind rustling through her hair.

If she had known when she'd run away from home that she was going to end up here, she definitely would have rethought her options.

Heather had been only fourteen when she'd run. Her life had been great up until she was ten and her father passed away. Her mom had remarried, and at first, everything had been fine, but then she'd hit puberty, and her big brother had gone off to college, and she'd been alone in the house with her mom and stepdad.

It started with so called "accidents."

He'd walk in while she was in the shower or while she was getting dressed. Then he had started to touch her, his hand lingering on her thigh, or on her chest close to her breasts.

She had told her mom, but she hadn't seemed overly concerned, telling Heather she must be imagining things. Her mom had said that her stepdad was a good man and that missing her dad wasn't a reason to make up stories.

For a while, she believed her mother.

But then one weekend while her mom was away on a girls' weekend with her friends, her stepfather had made himself comfortable in her bedroom and in her bed.

After that, he found frequent excuses for his wife to take trips to give him more time alone with her.

Heather couldn't take it any longer, but she didn't know where to turn.

Her mother wasn't going to believe her, and she didn't want to go to someone else for fear that they wouldn't believe her either.

Then the idea to run had occurred to her. She hadn't really intended to be gone forever, just long enough to scare her mom a bit. Then maybe she'd believe that Heather wasn't making up stories because she missed her father.

Instead, her second night away she'd been approached by a boy who looked to be only a few years older than herself. Stupidly, that had put her at ease, and she had walked right into his trap.

She had gone through all the usual steps when she realized she had been kidnapped. Fear, anger, shock, denial, acceptance. Now, she was mostly numb to the whole thing.

What hurt the most was the loss of her friends.

Joanna and Cara had already been here when she woke up in

her cage. Skylar had been here only a month. The girl had been unable to adjust. She'd just curled up in a corner, refusing to eat, refusing to do anything but cry. That had made the Scar Man angry, and one day Skylar had been removed from her cage never to be seen again.

Heather couldn't do that.

She couldn't give up.

She didn't fight like Cara had always been trying to do. She wanted to keep herself alive as long as possible. Surely, her mom had reported her missing, and people had to be looking for her.

But she'd had three babies now. Cara had gotten sick after her second, and after that, she kept having miscarriages. Since she couldn't carry a baby to term, she was of no use to their captors, so they'd killed her. Joanna had been killed after she'd had her fourth.

Heather knew they weren't going to keep her indefinitely. And according to what Joanna said, four babies seemed to be the most they wanted out of a girl. Lillian, Freya, and Tasha had all been killed after that.

That meant she only had one more to go.

Both her girls were gone. Sometimes she thought of them. Were they safe? Had whoever adopted them been good to them? Were they loved? Were they happy?

"Do you love him?"

Colette's voice ripped her from her thoughts. "The baby?"

"Yes. I mean, I know technically you weren't raped, although I still think what they did to us counts, but it's not like you wanted to get pregnant. You're their prisoner. What they did to you was wrong, but he's also half of you. So I was just wondering if you love him." Colette rested a hand on her stomach, no doubt wondering if she was already pregnant.

Heather wasn't sure how to answer the question.

Did she love her children?

She didn't know.

She didn't hate them. It wasn't their fault that they had been conceived the way they had any more than it was her fault. She hated what these people had done to her. She hated that she had been impregnated against her will. But did that make her hate her children?

No, she didn't think it did.

If someone rescued her this minute, would she keep this little baby lying in her arms? Or would she still give him up for adoption? No matter what, she truly wanted the best for him, and maybe he was better off without her. What did she know about raising a child even if it were possible she could keep him?

But it wasn't possible.

Any minute now, he was going to be taken away.

A tear slipped out and wound its way slowly down her cheek.

She hoped he got a good home.

"You do," Colette said softly. "You do love him."

Heather hadn't thought about it before. She couldn't. It was too painful to think about her babies. But she thought Colette might be right.

She pressed a kiss to her baby's soft little head, then put her finger in his hand. He immediately curled his own tiny little fingers around hers. She loved that.

She was going to miss him so much. In just one week, he had managed to work his way into her heart. How could something this small make such a big impact on her?

The clang of the basement door opening cracked her heart into a million pieces.

Footsteps boomed and then a moment later the Scar Man stood just outside her cage. "It's time, Heather," he said.

She clutched the baby tighter. "Can't I keep him just a little longer?"

"No," he said simply. The man never used more words than was necessary.

"But he's so little. He needs his mother," she begged.

"You're not his mother. You're merely the surrogate. Put him down and move to the back of your room."

She hated when he called it her *room*. Like she was a guest here. Well, she wasn't a guest, and she wasn't giving them her baby. She didn't think he would risk hurting the baby by using her shock collar, so she clambered to her feet, and eyed him defiantly.

He sighed.

He was always so calm. Scarily so. It was like nothing ruffled him. Heather thought that was what she hated the most about living here, that she really was nothing more than a tool in their moneymaking project. They didn't care about her. There was a never-ending supply of young runaways they could abduct. Knowing that made her feel like she was nothing.

"Put him down, Heather."

She weighed up her options.

She'd never made the Scar Man angry before. She didn't know what he'd do to her if she did.

There was one time she had seen him angry.

That's how she knew about the scars.

She was a little hazy on the details because he'd shocked the rest of their collars before he made his move, but she'd seen enough to know that he wasn't a man to be trifled with. After all, he had no problem plucking girls off the street, imprisoning them, and making them bear babies just so he could make some cash.

She couldn't do it.

She couldn't risk her baby being hurt.

Heather pressed a kiss to his cheeks, hugged him tightly, and set him down on the ground like she'd been told.

"I'll always love you," she whispered, then backed away.

As the Scar Man picked up her son and carried him away, she broke down.

* * * * *

11:13 P.M.

She probably shouldn't be here this late, but Daisy couldn't wait until morning.

She kept ping-ponging back and forth between thinking she should tell what she knew and thinking it was a horrible, terrible mistake.

Daisy knew she couldn't go on like this.

The constant second-guessing herself was making her sick. She had to make a decision and stick with it. She was starting to realize there were no right or wrong answers; there were risks no matter what she did.

So she was going to decide.

Tonight.

And there was only one place she could go to get the guidance she needed. With Caden gone, there was only one other person she trusted enough to help her make this decision.

She parked her car down the street and walked the rest of the way on foot. If she decided not to go through with this, then she didn't want anyone to know that she'd been here.

The door opened before she could knock.

"I wondered when you were going to show up."

"It's him," she whimpered. She felt like she'd been flung back in time twenty-five years and was the same scared kid she'd been when they'd first met.

"We don't know that for sure. And even if it is, we don't know where he is or even who he is anymore," Lieutenant Belinda Jersey replied.

Belinda had been her brother-in-law's boss up until she'd retired about two months ago. Belinda was in her early sixties and she was wiry, with smooth black skin, the blackest eyes Daisy had ever seen, and shoulder length dark hair. She'd never been married, up until she retired her job had been her life, and people had wondered what she would do once she gave it up, but it seemed like Belinda loved the freedom to devote more time to her hobbies.

As far as she was aware, no one knew that she and Belinda shared a past, and if she'd had her way, no one would ever have found out. But it seemed *he* was intent on bringing the past back to life.

"Who else could it be?" Daisy asked.

"I don't know," Belinda replied. "Come in, we shouldn't be talking about this out here."

She had never been to Belinda's house before and wasn't quite sure what to expect when she walked inside. It certainly wasn't what she saw. "Did you make those?" She looked in awe at the gorgeous cross-stitch pictures that covered the walls.

"I did," Belinda beamed.

"They're amazing." There were sunsets, animals, cottages set in beautiful gardens, castles, beaches, snow-covered mountains, and so many other gorgeous scenes.

"Thank you. Do you want anything to drink, or eat?" Belinda asked as they sat in the living room.

"No, thank you." Daisy perched on the edge of the sofa. She felt nervous, edgy, and she wasn't sure she could keep anything down. She hadn't been able to eat much the last few months, even less the last few days. It had been a struggle just to drink enough water to keep herself hydrated.

"So, you think it's him?" Belinda was watching her with cop eyes. Those probing, all-seeing, assessing eyes she remembered so well.

"Yes."

"It's been twenty-five years. Why now?"

"I don't know."

"He's had any number of opportunities to get his revenge."

"He has." Daisy shivered at the notion. She hadn't thought about it before, but she and her family had been completely vulnerable to him all along.

"He's killed three people already," Belinda said. Obviously she had been keeping up with what was going on despite being retired.

"He has four to go."

Belinda's eyes grew wide, then understanding dawned. "Because seven people died that day."

Daisy nodded. Tears burned the backs of her eyes, but she didn't want to cry again. Her face and throat were still aching from the tears she'd shed after seeing her family.

"Are you okay?" Belinda looked concerned.

She nodded quickly. She didn't want to think about that day. She didn't want to think about what had happened. She didn't want to think about any of it. She had shoved those feelings down deep, and she didn't ever want to let them come back up.

"Have you told anyone?"

Unable to speak just yet, she shook her head.

"So, they don't know any of it?"

"Nothing." She forced the word out.

"You shouldn't have to deal with all of that alone," Belinda said softly. "I know you got some counseling back then. Have you had anything more recently?"

"No." Daisy had hated those sessions. She hadn't wanted to deal with what had happened. She'd just wanted to forget about it. "Sometimes I would talk to Caden." Her voice broke when she said his name. It still didn't feel real that he was gone. It hurt so much like someone had grabbed hold of her heart and ripped it from her chest.

"I'm sorry. I know how much you loved him." Belinda reached over and patted her hand.

It was the first time someone had offered their condolences for her loss. It felt odd. Losing Caden wasn't something she could share because there was no way to explain their relationship without explaining her dark past.

"If there are seven victims, and he's already killed three, then there's you and me, and who else?"

"I don't know." She was so tired; this was exhausting; she didn't sleep. All she did was try to figure this out, and she couldn't.

"First was Caden." Belinda was looking thoughtful. She was in full cop mode now. "Then there was Devon." Daisy didn't miss the pain that flashed across Belinda's face as she mentioned the deceased cop. "Next was Maddie—"

"Maddie?" Paige had told her this morning there was another victim, but she hadn't had a chance to find out who it was. She hadn't had anything to do with the social worker since the day they'd met, but it made sense the killer would go after her.

"You didn't know?"

Daisy shook her head. This was all so overwhelming. Who was he going to go after next? "He sent me a letter," she confessed.

Belinda's eyes grew wide. "When?"

"Six months ago."

"That's why you moved out?"

"Yes."

"What did he say?"

"That if I open my mouth to the cops, he'll kill Mark and the kids. I don't know what to do, Belinda." She wanted someone to make this decision for her. "I don't even know anything helpful to tell the cops. I think I know who's doing this, but I don't have any proof. I don't know his name … I don't know where he is … I don't know anything …" she finished with a sob.

"We'll figure it out." Belinda came and sat beside her.

"What should I do?"

"I can't make that decision for you."

"But I need you to," she begged.

"It's you he's threatening. It's you he chose to let know what he was planning, and it's your family who's at risk. What is your heart telling you to do?"

She knew the answer to that.

If she were honest, she'd always known.

She was going to keep her mouth shut.

It made her feel horrible inside. People were going to die because she couldn't bring herself to open up about her past, but there was no way she was going to risk her husband and her children. She didn't have anything useful to give the cops anyway. Certainly nothing that could stop him.

She only had four days to live. She would use them to do whatever she could to find out anything she could about him, but when it came down to it, she would rather die herself than risk him laying a finger on her precious children.

"Have you decided what you're going to do?"

"Yes." She was oddly at peace with her decision.

"You're going to do as he said and keep your mouth shut, aren't you?"

"Yes. It might be the wrong thing to do, but I can't let him hurt my family."

"What if I say something?" Belinda raised a challenging brow. It was clear the retired cop thought she was making the wrong decision.

"That's your choice. Just likes it's mine to keep quiet. If you tell them about me, I won't cooperate when they question me," she challenged back. There had been so many times in her life when she had been powerless, but now she could make her own choices, and she was going to exercise that ability.

Belinda sighed. "I understand why you want to keep quiet, Daisy, but we can put all of you in protective custody. And if we can figure out who he's after, we can keep them safe, too."

"I can't take that risk."

"What if he goes after them anyway?" Belinda asked softly.

That was perhaps her biggest risk, but so far, he'd kept true to his word and stayed away from them.

Belinda sighed again. "Okay, you should go home—or wherever it is you're staying these days—and get some sleep. You look like you need it. Tomorrow we can regroup and see if we can come up with a plan."

If we're both still alive, Daisy thought to herself. "Be careful. He's saving me for last, but he could go after you next." She wished she was the only one to pay for her past sins and not all these innocent people.

"I was a cop for most of my life; I can take care of myself. *You* be careful."

"I will." She just wanted this to be over. She was tired of … well, she was just plain tired. Her past had chased her long enough. It was time for it to be over.

JANUARY 27TH

12:14 A.M.

He was getting close.

Only a few more left, then everyone who had messed with his life would be dead.

It gave him a special kind of peace he hadn't felt before to know that soon it would all be over.

Twenty-five years was a long time to wait. So many times he had wanted to hunt them all down and rip every piece of skin off their bodies while they were still alive and could feel every single cut. He wanted to beat them with his fists until they were a bloody, unrecognizable mess. He wanted to rip them limb from limb with his bare hands.

He hated them.

Hated them with a burning passion that ran deep through the very center of his being.

Something wet and slippery ran under his fingernails, and he looked down at his hands. Slowly, he uncurled his fingers from the tight fists he'd bent them into and saw that his short nails had dug into his palms and left four, crescent-shaped cuts on each palm.

His hate for them was so real. So alive. It lived inside him. Born that day twenty-five years ago when his life had exploded, festering every day since, to the point where he could no longer contain it. If he didn't let it out, then it would consume him, and he couldn't allow that to happen because that would mean that they won. And *no one* beat him. No one.

A figure appeared on the sidewalk, headed in his direction.

He hunkered down in his car to make sure he wasn't seen. A man sitting alone in his car, at midnight, with the engine and headlights off, was always a signal that danger was lurking.

Cautiously, he glanced over. He needn't have worried about them seeing him and wondering what he was doing. The person had their head bowed and was striding along purposefully.

As they got closer, his eyes grew wide.

It was Daisy.

What was she doing here?

She must have been visiting Belinda Jersey. He hadn't realized that they were close. He'd been watching them both for months now and hadn't seen them interact once. Maybe it was just that they knew he was coming for them and they were trying to find a way to stop him.

They couldn't.

Nothing was going to stop him.

He turned in his seat so he could watch Daisy. It had been so long since they'd been in the same room together. Did she still think about him? He thought of her every single day, but it looked like she'd moved on with her life. She had a husband and four children. She thought that he was her past, but she was wrong. He was coming crashing into her present whether she liked it or not.

So far, she'd been good. His threats had worked, and she hadn't gone to the cops. She had kept that pretty little mouth of hers shut, and so long as she continued to do that, then he would keep his promise. He had no interest in killing her family. They had nothing to do with this. He would kill them if he had no choice just like he had killed the man at the park yesterday, but he would only lay a hand on them if Daisy did something stupid.

Daisy was the one he wanted most of all.

He had even toyed with the idea of keeping her alive for a while.

Making her suffer for days or weeks or even months before he finally killed her.

That could be fun. Killing her slowly a little at a time. First her mind, then her soul, and then finally her body.

It would be risky, but it was certainly doable.

Before he even realized it, his hand was on the door handle. He wanted to grab her now. Knock her out, tie her up, stash her in his trunk and take her away with him. It would be so easy. She wasn't even paying attention to her surroundings. He would have her before she even realized he was there.

He stopped himself before he got out of the car.

He wanted her so badly it physically hurt, and to be this close to her was torture, but now wasn't the time. He wanted her out there, watching the people she had dragged into this killed one by one. Constantly debating what the right thing to do was, constantly second-guessing herself and her decisions, constantly waiting for him to come for her. That she was suffering watching helplessly as he took out those around her made his revenge all the sweeter

There would be time to get to her.

It just wasn't tonight.

Tonight was Belinda's turn, then there were only two more to go before Daisy would be his.

She climbed into a car half a block farther down from where he was parked, and a moment later, its engine revved, and it drove off down the street.

He had intended to wait another hour or two before striking, but now energy and excitement were buzzing through his veins. He didn't want to wait. He was ready to make his next kill now.

Grabbing his bag, he locked his car behind him and headed for Belinda Jersey's house. The retired lieutenant might be ready and waiting for him, and that turned him on more than anything else. He was growing bored with such easy kills. Caden Gervase, Devon Paddy, Maddie Pickle—they had all gone so smoothly. He wanted a challenge. Perhaps he really would keep Daisy alive for a while before he killed her just for the fun of breaking her first.

As he approached, he noted that the house looked quiet and dark. There didn't appear to be any lights on, and he couldn't hear the hum of a television or radio.

He circled around the house to the back door and quickly picked the lock. To the best of his knowledge, Belinda didn't have an alarm system installed.

Once inside, he paused to draw in a deep breath. The house smelled like victory. Some people might think that was odd. Most people didn't think that victory had a fragrance, but they were wrong. It did. And it was the sweetest thing he had ever smelled.

He slunk through the dark shadows, heading for the stairs. He'd been in the house before, and he knew that Belinda's bedroom was upstairs. As he crept, he was hyper aware of everything around him. His eyes constantly roved about, searching every dark corner and every place someone might hide. His ears strained to take in every noise, judging it for relevance and dismissing most.

He was just at the top of the stairs when he felt it.

His eyes hadn't seen anything, and his ears hadn't detected a sound, but he knew someone was there. She must have been looking out a window, seen him approaching, laid in wait for him.

Because he trusted his gut, he angled his body a split second before a bullet tore through the air and connected with his shoulder. Instead of being a direct hit, it skimmed the surface of his skin, causing minimal damage. Still, he allowed his body to drop to the ground.

Footsteps echoed in the quiet house as she came toward him.

She thought she'd got him right through the heart. There was no way she could have known that he'd moved just enough to avoid being killed, and he intended to use that to his advantage.

He waited until she stopped right beside him. He could feel the heat pouring off her. She was nervous, and it had probably been years since she'd shot to kill another human being. Too bad for her it wasn't the first time she had used her position as an officer of the law to shoot someone. Twenty-five years ago she had taken his family from him, and tonight he would take her life as punishment.

In one fluid motion, he lifted his gun and fired.

Unlike hers, his bullet connected squarely with its target.

It plowed through Belinda's abdomen.

Her eyes grew wide. She fumbled to point her gun at him again, but he stood and easily swatted it from her grasp.

She crumpled to the ground, her hands pressed to her heavily bleeding wound.

The sound of gunshots would bring the police running and send neighbors into a tizzy, putting them on the lookout for anything unusual. A strange car could draw unwarranted attention, and he didn't want it leading the cops to his door so he would have to move fast.

He rifled through his bag and pulled out the scissors. He would have liked to spend a little more time here, but he was satisfied knowing Belinda Jersey would die the long, slow agonizing death she deserved.

"You know who I am and you know why I'm here," he whispered as he bent down and grabbed one of her hands.

To her credit, she met his gaze squarely, her mouth drawn in a thin line as she battled the pain that must be crushing her.

He was about to make that pain a million times worse.

He snapped the scissors.

Belinda paled. He heard her suck in a breath, but she wouldn't scream. With each successive finger that came off, her color worsened and her teeth pressed into her bottom lip so firmly that blood began to trickle down her chin.

She thought she was too good to scream.

Let's see if she kept that up with what he had planned next for her.

He left her where she was. He wasn't worried about her getting away; her injuries left her mostly incapacitated. The wound to the stomach would kill her, but not right away. He didn't want her dead just yet.

Quickly, he tipped some gasoline about, then made a trail down the stairs.

With a smile, he lit the match.

Let's see if she could hold back those screams when the flames hit her.

He tossed the match and watched the fire spring to life.

Then he turned and walked away.

He was a murderer now—no longer just a killer—and he was proud of it.

* * * * *

12:45 A.M.

Ryan couldn't take his eyes off the dancing flames.

The house was an inferno.

He hated fires.

Sofia had almost been killed in a fire just after they met. He'd already been in love with her, and the thought of losing her had been soul destroying. He had literally walked through the flames to save her.

And the fire from a few days ago was still raw. When he woke in the middle of the night, he could still feel the heat of the flames. His lungs and throat were still rough from the smoke. The feeling of thinking he was going to die lingered.

And now, here he was watching another fire.

He felt so helpless.

He wanted to help, to do something, but there was nothing for him to do. The fire department was here. They were working on putting out the fire, so all he could do was stand back and try not to get in the way.

A blur to his left caught his attention, and he snapped an arm around Paige's waist as she ran past and dragged her up against his chest, holding her firmly.

"Was she in there?" Paige screamed, trying to break free.

He didn't answer.

He didn't need to; she already knew.

"Let me go." His partner fought to get away from him.

Keeping one arm around her waist, Ryan wrapped his other around her chest and held her tighter. She wasn't thinking clearly. If he let her go, she was likely to go running straight toward the burning building.

"Ryan," Paige cried.

"I know." He held her tighter.

"We have to get her out." Paige continued to struggle.

"She's out," he said quietly. The firefighters had been carrying her out when he'd arrived.

"Where is she?"

He knew his partner was in denial, so he answered gently. "She's dead, Paige."

"No!" The word was ripped from her throat, and she began to cry.

Belinda's death was going to hit them all hard. They'd known her for so long, and she had been their boss for over a decade. She had been there at his wedding; Paige's, too. She'd spent time with his kids. They hadn't just worked together, they'd been friends.

Paige had stopped fighting him and sagged in his grip. He could feel her body shuddering as she silently wept. Ryan turned her around and held her as she cried, tears pricking the backs of his own eyes.

At last, she fell quiet. "Arson?" she asked against his chest.

"We don't know yet."

"Another fire. Could it be him?"

He'd been thinking the same thing. So far, the killer had set fire to both Caden Gervase and Devon Paddy's houses, but not

Maddie Pickle's. He killed one victim a day, and usually in the early morning, so it was around the time he would be striking.

This could be him or it could be a horrible accident.

Paige pushed at his chest and straightened up. He slowly released his hold on her, making sure she wasn't going to do anything reckless.

"I'm okay," she assured him, shooting him a watery smile.

Ryan knew she wasn't.

None of them were.

They'd just lost a good friend, and whether it was murder or an accident, it was a huge loss.

"We should see if we can take a look at her body," Paige said. Pain was still in her eyes, but she had tucked it away and pulled her cop face back on.

He made himself do the same. "You want to see if she's missing any fingers."

She nodded. "It will either confirm that she's his next victim or not."

It would.

Without another word, they headed for the ambulance that was parked just a couple of houses down. When they reached it, his eyes locked straight onto the white sheet on the stretcher. Knowing that it was someone he knew underneath it was unsettling. Ryan was trying to keep his feelings and emotions carefully bottled away, but being this close to Belinda was making it difficult.

He turned to his partner and saw her eyes were also fixed on the sheet. He saw her swallow down another sob. Her eyes were shining brightly with unshed tears, but she pulled herself together and turned to the EMT. "Can we have a quick look at the body?" she asked.

The older man looked from her face to his. It was obvious that they were both upset. "I'm not sure you should," he said quietly.

Ryan shuddered. If the EMT didn't want them to look, then

Belinda must be in pretty bad shape. He wasn't sure he wanted to look. No, scratch that, he was *positive* he didn't want to look. "Was it the fire that killed her?" he asked.

"Yes," the man answered.

"But?" From the look on the man's face there was something else.

"But if the fire hadn't, the bullet to her abdomen would have," the EMT said in a rush.

So, it wasn't an accident.

It was murder.

"Was she missing any fingers?" Paige asked.

The EMT looked surprised by the question. "How did you know that?"

The confirmation they needed.

Belinda was victim number four. That meant there were still three to go.

"He's struck before," he replied. They'd kept that the killer cut off his victims' fingers from the press, so only those of them working the case were aware of it. Ryan wished they knew who he was so they knew who he was going to go after next and warn them. He hated feeling this helpless.

"I heard she used to be a cop. Did you know her?" the EMT asked.

"She was our boss before she retired a couple of months ago," Paige said softly.

"I'm sorry for your loss." The EMT's eyes were full of sympathy.

They nodded their thanks and slowly walked away, both lost in thought. Ryan's brain felt sluggish; it kept getting stuck on the thought that Belinda was dead.

"Ryan. Paige."

He looked up to see Jack and Xavier hurrying toward them. He hadn't known his brother and partner were here, but he shouldn't be surprised. Half the police department had turned up. Some were standing around looking at the still burning house in shock. Others were knocking on doors of the other houses in the street, trying to get information from the neighbors. No one would rest until Belinda's killer was found.

"We just spoke to a neighbor," Jack explained in a rush. His eyes looked frantic. Ryan felt his blood pressure jump.

"They saw something?" he asked.

"Someone visiting Belinda earlier tonight," Xavier replied.

"Who?"

"Daisy."

Blood drained from his face. "Could she still be in there?" Whatever had happened between Daisy and Mark, she was still his sister-in-law, and he thought of her as a sister.

They all turned to look at the house.

If Daisy was still in there, then she was already dead.

There was no way she could have survived.

The killer had used an accelerant, and the fire had spread quickly, consuming most of the house before firefighters even arrived on the scene.

Paige was already pulling out her phone, her hands shaking so badly she almost dropped it. She dialed and held it to her ear. A moment later relief flooded her face, and Ryan let out a breath he hadn't known he was holding.

"Are you okay?" Paige asked. She paused. "We need to talk to you later this morning." Another pause. "We'll explain when we see you. Be careful, Daisy."

"What did she say?" he asked as soon as his partner hung up.

"She asked what had happened. I didn't tell her, but I'm guessing since I'm calling her at this hour, she can figure it out."

Ryan nodded, feeling extremely disconcerted.

Daisy was involved.

They'd all been trying to deny the possibility, but after what had happened tonight, they couldn't any longer.

She and Caden knew each other, and it was seeming less and

less likely that the reason was because they were having an affair.

She had shown up on Paige's doorstep with a lame excuse to try and get information on the case.

She was here at Belinda's house tonight, even though as far as he'd known, the two didn't really know each other, and then just hours later Belinda was murdered and her house set on fire by the same person who had killed Caden and nearly himself and Paige.

That was too many coincidences to ignore.

She knew what was going on.

She had the answers they needed.

And she was going to share them.

Ryan didn't care that she was his sister-in-law; she wasn't getting any more special treatment. Four people were dead, another three were in danger, and everything seemed to keep pointing right back to Daisy.

He *would* find out what she knew, and if she was involved, sister-in-law or not, he would make sure she paid for Belinda's death.

* * * * *

5:33 A.M.

"Are you ready to leave?" He glared irritably at his boss.

He hated being stuck having to care for one of the babies. They were such disgusting little things. They smelled bad, they cried, they were always making themselves dirty, and they liked to share that filth around by throwing up on you or leaking from their diapers.

Why anyone would want one of them was beyond him.

The only thing he liked about babies was the money they brought in.

He didn't understand why they didn't get more girls.

Surely, the more they had, the better.

The more girls, the more babies.

The more babies, the more money.

If it were up to him, they would have dozens of girls and they would be perpetually pregnant. Teenage runaways were easy to find. There were hundreds of them. They could travel the country finding girls and bringing them here. It wouldn't be hard.

They should be raking in the cash; instead, they took in a safe amount. His boss was all about playing it safe. He never kept more than four girls at a time. He believed that if he brought in too many girls, it would draw undue attention to them. The occasional missing runaway was nothing. No one noticed that, but start kidnapping too many, and they could end up with the police on their tails.

So, they took just a few girls at a time and averaged three to four babies a year. Each infant could make upward of a million dollars. Black market babies were in high demand and not easy to procure, and if a bidding war was started, then the price skyrocketed.

They had a good reputation for providing healthy babies that were completely untraceable. The paperwork was always provided and looked legitimate. They'd never had anyone suspect that any of the children sold had come into their new homes via anything but legitimate means.

His boss was always careful about the families he chose to work with. They had to be able to keep the secret. They had to be able to hold up under interrogation should the need arise. And they had to be loaded with cash.

It all just seemed like such a waste.

They should be keeping more girls, producing more babies, bringing in more money.

But it wasn't up to him to make that decision. He wasn't in charge here. It was his job to lure the girls. It was a job he enjoyed. He loved tricking them. He loved the rush of knowing he could convince a vulnerable girl to trust him. And the moment where he showed his true colors and they realized they'd been conned was absolutely priceless.

He wouldn't be able to keep doing it much longer. He was looking older. He barely passed for a teenager these days, and once he no longer looked like a kid, he wouldn't be able to win the trust of the teen runaways.

What would his role be after that?

He brought food for the girls, and he was in charge of taking care of them, but he didn't want to spend his whole life doing that.

He wanted to be promoted.

He wanted to help run things.

He'd been at this for a long time now. He'd proved himself. He was a hard worker, and he'd successfully gotten every girl he set his sights on. Although it was sometimes hard to resist, he kept his hands off the girls because they weren't his to mess with. They were there to provide babies—nothing more, nothing less.

He had earned a promotion, and he would see that he got one.

He had no intention of tending to disgusting infants all his life.

"Let's go."

He looked up as his boss strode through the room. He didn't wait to see if his instructions were followed, just made for the front door.

With an annoyed grunt, he picked up the infant, trying not to get too close to it in case it decided to choose that moment to throw up, and headed for the car.

The baby was dressed in a yellow onesie that complemented his dark skin and fuzzy black hair. And along with him were several bottles of breast milk to get him through the next few days, a teddy bear, and a blanket with his mother's scent.

He set the baby in its car seat and then sat in the passenger seat, casting a cautious glance at his boss.

The man was all business, just like always. They had known each other for years, and yet they were virtual strangers. He didn't know any more about his employer than he had the first day they'd met. All he knew was that the man never said more than was necessary, never smiled, never talked about himself, never talked about anything he was interested in.

His boss scared him a little bit.

Not that he'd ever admit that out loud.

The man had been in this business for so long, nothing seemed to faze him. Screaming newborns, hysterical girls, the threat of the cops catching on to them. He took it all in stride. Snatching teenage girls off the street didn't bother him. He looked at them purely as merchandise—a way to make money. He didn't seem to have any negative feelings about forcing them to do things against their will. To him, they really were nothing more than a means to an end.

It had taken him a while to adjust when he'd first joined the team. He'd wanted in, but grabbing innocent runaways off the street niggled at him. These girls hadn't done anything wrong. They had simply been in the wrong place at the wrong time. They'd run because they were in trouble, but instead of finding help or peace, they were shoved into a cave and forced to bear babies who were then ripped from their arms.

But this was the life he had chosen. And taking those girls got easier each time. It was like a little piece of him deadened after each abduction. Now, he wanted more.

He drew in a deep breath. He may as well ask and get it over with.

"So, I was thinking …" He paused and cleared his throat. "I want to play a bigger role in the business. I can't play the part of a teenage runaway much longer, and I don't want to spend my life carrying food up and down the stairs to a bunch of pregnant girls, or changing diapers. So," he drew in a breath and stopped his rambling, "I would like to take on other responsibilities."

The man said nothing.

For so long that he actually started to squirm like a naughty child.

"Okay."

What?

Okay?

That was it?

He hadn't even asked a single question.

Was this a trick of some sort?

"Really?" he asked cautiously. This seemed too good to be true; there had to be a catch.

"Yes."

"I'd like to expand our business, add more girls." He had to force himself not to hold his breath as he awaited a response.

"Okay."

Okay?

Again?

He'd mentioned expanding several times and always been shut down because it was deemed too risky.

Part of him wanted not to push his luck, and the other part wanted to see how far he could go.

"At the moment, we have space for four girls. I was thinking we should up that to ten. Ten girls mean we can average ten babies a year, and depending on the timing, maybe a couple more. Ten babies a year at even half a million each totals up to five million a year. That's more than doubling our current income."

"All right."

Huh.

How about that.

Ask and you shall receive.

He was feeling pretty pleased with himself by the time they pulled to a stop in front of a local park. His boss liked to do the exchange in parks. He felt it was a neutral location, away from any potential prying neighbors of their clients, and a place where no one ever looked twice at anyone with a child.

Removing the baby car seat and bag, they both headed for the carousel. That was where they always made the exchange. As they got closer, he spotted them.

They stood together, arms around each other, and even from here he could see the fear and excitement battling on their faces. They couldn't quite believe yet that they were really getting the baby they had longed for, for so long.

Sometimes he wondered what these couples would think if they knew where their new babies had come from. Would they still want them? He believed people were inherently selfish, so he believed that they would sacrifice those girls' freedom so long as they got the baby they wanted.

"Is that him?" The woman dashed forward, closing the last few yards between them.

"Have you transferred the funds?" he asked, making sure to keep the baby car seat behind him. No money, no baby. It was as simple as that.

"Yes." The husband stood behind his wife.

Half of the money was deposited in their bank accounts when the couple contacted them. That money was nonrefundable. The rest of the money was due once the baby was born. If the couple didn't pay for it, the baby went to the next couple on the list.

His boss pulled out his phone, checking their bank accounts. When he gave the nod, he handed the baby over. The woman immediately pulled the child out of the car seat and cradled it to her chest, tears streaming down her cheeks as she and her husband stared at their new son.

He didn't feel joy that he'd brought happiness to an infertile couple.

He didn't feel guilt that he'd kidnapped a woman and artificially inseminated her, then stole her baby.

All he felt was hunger for more money.

* * * * *

146

8:08 A.M.

Belinda was dead.

The thought kept chasing itself around and around in her head.

Daisy felt like she was walking around in a daze.

Too many months of no sleep, not eating regular meals, the strain of being away from her family, plus the emotional upheaval of the last few days, and she was precariously close to losing it.

She couldn't think, she could barely function, and the cops were on their way here to interview her.

What was she going to tell them?

They knew she was involved. There was no use pretending otherwise.

It wouldn't take them long to figure out how.

Her entire world was about to come crashing down around her.

All of her lies would be exposed.

Her family would hate her.

Her friends would hate her.

This was her worst nightmare about to come to fruition. There was no way to stop it from happening. She could keep lying and tell them that she didn't know anything. That would buy her a little time, but it wasn't going to stop them. They had Caden ... they had Devon ... they had Maddie, and now they had Belinda. They had enough pieces to put the puzzle together and come up with the answers.

The knock on the door startled her even though she was expecting it.

She was shaking as she went to let them in. Daisy wanted to put on a mask of innocence, but she knew she wasn't going to be able to pull it off.

"Hello, Daisy," Ryan said as she opened the door. His eyes were different. Cold. This wasn't the brother-in-law she had known and loved.

"Daisy." Paige nodded. Her face was unnaturally pale, and her eyes were red with dark circles underneath.

It looked like they'd had a long night.

Paige hadn't told her what was going on when she'd called her a few hours ago, but as soon as she'd hung up, Daisy had switched on the news, and she'd seen that Belinda's house was on fire.

He must have been there while she and Belinda were talking, watching the house, waiting to strike.

Had he seen her?

She shivered at the thought of being that close to him.

"Can we come in?" Ryan asked the question, but he was already pushing past her into the hotel room.

She nodded numbly and closed the door behind them, trailing after them to the sitting area where they were already waiting for her.

"What is this about?" she feigned innocence as best she could.

Ryan just glared. He was so angry with her. In the almost twenty years they'd known each other, she didn't think she'd ever seen him look so angry. "How do you and Caden Gervase know each other?" he demanded.

If she had to answer questions, the best she could do was be as vague as possible. "We're old friends."

He rolled his eyes at that, and Paige reached over and rested a calming hand on his arm. "How long have you known each other?" she asked.

Daisy shrugged. "A while."

"You two were close?" Paige asked.

"I guess." She was trying to figure out where they were heading, what they were going to ask her, and what answers she was going to give them.

"Did he mention anyone watching him or contacting him before his murder?"

"No," she answered honestly. *She* had been the one who had

brought up the topic of someone leaving her a threatening letter.

"Do you know of anyone who would want to hurt him?"

"I don't have anything helpful that I can tell you, I'm sorry," she replied, wondering what she was going to say if they pushed her.

"You were at Belinda's house last night, why?" Paige was watching her closely. They knew she was lying.

"I wanted to ask her opinion on something." She was trying to be as honest as possible without giving anything away.

"What?"

"It was personal."

Paige arched a brow. "Did you see anyone hanging around?"

"No. No one." She might not have seen him, but he'd definitely been there. He could be watching her right now. Or her family. That was the most terrifying thought of all.

What if he knew the cops were here interviewing her?

Would he think that she had talked?

Would he go after her family?

"Daisy."

"Hmm?" She blinked. Had they asked her something? She was finding it increasingly difficult to concentrate.

"Do you know of anyone who might want to hurt Caden or Belinda?"

She just shook her head.

This was too much right now.

She needed to be alone.

She needed to think.

She needed to figure out what her next move was.

With Belinda dead, that meant there were only two more people for him to kill before he came for her. That gave her only three days left to live.

In ninety-six hours, Ryan and Paige would be investigating her murder.

Maybe she could run?

It was too late to save the others. Their deaths would forever be on her shoulders, but perhaps if she ran, she could draw him away, stop him from killing the next two people.

It could work.

She was the one he really wanted anyway, so if she ran, then she thought that he would probably follow her.

Maybe she should have tried that all along.

That might have stopped him from killing anyone.

She really should have thought of that earlier.

"Daisy."

The sound of her name snapped her attention back to Paige and Ryan. "Yes?"

"Did you know Devon Paddy?" Paige asked.

What did she say to that?

If she said yes, then she just gave them more ammunition to use against her. And if she said no, when they found proof that she did, she had also given them more ammunition to use against her.

"What about Maddie Pickle?"

Again, she just stared at them.

Her head was so heavy.

She wanted so badly just to lie down and sleep. Good sleep. Deep sleep. Sleep that was free from the haunting presence of nightmares.

She just wanted this to be over, but over meant being dead.

Dread had her stomach churning in a constant sickening series of revolutions like it was stuck on a fast spinning Ferris wheel.

Daisy knew she needed rest. She just didn't have much hope of getting any.

"Daisy, if you're in trouble, we can help you." Paige was looking at her earnestly. Fearfully. Like she somehow knew that she was one of the people on the killer's list.

"I'm fine." She tried to make her voice come out cool and confident, but instead, she sounded afraid and unsure.

"If you know who the killer is, you need to tell us," Paige pushed. Ryan just sat and glared at her.

"I can't help you, I'm sorry," she whispered. She wanted them gone. Now. She couldn't cope with this at the moment. All that mattered to her was keeping Mark and her children alive. She didn't care about herself. She'd be dead in a couple of days. Her family had to remain safe, and the only way to do that was to keep her mouth shut, but she was afraid that if they pushed her just a little harder, the answers would start tumbling out whether she wanted them to or not.

"Daisy, we're trying to help you." Paige looked exasperated.

She knew that, and she appreciated it, she really did. She was scared. She didn't want to be brutally murdered, and if there were a way to be one hundred percent certain that he would never lay a hand on her family, then she would tell them what they wanted to hear.

"If you know who he is, then that means he's coming for you." The look on Paige's face said she was ready to play hardball. The words she said next confirmed it. "Do you know what he does to them? He cut off their fingers. He cut off Caden's ear, stabbed him through the eyes, and cut all the way through his cheek and into his mouth. He used knives to secure Devon Paddy's hands to the wall then stabbed a knife up under his jaw and into his nose to silence him, then he cut him over and over again till he got bored and killed him. Maddie Pickle had her teeth knocked out, her tongue cut out, and her eyes gouged out. He shot Belinda then set fire to her house. She was still alive when the flames got to her. They were all alive when he tortured them."

Her stomach roiled.

She was going to be sick.

She'd known it would be bad. She knew he was angry, but she hadn't known it was this horrific.

"I don't feel well," she mumbled stumbling to her feet. "You need to leave."

"We can't keep you safe if you won't talk to us," Paige pleaded.

Daisy just shook her head.

"We know you know something, Daisy," Ryan growled. "And if I find out you had anything to do with Belinda's death, I don't care that we're related, I will make sure I see you rot in prison."

With that, he stood and stalked out of the room. Paige shot her an apologetic smile before following her partner out the door.

Daisy just stood there, her mouth hanging open in shock, staring after them.

She had never been spoken to like that before, especially from her beloved brother-in-law.

She wanted to cry, but tears wouldn't come. It seemed she was all cried out.

Instead, she just dropped to the floor, curled up in a ball, and debated for the millionth time whether or not she was doing the right thing.

* * * * *

9:26 A.M.

"She lied, straight to our faces," his brother grumbled as he and Paige joined them at the conference table.

"Daisy didn't give you anything?" Jack asked.

"Just lies," Ryan said bitterly.

He looked to Paige for some elaboration.

"She didn't answer most of our questions. She just kept saying she didn't know anything. She seemed distracted, and Ryan's right, she was lying, she knows something. I don't know what, but something." Paige rubbed tiredly at her eyes as she sank down into the chair Xavier pulled out for her.

"So we know she's involved, we just don't know how," he said.

"I know I haven't known Daisy as long as the rest of you," Xavier said, "but I just can't picture her being involved in murder or torture."

He agreed.

The Daisy that he'd known for approaching twenty years was sweet and kind and caring. She wouldn't hurt a soul. On the other hand, the Daisy he had known would never have moved out of her home without explanation and broken the hearts of her husband and children.

For Daisy to have done that, she had to have had a good reason.

Jack just wished he knew what that reason was. He was afraid that Daisy had gotten herself mixed up in something dangerous. She could be one of the seven people on the killer's list. Which at worst, gave them less than twenty-four hours to save her life, and at best, ninety-six.

They had to get her to talk.

"Belinda and Devon Paddy used to be partners." Xavier told Ryan and Paige what they'd learned while the two were interviewing Daisy.

Belinda's death hadn't sunk in yet.

He had known her for so many years, they had worked so many cases together; she hadn't just been his boss but his friend as well.

Since she retired, he hadn't made an effort he should have to keep in contact. He and Laura had kept intending to invite Belinda over for dinner so they could catch up, but things kept getting in the way. His job was busy and had unpredictable hours. Laura worked long hours at the women and children's center she helped run. They had a six-and-a-half-year-old son and a five-year-old daughter who always took priority over everything else. Plus a big extended family. Mark and his family, Ryan and his family, Laura's sister and her family, his parents, her parents, Paige and Xavier—who might not be biologically related but who were every bit a member of his family as those who were—and their families. Finding time for friends was hard.

But those were all just excuses.

They should have found the time to catch up with Belinda, and they hadn't. Now it was too late.

"Twenty-five years ago," Xavier continued, snapping him out of his thoughts.

Paige nodded. "So, this has to be related to an old case of theirs."

"Daisy was a kid back then," Ryan said. His face finally softened a little.

"We thought we might be looking for a case involving a kid because of Caden Gervase and Maddie Pickle," Xavier said.

"Maddie Pickle has been a social worker all her life," he said.

"And Caden Gervase was a teacher before he was a principal," Paige added.

"Everything lines up," he said. "This could be related to a case they all worked. Daisy could be the case."

"What do you guys know about Daisy's past?" Xavier asked.

"She doesn't talk much about her childhood," Ryan replied. "We would have to ask Mark, but I don't remember her ever discussing her family other than to say that they were dead. I don't even know how many siblings she had—if any."

"If something went bad with them, that would explain why she didn't want to talk about her family or her past," he said. He'd always thought it was a little odd that Daisy never mentioned her family. She had told them that they were dead but she'd never elaborated as to who exactly was dead. She hadn't invited any family to her and Mark's wedding, no aunts or uncles or cousins. No one. He'd thought it was sad that she was all alone in the world, and his entire family had made sure that she knew that she was one of them now, that she wasn't alone.

"If Daisy's family are really all dead, then who would be doing this now?" Paige asked. "We were assuming that the killer was someone who had had his children removed from the home, but Daisy said her family was dead. If she was telling the truth, then who would want to get revenge for her being taken and placed in foster care?"

"Some children who have been abused also feel shame and guilt over what happened to them. That might be why she never told any of us about it and why she said they were dead," Ryan suggested. "It might have been easier to accept what happened and move on if she pretended they were dead."

"Could also explain why she's not talking. If this is one of her parents—and we're assuming her father, given Tony's statement of seeing a man leaving the scene of Caden Gervase's murder—that she was taken away from, then maybe, even if there was abuse or neglect involved, she still loves them. Plenty of abused kids still love their abuser," Paige said.

"If we're right, then Daisy isn't a potential victim," Xavier said. "He would be punishing whoever took her away from him. He's done the cops, the social worker, the teacher that she might have confessed to. Which probably explains the relationship with Caden. If he was the teacher she first told, then she probably felt safe with him. They might have developed a sort of father-daughter relationship that continued into her adult life."

"If she was abused, and she suspected that her father was back, then she might be too scared to talk. She already knew what this man was capable of, and now she's seen firsthand how he's hunting down the people he believes to be responsible for taking her away from him. She might be too scared to tell us about it for fear that he'll come after us," he said.

"She looked scared," Paige said. "And the other day in my house when she was watching me and Elias and the girls, she looked sad. I don't think she wanted to move out of her home and away from her family. She looked like she missed them. But she did move out. Maybe he'd made contact, let her know that he was back and she was afraid he might come after her family."

"Daisy might not be a potential murder victim," Jack said slowly. "But if this is her father, then he could want her back, which means she's still in danger. This man is ruthless. He's going to take out anyone who gets in the way of him getting what he wants, just like he killed that jogger who interrupted him while he was with Maddie. That means everyone involved in this case is potentially at risk."

"Jack, maybe you should try talking to her," Paige suggested. "You're good at getting people to open up. Maybe you'll be able to get something out of her that the rest of us couldn't. We need to know if this is her father, and if it is, who else might be on his list. He's only killed four of his seven intended victims. If she can tell us who else was involved, we might be able to save the last three. And we need to know his name, where he might be staying, anything else she can give us. She's our only chance at stopping this before he finishes."

And the killer's end game might be Daisy herself.

If he viewed Daisy as his property, he wasn't going to give her up. Killing the people responsible for taking her away from him and then getting her back made sense.

He would not let that happen.

Losing Daisy would destroy his brother and his nieces and nephews.

This man had already killed one of his friends. He wasn't going to lose anyone else that he cared about. Not Daisy, not Mark or the kids, not his partner, not Ryan and Paige, no one. His family meant the world to him, and he didn't like anyone threatening them.

"You guys should go through Belinda and Devon's old files, see if you can find one with Daisy. If I have something concrete I can use, it might help me get her talking."

Paige was right. He seemed to possess some ability to get victims to open up and share things that they wouldn't with anyone else. His wife always told him that it was because he possessed this air of confidence that made people feel safe and secure around him. Jack didn't know if she was right or not, but if he could get Daisy to talk to him, tell him what she knew, then they might be able to end this before anyone else got hurt.

* * * * *

11:52 A.M.

She had been lying in the bath so long the water had turned cold, and yet she still didn't move.

It was more like she *couldn't* move.

Daisy felt like she had reached the end of her rope.

She had given up hope.

There was no way out of this. She was ready to just lie here in her hotel room and wait for him to come for her. It didn't matter. Nothing did. Nothing except making sure that he left her family alone.

Had he seen Ryan and Paige here earlier?

She was worried that he was watching her and he'd seen them and think that she hadn't heeded his warnings and had told all to the cops. She was so scared he would punish her for the perceived refusal to follow his instructions by hurting her family. She would warn them if she could, but none of them would answer her calls. Even if they did answer, what could she say but ask them to be careful? And without any explanation, they would just think she was crazy.

There was nothing she could do to stop him.

She couldn't find him, and even if she could track him down, that wasn't going to help her.

So, she was done.

When she got unbearably cold, she would drag herself out of the bath, dry off and collapse into bed. She probably wouldn't sleep, but she could at least just lie there and rest.

As exhausted as she was, her brain was too wound up for sleep. Probably the only way she was going to get any sleep right now was with the assistance of some sleeping pills.

Sleeping pills.

That was a thought.

One that hadn't occurred to her before now.

Maybe there was a way to stop him from killing her.

If she ended her own life before he got a chance to take it from her.

That would definitely solve her problem.

It would spare her from having to suffer horrifically before he killed her. Daisy knew he would do worse to her than he had done to the others because she was the one who'd started it all. She was the root of the problem. She was the cause of it all.

But if she were gone, it would be over.

Her death could stop it all.

End her family curse.

Perhaps she could go to the hospital. She could warn Mark and see if she could sneak some sleeping pills from somewhere.

Feeling a little better now that she had a plan, Daisy was just contemplating actually moving when she heard her hotel room door open.

Had she put the do not disturb sign on the door?

She didn't think so.

It was probably a maid coming in to clean and remake the bed, thinking that she was out.

"I'm in the bathroom," she called out, hoping the maid would leave and move on to the next room. "Sorry, I forgot to put the sign up."

She pushed herself up. For some strange reason, she didn't like to let the water out of the tub while she was still in it. Daisy was about to climb out when the bathroom door swung open.

Had Ryan or Paige come back?

Surely the maid wouldn't come in here looking for her.

But it wasn't the maid or one of her friends that stepped into the room.

It was a man, dressed all in black, his face covered by a black balaclava.

She stared in shock.

Was this really happening?

Was he coming for her now?

She'd thought she would be last.

Maybe he wanted her to watch him kill the last two?

Why disguise himself?

She knew who he was.

What should she do?

She'd never been in this position before.

Should she scream?

Should she try to run?

Should she look for a weapon?

Why wasn't she doing something?

Anything.

She was just standing there like an idiot waiting for him to come for her.

He took a step toward her, and her body suddenly sprang back to life.

She tried to jump out of the tub but slipped.

She fell, and it seemed to all happen in slow motion. Her head cracked into the wall and pain splintered her world into two. She landed with a splash, water sloshed everywhere, her body thudded onto the hard fiberglass floor of the bathtub.

Pain bounced around her skull.

She knew she had to move. She tried to, but her limbs wouldn't cooperate. They were sluggish and uncoordinated.

Then hands were on her.

One wrapped around her neck and shoved her head under the water. She thrashed frantically. She'd been wrong before. She *didn't* want to die. She wanted to live. She wanted her family back.

Then all of a sudden he let go.

Her lungs were begging for air.

She burst up out of the water and dragged in several gulps. Without pausing too long, she scrambled out of the bathtub, her eyes roving the room looking for anything she could use to defend herself.

Before she could do anything, she was roughly grabbed under the arms then tossed back toward the bath. She landed on the edge, her stomach taking the brunt of the fall, and again pain spiraled throughout her battered body.

Daisy thought he would shove her head back under water, but instead, he pinned her in place, bent over the side of the bath, her bare backside sticking up in the air.

She squirmed.

She'd never felt so exposed in her life.

Even the pain couldn't mask the fear and humiliation racing around inside her.

She knew what he was going to do.

He wanted to rape her.

Maybe this wasn't *him*.

Maybe the was just some random assault.

Maybe this was some sort of cosmic punishment for all the people she'd gotten killed.

If she craned her neck to the side she could keep her mouth and nose out of the water, but there was nothing she could do to get out of this man's grip. He had one hand pressed against her back, between her shoulder blades, holding her in place while his other hand found its way between her legs.

He touched her, and her stomach lurched.

His hands felt like flames setting her entire body on fire.

When she felt him touching her entrance, she let out the most pathetic, pitiful, whimpered moan.

The sound seemed to turn the man on because she felt him grow hard against her back, but it also snapped some sense back into her.

This was not happening.

It wasn't.

It simply wasn't.

He was distracted. He thought that he had her completely under his control. But he was wrong.

She wasn't giving up, and she wasn't letting him take her body from her.

Concentrating every single bit of energy she had inside her, she rammed her head back and connected squarely with his face. Pain almost shattered her, but the man groaned and released her.

Daisy didn't think twice.

She just ran.

She didn't know how, but there must have been enough adrenalin pumping through her system for her body to move on autopilot.

Out of the bathroom, through the hotel room, out the door, and into the hall.

She heard him coming behind her, but she didn't stop and look back.

A bullet whizzed by her.

She had tried to escape, but she was going to die anyway.

Then she bumped into something hard and bounced off it.

She didn't even have time to register what it was or what was happening before she was tackled to the ground. Something lay on top of her. No, some*one*. Someone was covering her body with their own.

That same person fired off a shot in the direction she'd just come running, then muttered a curse.

Jack.

It was Jack.

Somehow, her brother-in-law was here.

It hadn't really dawned on her that she was still naked until he carefully levered his body off hers and shrugged out of his jacket.

"Are you hurt?" he asked as he slipped an arm behind her shoulders and wrapped her in his jacket.

Injured?

Her brain seemed to have lost the ability to comprehend.

"Blood," she heard him mutter, then she was scooped up off the floor.

She hung limply in Jack's arms as he carried her back to her hotel room. He deposited her on the bed, spread the covers over her, then picked up his phone.

Phone.

He was going to call for help.

If he called for help, she'd be taken to the hospital.

If she were taken to the hospital then *he* would find out.

"Jack, no," she struggled to sit.

He frowned at her. "You're hurt, Daisy. You need to be checked out."

She was quickly growing panicked as shock set in. "No. Jack. No. Don't call anyone. Don't. Please, Jack. Please."

"Okay, okay," he soothed, gently laying her back against the soft pillows. "I won't call an ambulance, but I'm getting you help, and then we're going to talk."

A sense of relief settled over her. Things were out of her hands now. Daisy closed her eyes and let herself drift away.

*　*　*　*　*

12:47 P.M.

Daisy.

That one thought consumed him.

When Jack had called to tell him that Daisy had been attacked and that she was refusing medical treatment, Mark had dropped what he was doing and headed straight for the hotel.

Now he was standing in an elevator, waiting impatiently as it made the impossibly long journey to Daisy's floor.

That his brother wouldn't give any details about what exactly had happened to her was fueling his fear.

How badly was she hurt?

Who had attacked her?

Why had someone attacked her?

She was connected to Caden Gervase. Was her attack related to the murders?

The questions kept tumbling around inside his head, but he had no way of getting answers until he got there.

After what felt like an eternity, the elevator doors finally opened and Mark basically ran down the corridor. He had to see Daisy. His mind was conjuring up too many scenarios of what he was going to see when he got to her room, and the only way to stop them was to see her with his own eyes.

He expected to see the place crawling with cops and crime scene techs, but instead, when he entered the hotel room, all he saw was Jack in a chair beside the bed.

There was a small lump in the middle of the bed.

Daisy.

Her eyes were closed.

As he stepped closer, Mark felt his wildly beating heart begin to slow. She looked okay.

Then he stepped closer still.

Dark marks circled her neck. Blood streaked one side of her face where more bruises marred her skin.

A deep protective rage settled in his gut. Daisy had made mistakes, big mistakes, but she was still his wife, and he still loved her.

"What happened?" he growled at his oldest brother.

"I came to talk to her. We've had some developments in the case," Jack replied vaguely, and Mark bit down on the impulse to ask what those were. "I heard a gunshot," Jack continued, "and saw Daisy running toward me. I tackled her, fired off a shot, and the guy ran off. I couldn't leave her, so I didn't go after him. She was bleeding from her head, so I brought her in here intending to call an ambulance, but she freaked out and begged me not to, so I called you. Mark, she was naked," Jack finished quietly.

Mark's stomach dropped.

Naked.

Had she been raped?

Somehow, he managed to pull on a mask of clinical detachment and sat on the side of the bed. He couldn't look at Daisy as the woman he loved and the mother of his children. If he did, he was going to lose it. When he looked at her, he had to see her as the woman who had broken his heart. That was the only way he could function and treat her wounds.

"Daisy ..." He kept his voice calm and soothing as he perched on the edge of her bed and picked up her wrist to take her pulse.

Her eyelashes fluttered on her cheeks, and a moment later her large blue eyes opened to stare at him. It took her a moment before recognition flashed through them. Then she turned a weak frown in Jack's direction. "I told you not to call anyone." She winced as she spoke.

"And I told you, I was getting you help," Jack shot back. "You didn't want an ambulance, so you got Mark instead."

Slowly, her gaze swung back to his, but she refused to directly meet it.

Stamping down on his emotions, he shone a light in her eyes. "Headache?" he asked crisply.

She kept her eyes down but nodded.

"Dizziness?"

She gave another small nod.

Her pulse was weak but nothing to worry about. Her pupils were equal and reactive.

"Does she have a concussion?" Jack asked.

"I don't think so." Mark took hold of her face, and for a split second her eyes darted to his. He saw the fear in them, and the pain, but he also saw love. Daisy still loved him, so why did she leave?

Clinical.

Stick with clinical right now.

His emotions were too messy, and he still didn't know the extent of her injuries.

He tilted her head. The gash was above her right ear. It looked deep, and she'd probably need stitches. Right now, he didn't trust his hands were steady enough to do them.

Mark turned his attentions to her neck. The scumbag who attacked her had wrapped his hand around her throat. It took every bit of control he had not to scream and track the man down and see how he liked it when someone strangled him. The bruises were still darkening. When he probed them, she winced, her eyes scrunching closed.

"She should go to the hospital, shouldn't she?" Jack asked.

"Her neck is badly bruised. It could keep swelling, cutting off her air supply, so yes."

"No." Daisy bolted upright. She flinched at the obvious pain she was in, but it wasn't enough to stop her from trying to climb out of bed.

She was fast and already on her feet before he could react. She swayed, and her knees buckled. Mark caught her before she could hit the floor.

Jack's jacket dropped from her shoulders, and the full extent of her injuries became obvious.

"Daisy," he whispered, horrified. There were bruises across her stomach, down one side of her body, and a handprint shaped one on her back.

She tried to struggle out of his grip, but he simply tightened his hold and gathered her up into his arms. She needed x-rays and scans; she needed the hospital.

"Mark, no." Her struggles intensified when he started walking toward the door, and she realized where he intended to go.

The pure panic in her voice made him stop. What had she gotten herself into that she was this afraid of a trip to the hospital?

"Please, Mark," she begged. "If you still love me, then don't take me to the hospital."

She knew just how to get to him.

With a growl, he stalked back to the bed, deposited her with a gentleness that belied the anger inside him, and proceeded to check all of the bruises covering her body. When he had confirmed that nothing looked too serious, he covered her with the blankets.

Then he just stood there staring at her.

He could have lost her tonight.

Despite everything that had happened, everything that she had done, he still loved her utterly and completely.

The thought of someone hurting her filled him with so much rage, he saw red.

Daisy was shaking. She was in shock, and she really should be in the hospital, but if she was going to refuse to go, then he'd do whatever he could for her here. Starting with stitching her head wound.

Readying his supplies, he got to work.

She kept her eyes closed, refusing to look at him.

Touching her again after so long felt so good.

When he was done, he let his fingers trail down her cheek, settling on her jaw.

He couldn't help caressing her soft skin.

Her eyelids flickered, and she opened her eyes to meet his, confusion shining brightly in their bluey depths. She looked so sad. Just like she'd look when she'd come by the house while they'd been outside building snowmen. He'd taken pity on her then, felt bad that the kids were shutting her out. At least, that's what he'd told himself. But really, he just hated to see her sad; her pain was his pain.

His eyes dropped to her lips.

He wanted to kiss her.

Like magic, her gaze dropped to his lips, her own parting.

"Daisy, do you know who attacked you?" Jack asked, breaking the spell.

Mark threw his brother a dirty look. He had the worst timing.

"Daisy?" Jack prompted.

"No," she whispered. She looked so small and vulnerable. How could someone hurt something so beautiful, so precious?

Jack came and sat on the bed on Daisy's other side. "Did he rape you, Daisy?"

Her eyes darted about, settling on nothing, and she gave a single shake of her head.

The bottom fell out of his universe.

She was lying.

It was written all over her face.

He needed to get out of this room.

He was suffocating in here.

He had done what he'd come here for. He'd checked Daisy out as a doctor. The rest was up to Jack.

Mark was going to leave when he felt his brother's eyes on him. The look Jack gave him was clear. *Stay.*

He uncurled his fists and didn't move.

Jack was right. This wasn't about him. Eighteen years of marriage, four children—surely he owed her this at the very least.

"Daisy," Jack prodded gently. "Are you sure that he didn't sexually assault you?"

How did his brother do this every day?

He had been in this room for less than thirty minutes, and he was sick to his stomach.

He had dealt with victims before, even sexual assault victims, but this was his *wife.* He was going to lose his mind.

"He …" Daisy's tongue peeked between her lips and wet them. "He t-tried. He-he t-touched me w-with his h-hand." She lifted her own hand and stared at it.

Mark quickly grabbed her hand and held it tightly before he let out all the anger stewing inside him. Being clinical was out the window. He couldn't pretend she was just some patient. Daisy looked from their joined hands up to his face, her expression confused.

He was equally as confused.

He didn't know what he was doing. He wasn't sure he should be sending her mixed signals in her current condition, but all he knew was that he couldn't let her go through this alone.

"Could this have something to do with the murders?" Jack pressed on.

Mark expected Daisy to offer a denial. Tell them that she didn't know anything. That the murders were nothing to do with her.

Instead, she met Jack's gaze squarely. "I don't know."

* * * * *

1:23 P.M.

She knew that she was done.

She couldn't do this alone.

She had to take that leap of faith and put her trust in her family.

Daisy met Jack's gaze squarely and answered honestly. "I don't know." The man who had attacked her wasn't who she'd been expecting to come after her.

"We know you're involved, Daisy," Ryan said from the door.

He was right. They already knew too much, and it wouldn't take much longer before they figured out the rest. She may as well speed things up a little and fill them in.

She drew in a deep breath. This wasn't going to be easy, but she'd been in this place before, and she'd done the right thing. It was time to do the right thing again.

"I'm sorry," she said to Mark. She prayed that he didn't get hurt because of what she was about to say.

"What? Why?" He looked confused.

Ignoring him, she turned to Jack. "You'll make sure that you put him and my kids into protective custody?"

"Protective custody?" Mark jerked to his feet. "Daisy, what is going on?"

Ryan, Paige, and Xavier had closed the hotel door and all pulled up chairs around the bed. She felt boxed in. Bordering on claustrophobic. If she weren't so sore from the attack she would have gotten up and paced.

"He threatened them?" Xavier asked.

"Yes."

"Is that why you left?" Mark asked.

She couldn't look at him. "Yes."

"We don't think that Mark and the kids are the only ones in danger, Daisy. We think he might try to kidnap you," Jack said. He still sat beside her on the bed, and his blue eyes were full of sympathy and concern.

"He doesn't want to kidnap me," she sighed. "He wants to kill me." She didn't have to be looking at Mark to know he'd visibly paled. She could feel it. "What did you already find out?" The more they knew, the better, at this point. It was less she had to say out loud.

"Caden Gervase used to be one of your teachers when you were a kid," Ryan said.

She nodded. She was so thankful he had been. If he hadn't—if there hadn't been someone she trusted—who knows what would have happened to her.

"Maddie Pickle was the social worker who worked your case," Ryan continued.

She nodded again.

"You were in foster care?" Mark asked incredulously. She knew this was a lot for him to take in and unfortunately, there was a lot more to come.

Daisy gave another nod in response to Mark's question.

"Belinda and Devon Paddy were the cops involved," Ryan said.

Oh yeah, they'd been involved, all right. "Yes."

"Your father was abusive." Ryan's confidence faltered a little on that. They knew something had happened to have her removed from her home, but they had no idea what.

"My father never laid a hand on me," she replied.

"Then why were you taken away?" Jack looked confused.

This wasn't easy, and part of her brain still screamed at her to play it safe and keep her mouth shut, but she'd come this far. She had to push through her fears. "You're sure that you'll keep Mark and the kids safe?"

"Positive," Xavier promised.

"Just tell us what happened to you," Mark said tightly.

Okay.

She could do this.

"My parents dealt in black market babies." She could tell by the looks on their faces, they hadn't been expecting that. "They kidnapped young runaways, kept them in the basement, got them pregnant, then sold the babies," she explained in a rush, letting out a sigh of relief now that she'd said it.

"How did you find out?" Paige asked. Her face had gone pale, and Daisy assumed it was because Paige's adopted daughters had been held prisoner in the early years of their lives, so it was a sensitive topic for her.

"They showed me the basement," she replied. She cast a glance at Mark, trying to gauge his reaction to what she was saying.

"Who did?" Jack looked confused.

"My parents. It was a family business. It wasn't just my parents, my mother's sister and her husband were involved, too. And my older brothers." She looked at Mark again. He was sitting like he was made of stone. She couldn't read his face at all.

"They wanted to bring you in on it, too," Ryan said. A statement, not a question, but she nodded anyway. "How old were you?"

"Thirteen. It was the day after my thirteenth birthday. They took me down to the basement, explained to me what they were doing, and what my role was going to be. They wanted me to lure teenage girls. I was a kid. They said other kids would trust me."

Why wouldn't Mark look at her?

Was he repulsed by what he'd learned about her family?

This was why she'd never said anything about her past. Mark's family was full of cops. They were good people. If he'd known what her family was really like, he would never have been interested in her.

Her family kidnapped vulnerable teenage girls, held them prisoner, and forced them to have babies that were then ripped from their arms.

She needed Mark to look at her.

She needed to know what he was thinking.

She needed to know if she had already lost him forever or if there was a chance for her to make up for hurting him.

Obviously noticing that Mark was distracting her, Ryan moved his chair so that he blocked her view of her husband. "Were there girls there in the basement while you were there?" he asked.

"Yes. Four of them. They were a little older than me." Daisy would never get the terrified faces of those girls out of her mind. They'd been so scared. And they were so young. One of them had been heavily pregnant; another had been holding a tiny infant in her arms. She had been so overwhelmed. Overwhelmed and sick to her stomach.

"What did you do?" Jack asked.

"I took a photo. It was of one of the girls holding a baby. My parents said it was what they showed to prospective buyers to help them get an idea of what the baby might look like, and I went to the teacher I trusted most at my school."

"Caden Gervase," Ryan said quietly.

"Yes. He called the police. I was scared he wouldn't believe me, but he did. I probably looked shaken enough that he knew I wasn't lying. And I had the photo. I don't even remember taking it. I just had it in my hand when I went to him. It turned out the girl had been reported missing two years earlier. Belinda and her partner came, and I told them everything I knew. Then Mrs. Pickle came, and she took my younger brother, Thorne, and me to a group home."

"What happened to your family?" Paige asked.

"I didn't lie when I said they were dead. When the cops showed up, my family decided they weren't going to prison. They shot at the cops who fired back. Both my parents, my two older brothers, my Aunt Kerryn and Uncle Drew, and their fifteen-year-old daughter, Xaria, all died that day."

"Seven people," Jack said.

Daisy nodded. "That's why he has seven people to kill now."

"Do you know who it is?" Xavier asked.

She hesitated. She knew who she *thought* it was, but she wasn't positive.

"Daisy?" Xavier prompted.

"I don't know for sure. There was another cousin, Liam. He escaped somehow. He didn't die with the others. The cops thought he burned down the house and ran."

"The house was burned down?" Jack asked.

"Yes. I know this killer has been doing the same thing."

"So, you think it's your cousin?" Paige asked.

"I think, but I don't have any proof, and I'm not one hundred percent certain. For all I know, it could be one of the parents who lost their baby when the truth came out. I think the cops were able to ID a couple of the babies from what little they got out of the house after the fire. Or it could be a relative of one of my family's victims. It could be the woman who survived. I really don't know." Daisy sunk wearily down against her pillows. She had blocked out what had happened in here tonight by distracting herself with retelling her childhood horror, but dark thoughts were creeping in.

"Someone escaped?" Jack asked, drawing her attention back to him and their interrogation.

"Yes. I don't know who she was, and I don't know how she got out. All I know is that one of the women from the basement got out of the house alive before it burned down."

"You have a younger brother. Could he be involved?" Jack asked.

"No," she replied empathically. "Thorne didn't even know. They didn't tell me about the family business until I was thirteen. Thorne was only eleven. As far as I know, he still doesn't know all the details."

"You two aren't close?" Ryan asked.

"Not really. We had another aunt. My dad was an only child. I didn't have any grandparents, but my mom had another sister. She wanted to take both of us, but I couldn't go with her. I couldn't be sure she hadn't been involved, and I freaked when she arrived to pick us up." She dropped her eyes to her lap and twisted her hands together. She'd always felt guilty about how she had treated her aunt who as far as the cops could tell had not been involved in the black-market sale of babies. The woman had just learned the truth about her sisters, then Daisy had all but accused her of being the same. The look of hurt on her aunt's face when she had freaked out upon seeing her still had the power to bring tears to her eyes.

"So, you grew up in foster care," Jack said.

"Yes. The family was good to me. They made sure I was fed and clothed. That I went to school, did my homework, attended extracurricular activities. They made sure if I was out at a party with friends, that I knew I could call them if I got into trouble. They took good care of me, but they didn't love me. They took care of me because it was their job. They were my caregivers, not my family." She had never had a real family until she met Mark. His parents, his brothers, they had all welcomed her with open arms. Making it clear that she was one of them now, and never pressing her on her biological family when she made it clear she didn't want to talk about it.

"Why did you go for help?" Paige asked.

"Because it was wrong. What they were doing was wrong. I had to do whatever I could to stop it."

"You had to turn your family in, though. That's a big thing for a thirteen-year-old girl to do," Jack said.

"I did what any normal person would have done," she said simply. And that in saying—and believing—that she had to admit that her family was not normal.

She was tired now.

Her entire body ached with a dull thumping pain, and memories of the attack, of the man holding her under the water, of his hands touching the places on her body that no one but her husband had ever touched, were all hammering at her mind.

She wanted to sleep.

She wanted to just close her eyes and let sleep consume her.

Sensing this, Jack said, "You should get some rest now. You've been through a lot tonight. Mark can give you some painkillers and something to help you sleep."

Mark.

She couldn't bear to look at him.

How could he still want a life with her now? He knew who she really was. He knew why she'd broken his heart and walked away from him and their kids, and he knew she'd placed them in danger by talking to the cops.

"He'll kill anyone who gets in his way," she said sleepily, letting her eyes fall closed. "Quickly and painlessly. They snapped the girls' necks. They weren't murderers. They only wanted the babies for money. They killed the girls so there would be no loose ends. I'll be his last kill. Thorne will probably be number six. I don't know who his other one will be."

Sleep had already grabbed hold of her and dragged her under

before Mark could give her anything for the pain.

JANUARY 28TH

3:16 A.M.

Something woke her.

It took a moment to realize what it was.

Her security alarm.

She had installed a top-of-the-line security system as soon as she'd bought her house. Her safety was her number-one priority. She had been weak once before, not paid attention to what was going on around her, not been smart. She would *never* make those mistakes again.

Now, she was vigilant. Every single second of every single day. She would never give another human being a chance to hurt her.

So, she had made her house a virtual fortress, and she'd done the same with her heart. She didn't let people get close to her. She didn't trust them. She didn't trust anyone. It made for a lonely life—lonely but safe, and safety was what she craved most in the world. In her own way, Katrina was happy.

She picked up her phone and glanced at it to see what had tripped the alarm.

Someone had opened the kitchen window.

Someone was inside her house.

As well as alerting her, the security system would also have sent out warnings to the company who installed it and the local police. They would both be here within minutes. She could go to the safe room, barricade herself inside and wait for help, or ...

She could go after the intruder herself.

He wouldn't be expecting her. The security system was very good. Unless you knew what to look for, you would never notice the censors or cameras dotted throughout her house.

Touching her phone's screen, she brought up an image of her stairs. A man was slowly creeping up them. He thought he could come for her, he thought he could get her, but he had another thing coming.

Picking up the gun that she kept on her nightstand, she slid out of bed. Katrina was always armed. *Always.* She was a perfect shot and had a permit to carry a concealed weapon. She was heavily trained in self-defense, a black belt in karate, a boxer, and she spent hours a day at the gym training as a body builder. Never again would she be a small, weak, easy target.

The man was getting closer.

Hide or stay and fight?

She asked herself the question, but she already knew the answer.

She would stay and fight.

She wanted to teach this man a lesson.

He had picked the wrong house and the wrong woman.

Katrina kind of liked the idea of teaching this man a lesson and getting him off the streets so he couldn't hurt anyone else. At one time in her life, she had toyed with the idea of becoming a cop, but she would never have passed the psych exam, so instead, she'd focused her energies on becoming strong. She taught self-defense classes, worked as a personal trainer, and focused on her boxing and body building. In her own way, she was helping others to be strong, so they could fight for themselves.

A strange sort of rush flooded through her veins.

Adrenalin mixed with excitement and something else. Something she couldn't entirely name. Katrina would never hurt another human being, not after what she had been through, but the idea of hurting someone who wanted to hurt her first held a certain appeal. The same appeal boxing held. It gave her the ability to work out all her pent-up frustrations in a safe environment.

She liked that—needed it, even—and this would be so much better because this man was a predator and that's who she was really angry with. That's what her anger longed to latch on to. That's what her anger wanted to grab hold of and pummel and pummel until there was nothing left.

Hiding behind the door, she clutched her gun and waited.

It felt so empowering to be the one with the control.

Her body tensed as the door opened.

She held her breath and waited while he took a step into the room.

She could feel his confusion as he took in the empty bed.

She waited another second or two, and then she pounced.

"Don't move," she growled.

The man froze.

"I have a gun, and I would be all too happy to use it, so drop your weapon," she ordered. She almost vibrated with the need to hurt this man. He was the personification of every person who had ever hurt her. She wanted him to ignore her. She wanted an excuse to be able to hurt him.

The man didn't listen.

Katrina tightened her grip on her weapon. "Either you drop your weapon, or I will shoot you. I'll start with your knee and work my way around your body. I wonder how many shots I'll get in before the cops show up. They're already on their way."

"I don't have a weapon," he said.

She laughed at that. "As if. I'm not going to ask again."

With an irritated grunt, he tossed his gun onto her bed.

"Now turn around."

He grunted irritably again like she was the one annoying him, yet he was the one who had broken into her home at three in the morning.

"I don't like repeating myself." Even as she said it, Katrina hoped he disobeyed. Her finger was dying to pull the trigger.

The man turned. So slowly she almost snapped at him to hurry up, but then she caught a look at his face.

The world stopped spinning.

Her brain froze … her body with it.

It was him.

She didn't know how, but it was.

Her worst nightmare had come back to bite her.

Just like that, it was like the last twenty-five years of growing strong evaporated in this one instant.

All over again, she was that terrified teenager who had been tricked and kidnapped.

She was back in that basement in that cage.

She was scared and cold and hungry and hopeless.

She wasn't strong … she wasn't tough … she wasn't fearless … She didn't want to take her anger out on anyone. She just wanted to curl up in a ball and let fear consume her.

The man cocked his head, sensing her growing fear, and took a step toward her.

Katrina still held the gun, but now it shook.

Only he had the power to do this to her. To turn her from the strong, independent woman she had become to the trembling little girl she had been back then.

He advanced on her. He was going to kill her. She'd been paying attention to the news, and she knew someone had been killing all of them who'd been involved in the black-market baby case. That's why he was here. Revenge.

Sirens.

The night suddenly filled with sirens.

Help.

Help was coming, but was it going to get here in time? He could still kill her and make a run for it.

The gun was still pointed at him, and maybe that made his decision for him because he ran at her, but instead of wasting time killing her and risking getting caught, he just shoved her and ran out the door.

Shaky and wobbly on her feet, the force of the blow sent her sprawling backward and into the wall before she slid—as if boneless—to the floor.

Her head was a swimming mess.

That couldn't have just happened, could it?

It must have been a nightmare.

Just a horrible, bad dream.

She had dreamt about that time in her life so many times before.

If pain weren't zigzagging through her skull, she really would have thought that she was just dreaming.

Voices shouted, footsteps pounded, people came running toward her.

Katrina shrank away from them.

It had to be him.

He was back.

And this time, he would kill her.

"Ma'am, are you hurt?" A figure hunkered down in front of her.

The voice wasn't his, and when she made herself look at the face, it wasn't his either.

She sighed with relief.

"Ma'am?" The cop was eyeing her with concern.

Pull yourself together, she reprimanded herself.

He can only break you if you let him.

"I'm okay, he ran." She struggled to her feet, brushing away the cop's well-meaning hands.

"We're chasing him; hopefully, we catch him," the cop assured her.

Katrina nodded, but she didn't hold out much hope. He would get away, and then he'd just wait and come back for her.

It wasn't fair.

She had fought so hard to get strong, to recover, to build herself back up so much tougher than she had been before.

How could he shatter her in one single second?

* * * * *

4:00 A.M.

She sprung awake on a strangled scream.

Still half stuck in her nightmare, Daisy expected to find herself in the bath, her head fully submerged, water flooding her mouth and nose, drowning her.

Instead, she found herself in a bed.

A strange bed.

She was no longer at the hotel, and she wasn't back at home, either.

The unfamiliar setting did little to calm her wildly thumping heart. She felt like she had just run a marathon rather than just woken up.

Fear coiled inside her. It wanted to spiral out and consume her. Fear about the attack and what had almost happened battled with fear that her cousin would soon come for her, which battled with fear that Mark would never be able to forgive her, even if she survived.

Daisy didn't want to be in bed any longer. The thought of sleep was too overwhelming. There were too many monsters waiting to haunt her dreams.

Carefully, she stretched out. She was stiff and sore from the attack. Plus, she had no idea how long she'd been asleep, but it was definitely long enough for every muscle in her body to tighten, and every single bruise to settle in.

She needed to move.

Although she didn't remember being brought here, she assumed that "here" was the safe house. It made her breathe a little easier to know that her family was safe. At least, whatever happened next, Liam wouldn't be able to get his hands on them.

If Liam was the killer.

She really wanted to believe that he wasn't. She wanted to believe that her entire family wasn't insane.

Padding quietly through the bedroom she'd been placed in, Daisy tried not to feel hurt that Mark hadn't stayed with her. He was angry, she got that, she really did. She had always known that if the truth came out, he would be. It was a huge blow to learn that your wife's family kidnapped runaway teenage girls and made them get pregnant so they could sell the babies for money. She just wanted to know if there was hope for them if he would give her a chance to make things up to him.

When she opened the bedroom door, she found herself at one end of a long hall leading to a stairway. Once she reached the stairs, she headed down them.

Voices sounded from a room at the front of the house, and she assumed they belonged to whichever cops were keeping watch over her family. She circled around to the back of the house hoping to find the kitchen; she badly needed some coffee.

Daisy froze at the kitchen door.

Mark sat at the table.

She wasn't sure she was ready to see him just yet. She couldn't face his anger on top of everything that had happened yesterday.

Forcing herself to keep moving, she flipped on the light and walked over to the coffeepot. "Couldn't sleep?" She tried to keep her voice light.

Mark grunted.

Her heart clenched. He was angrier than she'd thought. What was the point of being safe from a killer if she was going to lose her husband and family? She may as well be dead. She *was* dead without them.

She couldn't give up, though; she had to give him time. She had to be patient. He'd had a lot to take in over a short amount of time—*that* on top of her recent out-of-character behavior. He had to be so confused, as well as angry and hurt. She had to do whatever she could to fix things while she still had a chance because the death sentence hanging over her head hadn't gone anywhere.

"Can I sit?"

He glowered at her, but she interpreted his grunt as an affirmative.

Fighting her instincts to run, Daisy sat. She had to stop running from her problems and face them. Gathering her courage, she took a long sip of her boiling coffee. The hot liquid felt like heaven sliding down her aching throat.

"Are the kids here?" she asked. She assumed they were, but it seemed like an easy way to get him talking.

"Yes," he replied curtly.

She almost chickened out but made herself ask, "Do they know?"

Mark said nothing.

Daisy didn't know how to interpret that. She wasn't used to seeing her husband like this. Mark was usually so easygoing. He was sweet and kind and caring, and so much more than she deserved.

"I'm sorry, Mark." She shoved back from the table, unable to look at her husband's angry face any longer. "I know you're angry with me, and I never expected you to just forgive me when you found out. I know it will take time; I just hope I have enough time to make it up to you."

"That's not funny," Mark snapped.

She hadn't intended it to be. She didn't like living knowing someone wanted her dead. And not just wanted her dead but was simply biding his time until he could make it a reality.

Before she even realized he'd moved, Mark had spun her around and shoved her up against the wall. His mouth descended on hers, his hands wrapped around her stomach, their grip almost crushing, as he kissed her like he was starving and she was his only sustenance.

Abruptly, he let her go and stalked back to the table, leaving her panting and more confused than ever.

She knew he was hurting; she knew he was angry. She wouldn't be surprised if he hated her for everything she'd done and all the pain she'd brought on him and their kids, so why had he kissed her?

"The kids know that someone wants to hurt you and that they threatened us and that's why you moved out," Mark muttered.

So he hadn't told them about her family. Not that she expected he should be the one who had to tell them, but that he had kept that quiet let her know how ashamed he was of her.

It hurt.

More than the bruises decorating her body.

Hurt more because the pain was in her heart.

But she understood.

She was ashamed of herself, that's why she'd never told anyone who she really was. That's why she had done everything she could to keep her past firmly in the past where it couldn't taint her future.

Now her future might be tainted beyond repair.

If she had been honest from the beginning, then maybe none of this would have happened. Maybe Caden and Belinda and the others would still be alive. Maybe her husband and children wouldn't be in danger. Maybe she wouldn't be about to lose everything she'd clung to so tightly trying to let them make her a better person.

Numbly, she returned to the table, and with her eyes fixed firmly on her neatly folded hands, she apologized again, "I'm sorry, Mark. I know that you must see me differently now that you know the truth. I know I should have been honest from the beginning. I shouldn't have tricked you into marrying someone like me. I know you must be angry. I know what a shock it is to know the truth about my family and what they did. I'm sorry," she finished helplessly. She didn't know what else to say.

"You think *that's* why I'm angry?" he exploded, his blue eyes like two sharp icicles stabbing into her chest. "Because your family dealt in black-market babies? I don't care about that. They were scum. Worse than scum, but you're nothing like them, Daisy. You were just a kid, and yet you risked yourself to do the right thing. I'm so proud of you and what you did. But you lied to me. Every single day since I met you. You lied because you didn't trust me, and that's what hurts."

Tears blurred her vision.

She had been so stupid.

She knew she could have trusted Mark, but she was so ashamed for him to know where she came from when his family was so perfect.

She didn't deserve him.

"Don't ever think that." He reached across the table and pinched her chin between his fingers, forcing her head up, so she was looking at him.

Some of the anger in his eyes had dimmed, but it was still there, and it was still directed at her, and suddenly she felt so old and so tired. Carrying the burden of her family's guilt around for so long had taken a toll on her she hadn't even realized until this moment.

"You are a beautiful woman, inside and out. You are good and sweet and kind and sensitive and thoughtful. You are an amazing mother, a great friend, and a wonderful wife."

A glimmer of hope ignited inside her. Could they find a way to get past this? Could they rebuild what she had single-handedly shattered? Could they get back to what they'd had before?

Pain replaced the anger in Mark's eyes, and her heart jackknifed in her chest. "I love you ... I'll always love you, but you don't trust me. I'm trying, Daisy, but I don't know where that leaves us."

For a long moment, they just stared at each other.

She wanted Mark to pick her up, to hold her on his lap, to

make her feel safe and loved. To make her feel like she wasn't alone.

But that was stupid.

Of course, she was alone.

She was always alone.

Part of her had believed that if Mark learned the truth, then he would understand why she hadn't been able to tell him and forgive her. She'd told herself that she knew it would take time, but deep down, she hadn't really believed that. She'd thought that they could just pick back up where they'd left off six months ago.

Now she knew that could never happen.

Leaving her mostly untouched coffee cup on the table, she stood. She had to leave. She couldn't be in here with Mark any longer. It was going to rip her already battered heart to shreds.

In the morning, she would talk to Paige and Ryan. Maybe they could use her as bait to catch her cousin before anyone else was hurt or killed. Then, at least, she'd feel like she was doing something useful instead of just bringing pain to the people she loved.

As though sensing what she was thinking, Mark said, "I need time, Daisy. I don't want anything to happen to you; don't do anything stupid. You should rest. Your body needs sleep to heal. I left you painkillers on the nightstand in your room when I put you in there earlier. Take them, sleep, think about everything that you'd lose."

Lose?

What did she have left to lose?

She'd already lost everything that was important to her.

* * * * *

9:32 A.M.

Before this, Colette had never realized what being cold actually

187

was.

She thought she had. She thought she knew what it was like to be cold, but she'd been so wrong. Here, the cold seeped inside her, reaching deep into her bones, into her blood, into her internal organs. It claimed her; it owned her; it burrowed into her brain until she could think of little else.

Colette didn't care that she hadn't had much to eat; she wasn't hungry anyway. She didn't care that her body ached from sitting on the unforgiving concrete floor; she just wanted to be warm.

She needed a distraction.

Otherwise, she was going to drive herself crazy.

Heather had folded in on herself after her baby had been snatched away. The other girl had curled up on her mattress, pulled her tattered blanket over her head, and stayed there.

That was over twenty-four hours ago.

The only way to tell how much time was passing down here without any access to the outside world was by their meals. They came three times a day; there had been a dinner right after the baby was taken, then a breakfast, lunch, and dinner, and one more breakfast.

At first, she'd tried to give Heather space, knowing that the girl had suffered a major loss and that she needed time to process it. Despite Heather never answering her question about whether or not she loved her son, Colette had been able to tell that she did. Love for the infant was written all over her face.

How could Heather love a baby she'd never chosen to have?

She had been raped. It might have been all sterile, but as far as Colette was concerned, sticking tubes up a woman's vagina to impregnate her was rape. She couldn't imagine loving a child that was conceived like that.

For the millionth time, her hands fell to her own stomach. What if there was already a baby growing in there? She didn't want to be pregnant. She didn't want to be here in this horrible cage. She didn't want any of this to be real.

So, why was it?

Why, for once in her life, couldn't she have things the way she wanted? What she wanted wasn't anything special. Just to be safe, to be able to go to school, study hard, get a good job, have a normal life. That was all. It was what everyone else had.

It wasn't fair.

She wanted to pretend that someone would be looking for her, that any moment the cops would come rushing in and save her. But the reality was that was never going to happen. No one cared that she was gone.

She was on her own.

If she weren't already pregnant, she would be soon.

They would keep trying until she was. And then she would be like Heather, mourning the loss of a child she didn't want because a maternal bond tied her to it anyway.

No.

No.

She couldn't do it.

She couldn't do this.

She launched to her feet and began to pace frantically around her cage.

Her panic was growing.

It was going to keep growing until it filled her up inside, and then it was going to come bubbling out.

What would she do when that happened? She had no control over what was happening to her. She couldn't escape her cage. She couldn't stop them from getting her pregnant. Even if she decided she wanted to end her life, her options were limited. Maybe there was something she could do with her blanket. People in prison sometimes strangled themselves with theirs, right? Maybe she could figure out how to do that.

Was she really considering suicide?

She was losing her mind already.

A few days and she was ready to give up and die.

No.

She had to stay strong.

Earlier, she'd tried to get Heather to talk; this time she was going to make her. She couldn't do this on her own. They needed each other to survive. Heather couldn't just give up on her.

She dropped to her knees at the bars between their cages, ignoring the pain that spiked up her legs. She had no time for pain right now.

"Heather."

Nothing.

"Heather."

Silence.

"Heather!" This time she bellowed the girl's name at the top of her lungs.

The sound echoed through the basement but had the desired effect. The bump under the blanket shifted, slowly rising like some sort of weird, gray ghost. A human emerged from underneath, a hand poked out, and pulled the blanket down. Although she'd shed the blanket, Heather still looked like a ghost. She was pale, and her red-rimmed eyes were vacant.

"Come on, Heather, please don't give up on me," Colette begged. How could she survive this on her own? She knew the answer already. She couldn't. She needed Heather. So badly. Together they could encourage one another. Maybe they could even figure out a way to escape. "Heather?"

She blinked and tried to pull herself together. "Yeah."

"Yeah?" Colette wasn't sure that her new friend was back with her yet.

Heather drew in a long, shaky breath, then nodded. "Yeah."

Colette released a sigh of relief and forced a smile to her lips. "We can do this. We can survive this. We can figure a way out."

Heather nodded encouragingly, but she saw that there was no real hope in her eyes. She had lived through this for years already. She knew no one was coming. She no longer battled denial. Was that going to be her one day? How long would she last before she became hopeless? Weeks? Months? Years?

Before she could say more, try to force her own hope into Heather, she heard the clunk of the basement door that meant someone was coming.

Immediately, she was on edge.

Breakfast had already been delivered, and it couldn't be lunch already, so why was someone coming? Maybe they wanted to see if she was pregnant? They couldn't check for pregnancy this soon, could they? She wasn't sure. She'd never really known anyone who was pregnant, so she didn't know much about what to expect.

The man who had tricked her stalked down the stairs. It drove Colette crazy that she didn't know his name. She hated not knowing even the most basic information about her captors. Without it, she couldn't form a connection with them and talk her way out.

"It's shower day," he announced without preamble.

Heather knew what that meant and immediately stood and shed her oversized T-shirt.

Colette didn't move.

She wasn't stripping in front of this man or anyone else. That he had already seen her naked when he'd brought her here and removed her clothes, or when they'd performed the artificial insemination procedure on her, didn't factor in. Those times someone else had stripped her, this time she was expected to remove her clothes in front of him of her own free will.

"Hurry up!" he snapped. "I'm not in the mood for this today."

Desperately, she shook her head. He didn't really expect her to get naked in front of him did he?

"Now, Colette. You don't shower today, and you won't eat until next week's shower day."

"Do it," Heather hissed. "He means it."

She weighed her options. Was it worth risking having nothing to eat for an entire week just to cling to her pride? What good was pride in a place like this? She lived in a cage. She had to let go of stupid notions of modesty.

With tears burning the backs of her eyes, she yanked her T-shirt off and threw it on the floor, then did her best to cover her breasts and private parts from his prying eyes.

He smiled meanly. "Good girl." He went to the wall and turned a tap. A moment later, water sprayed out of the hose in her cage and Heather's. "Five minutes and not a second more."

Although she fought against it, the prospect of being able to get clean—even if it was like this—was too great, and her feet led her to the water. The water was icy cold, but at least it was water, and she quickly used her one cake of soap to scrub every inch of her body.

The man watched.

With his hand down his pants.

She tried to keep her back to him, but it didn't seem to faze him.

This was what her life had come down to. Living in a cage, showering naked in cold water from a hose, while some despicable man watched and got off on it.

Her humiliation was complete.

She was nothing.

She was never going to be anything.

This was her life now; the quicker she accepted that, the better. Clinging to childish hopes of white knights coming running to her rescue was only going to cause her more pain.

Colette had been wrong.

She hadn't lasted weeks or months or years before she gave up hope. She had only lasted days.

* * * * *

11:04 A.M.

Why was he doing this?

Mark watched Daisy as she did her best to explain to their children about her past and her family and why they had been brought here. He should be trying to help her. He should be putting his arms around the woman he loved and making sure that she knew how much he loved her.

And he did love her.

But last night he had hurt her when he'd told her that her lack of trust in him meant he didn't know if they could work things out.

He had lied.

It wasn't that Daisy didn't trust him. It was his own stupid ego that was the problem.

Why hadn't she told him?

Didn't she trust him?

The question that had been haunting him the most was, would he have done the same thing in her situation if their positions were reversed?

Mark may not want to admit it, but he knew the answer to that.

If he had lived through what she had, and he'd met someone he felt a connection to, he might be scared enough to keep quiet about who and what his family was.

Daisy had only been a kid, and her family had been dangerous. He'd never met them, but he suspected they were dangerous enough to kill her if it meant keeping her quiet. And yet, still, she had done the right thing. In doing so, she'd lost everything. She had been completely alone in the world. She'd had people who cared for her physical needs but no one to love her.

She amazed him. That she had been so strong despite being so young, and that she had single-handedly stopped her family's operation by going to the cops made him blaze with pride.

He understood why Daisy hadn't told him.

So, why couldn't he tell her that?

Did he want to punish her?

It had hurt that she'd walked away, that she'd thought that his safety was more important than her own, that she'd decided to handle things on her own rather than coming to him.

But it was time to man up.

Mark was afraid that if he continued to let Daisy think that he was angry with her and that their relationship might be over, then she would think that she had nothing to lose. And if she thought that she had nothing to lose, then she might try to use herself as bait to catch her cousin or whoever it was who wanted her dead.

He really could lose her.

If he did, it would be his fault.

It was time to shove away the anger that Daisy had kept secrets and be the husband that she needed. She'd dealt with a lot on her own for a long time; she deserved to have someone to lean on. She had sacrificed her home, her happiness, and she'd been willing to sacrifice her life. Surely, brushing away a few hurt feelings wasn't too much to ask.

"Okay, guys, Mom needs to get some rest now," he announced. Once he got her alone in her room, they could talk. "You can watch TV or hang out in your rooms, but no going outside."

"We really have to stay here?" Brian looked annoyed. "I have a party I was going to go to tonight."

"I never gave you permission to go to the party," he reminded his oldest son. "And yes, other than school where someone will escort you and pick you up afterward, you have to stay here." Mark didn't know why Brian was being so hard on his mother. The other kids had been relieved to learn why Daisy had left, and any lingering hurt feelings seemed nonexistent. But Brian just couldn't let it go.

"That's not fair. Just because Mom has deranged relatives, why should I have to suffer?" Brian glowered.

"Hey!" He made sure his son was looking him in the eye. "You don't speak about your mother that way."

"Well, it's true," Brian sulked. "How do we even know that Mom wasn't involved in selling babies like the rest of her family? Maybe she deserves what this killer is going to do to her."

Daisy's head dropped as though she believed she deserved the anger Brian was directing at her. Was this why she'd never said anything? Because she was afraid that people would think she was like the rest of her family?

Anger surged through him. *No one* spoke to his wife like that—not even his son. "You're out of line, Brian. Apologize to your mother. Immediately."

"Sorry," Brian muttered, but Mark saw the shame flare in his eyes. He'd let his anger get the best of him, and if he didn't learn to control it, then he was going to get himself in trouble.

"Go cool down," he ordered.

Brian stood, stormed to the door, then came to a halt. "I'm sorry, Mom. I know you would never hurt someone on purpose." Then he was gone.

Daisy hadn't moved.

She remained hunched over on the sofa, her long, blonde hair providing a curtain around her head that she could hide behind. He didn't want to see her like that. She was too strong for that. She didn't run from anything. She faced everything thrown her way with more grace and strength than he could ever muster.

"Hey." He eased onto the couch beside her. He wanted to tell her everything he was thinking, but he wasn't sure where to start. Deciding on something easy, he asked, "How are you feeling?"

"Fine," came the whispered reply.

Mark reached for her wrist, cursing his own cowardice, and checked her pulse. It thumped strongly beneath his fingertips. She was already recovering from her injuries—at least physically. Psychologically she was withdrawing.

"Let's get you upstairs and into bed. Your body still needs

rest." He took her elbow and helped her stand. She tried to tug herself free, but he wasn't letting her go. Not now. Not ever. He let his hand trail from her elbow down her arm to clasp her hand. He wasn't her doctor; he was her husband, and he should hold her as such.

When his fingers curled around hers, her head darted up to look at him in surprise. "What are you doing?"

"Holding your hand." He shrugged.

"But I thought—"

"Then you thought wrong." He cut her off. "I'm not angry with you. A little hurt, maybe, but I understand why you didn't tell me about your family. You think it will make me see you as one of them, but it doesn't, Daisy. You're nothing like your family."

"You never met them," she reminded him.

"What they did was deplorable. What you did was amazing, and I couldn't be prouder of you."

"Really?" She looked confused.

"Of course." He squeezed her hand and led her through the house back to her room. As soon as he closed the door, he pushed Daisy up against it and kissed her. This kiss was different than last night's kiss had been. That had been full of six months' worth of pent-up confusion and emotion. This one was softer, sweeter. He wanted her to know how much he loved her.

"You've kissed me twice now," Daisy said when he finally managed to pry his lips away from hers.

"I can make it three if you like." He smiled.

"I don't understand." She pushed away his hands which rested on her hips and paced the room. "I thought you'd be angry with me. You were angry last night. I lied to you, Mark. Our whole relationship. And I moved out and broke your heart," she said sadly. Her eyes were full of so much pain, he wanted to do whatever it took to erase it.

"To keep us safe," he reminded her. "Did you really believe he would hurt us if you went to the cops?" He already knew the answer but wanted to make her see that she had been put in an impossible situation where there wasn't an easy right choice.

"Yes. He was watching the house. He sent me a picture of you the other night bringing groceries in."

"The car," he murmured, remembering the one that had been parked outside the house.

"You saw him?" Daisy's eyes grew wide.

"No, I just saw a car. He drove off when I got too close."

Daisy shuddered so violently it seemed her tiny frame would shatter into a million pieces. She hadn't been taking care of herself since she left. Her frame was too bony, and the dark circles under her eyes told the story that she rarely slept. No wonder she'd slept over twelve hours after her attack, even with the sedative he'd given her before they moved her to the safe house, he hadn't expected her to sleep so long. He hated seeing the bruises on her face; they reminded him that he had nearly lost her and that he still might.

"Don't play bait, Daisy," he begged, going to her and wrapping her up in his arms. "Please. We can work through this ... we can figure things out ... I love you."

She relaxed in his arms, hers wrapping tightly around his waist, and she pressed her ear to his chest, snuggling into him. "I love you, too. So much. I'm so sorry for lying to you."

He'd be stupid to throw away what they had. He could work through his bruised feelings. "I forgive you, okay? I forgive you. Let the cops find your cousin or whoever it is who wants to hurt you, but please don't put yourself at risk. I love you; I don't want to lose you. Please, Daisy, promise you won't do anything rash."

* * * * *

2:39 P.M.

"After Liam Hayden set fire to the Allen house, pretty much all evidence was lost, so no one ever knew how many girls they kidnapped, how long they'd been doing it, how many babies they'd produced and sold, or those babies' identities," Ryan said.

"Going back through the twenty years before the fire, there were at least twenty thousand teenage girls reported missing in the area that could have wound up victims of the Allen/Hayden family. If Daisy hadn't told someone what she'd found out then, they probably would have continued indefinitely," Paige said. Daisy had probably saved hundreds of lives by being brave enough to know what her family was doing was wrong and turning them in.

"They never found the bodies of any of the girls other than the ones who were in the house that day."

"No one even knew those girls were in trouble," she said, more to herself than her partner. Paige hated that. Someone should have noticed; someone should have done something. Maybe then, it wouldn't have come down to a thirteen-year-old kid to end the trafficking ring. "If Daisy had slipped up, let them know that she wasn't going to be part of the family business, they would have killed her."

"They would," Ryan agreed. "I doubt she thought about the risks. She was thirteen. She just acted on instinct."

"Taking the photo with her was a stroke of genius. Without it, they wouldn't have been able to ID the baby. They contacted doctors and pediatricians and asked about anyone bringing in an adopted infant baby boy. Since they had identified the girl in the photo, they got a DNA sample from the family, and they used it to find the baby. The couple led them to another couple who had told them about the babies. They'd adopted several years earlier. Their son was six, and he ended up in the system. His parents did some prison time, and the adopted mother ended up committing suicide. Those were the only two babies they were able to identify."

"Fawkner Miller is thirty-two now, he's married, no kids, he's an electrician. Wade Jeebes is twenty-five, married, has a little girl. After the fire, he was reunited with his mother's family and raised by them."

"Who's fathering these babies?" she asked. "DNA tests showed that neither the Allen men nor the Hayden men were the father of Fawkner or Wade, so it goes to reason that they weren't the father of any of the other babies either. So who is?"

"Maybe they kidnapped male runaways, too?"

"Daisy never mentioned any teenage boys," she reminded her partner. "They were getting sperm from somewhere, maybe a sperm bank? Or medical facility of some sort?"

"Daisy's uncle was a mortician," Ryan said slowly.

Her eyes grew wide in horrified shock. "You think they were getting sperm from recently deceased bodies?"

"Could be. It would solve all their problems. Dead guys aren't going to worry about you stealing their sperm."

"That's disgusting," Paige shuddered.

"It is," her partner agreed. "We'll speak to both Fawkner and Wade and see if it's possible that either of them could be involved."

"I know Daisy isn't positive that it's her cousin who's the killer and suggested that it could be one of the couples who lost their baby. Or one of the families of the victims, but I don't know. Only two babies were ever identified, and one of them only had the baby for a couple of weeks. And only four girls were ever identified as victims, one of whom survived. The others died in the fire. That doesn't leave us a lot of suspects. And," she continued, "let's say it *is* one of them. Why kill Belinda and Devon Paddy? Why kill Caden Gervase and Maddie Pickle? If you wanted revenge for your daughter being abducted, it doesn't make sense that you would go after the cops or the teacher Daisy told, or the social worker who removed her and her younger brother from the home. None of them are to blame. And even if we say that it's one of the adopted parents who had their child taken away; okay, maybe they'd blame the cops, but the teacher and the social worker? That makes no sense."

"Going after Caden and Maddie makes it seem much more personal," Ryan agreed. "Like the focus is anyone who had anything to do with the events leading up to the fire. The cousin would have reason to be angry with them. He lost his family that day because they would rather have died than faced criminal charges. And he lost his business. You think he started it up again?"

The idea of more girls suffering the same fate and more innocent babies being sold didn't sit well with her. They had to find out if Liam Hayden was still running this operation. No one had done anything last time to help those girls. If there were more victims, then they had to do whatever it took to find them and save them.

"He burned the house down so no one would have records of the victims or the babies," Ryan said. "But that also means there was no way to tell what he took with him. He could have had access to the money they got from selling the babies. He was eighteen then. He could easily have started the business up again. He already knew what to do, and assuming that the kids were all brought in at thirteen, then he had been involved for five years."

"Once we've interviewed Wade and Fawkner, we should go through missing persons reports, see if any teenage runaways pop as potential victims. If this *is* Liam, then we should talk to Daisy again. See what she thinks her cousin would do, where he might set up the business again, what kind of girls are more likely to catch his attention."

"And we still have to track down the only survivor of the fire," Ryan reminded her.

Katrina Finnish had, for all intents and purposes, disappeared off the face of the planet. After being discovered unconscious in the neighbor's yard by firefighters, she had been rushed to the hospital. She had refused all attempts to reunite her with her family, and because she was no longer a minor, they hadn't been able to force her. She had disappeared from the hospital in the middle of the night, and no one had seen or heard from her since.

"Think she's still alive?" Paige asked.

"From the transcript of the interview she gave the cops after she was found, she was strong but withdrawn. I guess it depends on how strong her will to live was."

"Daisy was only thirteen, and she'd only just learned the truth about her family. She thinks her cousin is the killer because he was the only one who survived the fire, but she doesn't really know anything about the situation. If we can find Katrina, she would be more likely to be able to give us the insight we need into Liam Hayden. We need to try to figure out if she's still alive, and if she is, then where she's hiding."

Katrina might be the only one who could give them enough insight into Daisy's cousin to find him before he finished his murderous crusade of revenge. She might have spent time with him during her captivity. She might be the only one who could tell them something that would lead them right to Liam.

Stopping him was their number-one priority.

Daisy's life counted on it, along with who knew how many other teenage girls and their babies.

* * * * *

5:41 P.M.

"Try to relax."

"Relax?" Daisy repeated. "I can't." Instead, she continued her pacing, up the living room, around the sofa, and back down to the other end of the room. She had been repeating the circuit over and over again so many times she was starting to feel dizzy, but still she didn't stop. Sitting and doing nothing would make her feel so much worse.

"Daisy, it's only your brother," Mark said. He was watching her nervous pacing, but he clearly didn't understand the root of it.

Her baby brother wasn't just her baby brother. He was the only person left from her family, and the prospect of seeing him after so many years left her stomach all jittery, and not in a good way.

"He's not *only* my brother," she told her husband. Daisy was so unbelievably relieved that Mark had found a way to forgive all her lies. She needed him so badly right now, and while she didn't deserve his forgiveness, she was so grateful for it. The black cloud that floated around her head had lifted a little. "Thorne is it. He's the only link I have to my past, to my childhood, my family. I know it's weird, that I shouldn't want to remember them, but I can't help it." She didn't know how to explain the mixed and messed up feelings she had for her family.

"I understand, Dais. They're still your family; of course you still love them."

Mark was trying so hard, but he didn't get it. How could he? He'd grown up with a perfect family—parents who loved each other and their kids unconditionally and brothers who all got along and who remained close into adulthood. He didn't know what it was like to come from such a twisted group of people.

"How can I love them after what they did?" she asked, more to herself than her husband. "How could I have never noticed what they were really like?" That had haunted her every day since her parents took her into the basement and showed her what was down there.

"Because you were just a kid," Mark reminded her. "Kids don't pay attention to what their parents are doing."

"They died because of me," she said softly. Maybe she shouldn't feel guilt over her parents and older brothers' deaths, but she did.

"No." Mark stood and came to her, grabbing her shoulders and forcing her to still her restless pacing. "Don't ever say that again, Daisy. I don't know why your parents would rather have shot at the cops until they shot back, but their deaths are not your fault. What you did was amazing."

"I didn't even stop to think about what I was doing. I just acted on instinct," she rebutted. She hadn't made a conscious decision to take the photo and go to Caden; she'd just done it. She had flipped into autopilot when she saw those girls in cages in her basement, and her brain had somehow just known to do the right thing no matter what.

"That's what makes you so amazing." Mark lifted a hand and ran his fingers through her hair. "You did the right thing without even thinking about it."

"Thorne doesn't think I'm amazing. He blames me."

"You said he doesn't know the truth about your family."

"He doesn't. At least, as far as I know, he doesn't. That day, when Belinda and Devon sat Thorne and me down and told us that our parents and brothers were dead, he was so angry. He blamed me. When Mrs. Pickle took us to a group home, he didn't want anything to do with me, he wouldn't talk to me; he wouldn't even look at me."

"He was a kid who had just lost family. He was lashing out at the nearest person who just happened to be you," Mark soothed.

"I know, it just …" She trailed off, not wanting to complain.

"Just that it hurt," Mark finished for her. "It's okay to be hurt. You went through something traumatic, and it all happened too quickly. You didn't get a chance to process any of it, and because your parents were dead, you didn't get a chance to talk to them to try to get answers."

There was one thing that she'd always wished she'd been able to ask her parents. Something that she wasn't entirely sure she wanted to know but that constantly hovered at the corners of her mind. Maybe if she'd been able to get an answer, it would have helped her reconcile the distant, but kind, parents she had known with the cold people who stole teenage girls and treated them like property that they could use as they pleased to earn money.

"What are you thinking?" Mark tucked a lock of hair behind her ear.

She looked at her husband, wishing she was like him and had never known what it was like to doubt that the people who created you loved you.

"You can tell me, honey." Mark's hand still rested on her shoulder while his other smoothed her hair. His touch grounded her. Whether her parents loved her or not, her husband did. And their children. Despite Brian's anger, she knew her son loved her, too; he was just hurting. When this was over, if she was still alive, she was going to make him her number one priority.

"Daisy?" he prompted.

Her husband might not understand, but she knew he would try. "Would they have done the same to me? That's what I was thinking."

"Would who have done what?"

She sighed, then said in a rush, "Would my parents have ended up sticking me in a cage in the basement and making me have babies, too? Was I any different than the girls they kidnapped? Did they love me?" Her voice wobbled a little, and she felt just like she had as a scared, confused kid.

"Oh, baby." Mark drew her to him, holding her tightly against his chest, his arms locked around her. "I wish I could answer that for you."

"I don't want to lose Thorne, too," she whispered into his sweater. "It was easier to stay away. Even after we grew up, we haven't really had anything to do with each other. I kind of liked it that way because it was safe. I didn't have to worry about him leaving me too. But now he's coming, and I don't know what to expect. What if he's still angry? What if he doesn't want to be stuck here with me? What if he still blames me? What if he thinks it's my fault that he's in danger now? What if he hates me?"

Mark couldn't answer any of those questions, so he just held her. That helped her more than platitudes because it was honest, and she needed a big dose of honesty right now to remain grounded.

"They're here," a voice announced from the door.

Resolutely, Daisy straightened her spine, readying herself for the tirade she was sure her estranged brother was going to deliver. She understood that, from his point of view, it looked like she was responsible for the destruction of their family. Part of her even agreed with him. Maybe if she had thought about what she was doing and done things differently, there would have been a different outcome. But she hadn't, and she couldn't go back and redo it. Both of them had to live with the consequences of her choices.

"I'm right here with you," Mark murmured in her ear. She reached for his hand and squeezed; his support meant everything to her.

It had been almost twenty years since they'd last seen each other. Thorne had been only eighteen then, but she recognized him the second he walked into the safe house's living room.

She would recognize him anywhere.

He looked just like their father. Ridge and Forrest had looked just like their dad, too. She was glad that Thorne hadn't followed in their older brother's footsteps. If nothing else, she'd saved him from being dragged into the black-market baby business.

Slowly, her eyes traveled to meet his.

They stared at each other.

Neither of them moved.

She was too afraid, and from the stone hard look on his face, Thorne was too angry.

Finally, he took a step toward her and she subconsciously took one back, bumping into Mark, who stood firm and solid behind her. His strength seeped into her, and she steeled herself. Her little brother deserved a chance to unload his anger. She would stand here and take it. She owed him that, at the very least.

Forcing herself to maintain eye contact as he stalked toward her, she felt Mark tense protectively, but he kept quiet.

When Thorne reached her, he did the last thing she had been expecting.

He threw his arms around her, lifting her feet right off the floor, and squeezed her. "I owe you a huge apology, Daisy."

JANUARY 29TH

Daisy couldn't sleep. She was too wired.

Her brain was on overload. Mark wasn't angry with her, Thorne wasn't angry with her, and even Brian was thawing out. She felt calm and relaxed. Almost *too* calm and relaxed. She wasn't used to feeling this way.

The more relaxed she felt, the more her mind wandered. And it wasn't wandering to a good place.

Images from the hotel bathroom kept trickling in.

The feel of the man's hand on her back, holding her down, was imprinted on her skin, like it was still there. The feel of his hand between her legs, trying to force its way inside her was still there, too.

Memories of the assault wanted to invade her dreams. During the day she could focus on other things, but at night she was vulnerable to them. They could get to her while she slept, and the knowledge was enough to keep her awake.

Trying to move as carefully as possible, she rolled over onto her other side. She didn't want to disturb Mark; he needed his rest. She'd spent months barely sleeping. Her body was used to it, and she'd rather stick with that than risk nightmares.

She rolled over again—onto her back this time. She wasn't used to spending this much time in bed, and her achy body couldn't get comfortable. The stitches Mark had put in to close the gash above her ear were starting to itch as the wound began to heal, and it was driving her crazy. Daisy hated to be itchy. She much preferred pain and usually dug her fingernails into any itchy spots till they hurt rather than itched, but the bruises around the wound made doing that difficult.

With a frustrated sigh, she rolled back onto her side, wincing as her bruised body protested.

"Daisy, try to sleep." Mark's voice floated through the dark.

"Sorry, I thought you were asleep," she whispered back.

"I can't sleep with you wiggling and squirming like that. It reminds me of the days when the kids used to sneak into the bed in the middle of the night then toss and turn all night long."

She remembered those days; they'd been the happiest of her life. Raising their children with Mark, all the simple little family things that most people complained about, but that she relished every second of because they were so normal.

"I'll get up and let you rest."

"No, stay here with me. You need to sleep … your body is still healing," Mark said, curling an arm around her waist and tugging her closer.

"I'm too wired for sleep. I'm going to go downstairs, drink some warm milk, then come back and see if that helps relax me."

"Want me to come with you?"

"Thanks, but you should sleep." She didn't want to disturb her husband any more than she already had.

"I don't mind."

Daisy leaned over and kissed Mark. She could never express how grateful she was for his support. "I won't be long; you can keep the bed warm for me." She loved that he wanted to be with her, but she needed to process things, and she needed to be on her own to do that.

Liam was still out there somewhere, and he hadn't killed anyone last night. She didn't know why, and it made her nervous. She had to decide if staying here was the right thing for her. She was glad her family was safe, but she was the one Liam wanted. She still thought trying to trap him was a viable option, but she knew her family wouldn't be supportive of that. She needed to come up with a way to convince them. She wanted the threat hanging over her family's head gone. She couldn't live like this, knowing they were in danger because of her. She would do whatever it took to end this so they stayed safe.

"Call me if you need me." Mark sounded disappointed she needed time alone, but she appreciated that he didn't push her.

"Always," she promised. She wouldn't shut him out again, although she'd had her reasons, and still believed those reasons were valid. She wouldn't hurt Mark like she had by keeping him in the dark.

Climbing out of bed, Daisy grabbed her robe and wrapped it around herself as she hurried downstairs. Maybe if she could just clear her head, she could go back to bed and actually sleep.

It was quiet downstairs. She heard voices in the living room, but bypassed them, not wanting company right now. In the kitchen she quickly made herself a mug of hot milk. It had always helped her to sleep when she was having trouble shutting off her mind.

When she was a little girl, her mother used to make her hot milk when she had bad dreams, then she'd tuck her back into bed and sit beside the bed until Daisy drifted back to sleep. Why couldn't her parents have stayed like that? Normal. That was all she wanted—not perfect parents, just normal ones.

Before she'd learned the truth, Daisy had always thought her parents were normal. They never laid a hand on her or her brothers physically or sexually. They were never psychologically abusive. They didn't impose a million rules, and yet, they made sure she knew to do as she was told.

She had thought her home was like everyone else's, which made learning the truth that much worse.

As she reminisced, she wandered to the back door. Her dad had loved camping. They'd gone every summer up to the mountains and spent weeks sleeping in tents, cooking over a fire, hiking, and playing in the great wide outdoors. She had loved those times, they were among some of her best childhood memories.

Her dad's favorite thing to do had been to lie on the grass and stare up at the stars. She had always loved joining him, lying at his side watching the stars twinkle like tiny happy sparkly people and searching for shooting stars.

Without even realizing what she was doing, Daisy opened the back door and stepped out into the freezing night. The sky was clear, and millions of stars stared back down at her.

How could her parents have seemed so normal and yet done such horrible things?

Shouldn't she have been able to tell that they were evil?

They were evil, she knew that, but how hadn't she seen it?

Had Ridge and Forrest been evil, too, or had their parents made them evil?

If she hadn't been brave enough to get help, would her parents have made her and Thorne evil, too?

What would her life be like now? She knew she wouldn't have Mark and their kids, but would she be kidnapping runaway girls and holding them hostage, forcing them to have babies just so she could get money? Would she think it was okay to do that? Would her sense of right and wrong be so mixed up that she actually thought that she could imprison and hurt others just so she could get what she wanted?

Daisy shuddered. She was so glad her life hadn't turned out like that. Because of Caden and Belinda and all the others, she wouldn't have the life that she did without them. She was eternally grateful.

She was about to turn around and go back to bed, suddenly yearning to have her husband's arms wrapped around her, when she saw movement over by the back fence.

A cat?

No, it was too big to be a feline.

Horror washed over her.

It was a person.

Climbing over the fence.

Maybe it was just a neighborhood kid sneaking out, or going back home after getting up to mischief.

Although she knew she should go back inside, lock the door, and tell one of the cops what she'd seen, her feet remained frozen in place.

The person looked at her.

Their eyes met.

Even in the dark, she could see who it was.

It was Liam.

How had he found her?

Finally, her feet regained the ability to move, and she spun around, screaming as she ran back inside.

She didn't want to die.

More than that, she didn't want Liam to get his hands on her family.

By the time she stepped back into the kitchen, the cops had heard her screams and materialized.

"It's Liam," she announced without preamble. "Coming over the fence."

They ran past her out into the yard as the kitchen filled with people.

"Daisy?" Mark grabbed her, his frantic gaze searching her for any signs of injury.

"Liam," she said as she pressed herself against him, suddenly icy cold, and needing to soak up Mark's warmth.

"Where?" Thorne demanded.

"In the yard." Her teeth began to chatter, and her shivering increased. It was one thing to know that Liam was coming for her but another to know her cousin had tracked her down and was just yards away.

But if they got him, it was over.

It would finally be over.

No one else would die.

She hardly dared to hope it was true.

Her overwhelmed mind and aching body gave out simultaneously, and she collapsed, fainting dead away in her husband's arms.

* * * * *

2:13 A.M.

Leaving Daisy in the safety of the kitchen, Xavier ran out into the dark night, Paige on his heels. They had been in the living room. Paige had been reading while he'd been on the phone with Annabelle who was recovering from another bout of morning sickness that continued to plague her pregnancy. They were both counting down the days until their baby would be born when they'd heard Daisy's screams.

They had immediately gone running to see what had happened, and when Daisy said that Liam was in the backyard, they had rushed outdoors.

This could be it.

The break they had been waiting for. The killer hadn't struck yesterday, maybe he'd wanted to go after Daisy or her younger brother Thorne next but couldn't since they had placed the two in protective custody.

If it really was Liam Hayden whom Daisy had seen in the yard, then this could all be over in just a couple of minutes. They would catch him, arrest him, and no one else would wind up dead.

Scanning the yard, he noticed movement—a shadowy figure trying to scramble up and over the back fence.

"Paige," Xavier pointed at the fence. "There."

"I see him."

Both of them took off, guns drawn. "Liam, down on the ground," he yelled as they ran.

The man ignored them, and continued to try to struggle to get up and over the nine-foot-high wooden fence.

By the time they reached him, Liam was halfway over, bent across the top. His legs were still on their side, and Xavier grabbed hold of them and yanked as hard as he could. The man lost his balance and came tumbling down. Xavier fell with him, landing on top and pinning Liam to the ground.

While Paige kept her gun trained on Liam's head, he snapped on a pair of handcuffs and dragged the man to his feet. In the half light, he couldn't read the expression on Liam's face, but as they started to lead the man back inside, Xavier noticed he was limping. After everything Liam had done, he got a certain amount of satisfaction seeing him hurt.

The first thing he saw as they entered the kitchen was Mark scooping Daisy's limp body into his arms.

"Is she all right?" Liam asked, trying to take a step toward his cousin.

"Stay away from her," he growled, yanking Liam back. "Is she okay, Mark?"

"I think she just fainted. She's so exhausted from the stress of the last few months, then the attack at the hotel. I think her body just reached its limit. Seeing *him*," Mark glared at Liam, "probably pushed her over the edge."

Mark carried a still unmoving Daisy over to a couch on the other side of the room. Liam tried to get closer, but Xavier wrapped his hands around the man's biceps and held him back. "I just want to know she's okay." Liam struggled in his grip.

"So you can kill her?" Paige demanded.

"I don't want to kill her," Liam said. His eyes were fixed on Daisy's still form as Mark laid her down on the sofa and picked up her wrist to take her pulse, then tilted her head to the side and examined the gash above her ear.

"She's all right," Mark announced. "But she needs rest. I'm going to give her something to make sure she sleeps. Get *that man*," he jerked his head in Liam's direction, "out of here as quickly as you can."

"Let's go." He tugged Liam toward the door. They'd take him down to the station, interview him, get Tony to ID him as the man he'd seen walking away from the scene of Caden Gervase's murder.

"No, wait, I need to talk to Daisy." Liam once again struggled in his grip.

"Does it look like she's in any condition to talk to you right now?" Paige asked.

Daisy didn't need to be subjected to having to talk to her insane cousin. She'd been through enough, and there was nothing Liam had to say to her that she needed to hear. He was just going to make a string of excuses.

Liam's head hung down, looking at his feet but suddenly he squared his shoulders and lifted his head to look them directly in the eye. "It wasn't me. I didn't kill anyone. I'm not who you're looking for."

"Then why are you here?" Xavier asked, not believing the man's protestations of innocence. He heard it every day; criminals never wanted to take responsibility for their actions.

"I came to talk to Daisy," Liam replied. "I heard about what was happening, and I thought she would think it was me because I was the only one who walked away that day alive. I had to convince her it isn't me. I haven't been killing the people involved in what happened to our family. If I don't make her believe me, then she won't be prepared. When he comes for her, she won't be ready."

"When who comes for her?" Paige asked, looking as unconvinced by Liam's claims of innocence as he was.

"I don't know." Liam dropped his gaze again.

"I think you do know," Xavier contradicted. "It's you. You're the one who's coming for Daisy and Thorne, just like you came for everyone else who was involved in the deaths of the rest of your family."

"You killed Caden Gervase because he was the one who Daisy confessed to," Paige continued. "You killed Maddie Pickle because she was the one who took Daisy and Thorne away. And you killed Belinda Jersey and Devon Paddy because they're the ones who shot your parents, sister, cousins, aunt, and uncle. We know you intend to kill seven people. Daisy and Thorne are two of them. Who's the other? Is it the girl who escaped that day?"

"She didn't escape," Liam said quietly, still refusing to look at them.

"Then how did she get out?" he asked.

"I got her out."

"What?" That wasn't what he had expected to hear. A glance at Paige confirmed that she was just as surprised.

"What are you saying?" Paige asked. "That you weren't involved in the black-market babies business? That you didn't set the house on fire?"

Although he still kept his head down, Xavier could see Liam's cheeks tint pink presumably with embarrassment. "No," came the soft reply.

"No, what?" he pressed.

Liam shuddered, and Xavier didn't know what to make of the man. He certainly didn't seem like the kind of person who had so viciously and methodically tortured four people, then snapped the neck of a man who interrupted one of his killings. This Liam was jumpy and nervous, and he seemed genuinely concerned about Daisy. It didn't make sense. He'd been expecting a smug, cool, calm-and-in-control killer. Not this jittery mess.

"You better start talking," Paige snapped.

"I did set the fire."

"To get rid of any incriminating evidence against your family," Xavier said.

"Because I thought it would help."

"Help with what?" Xavier couldn't get a read on this guy.

"I thought the fire would make them stop shooting at the cops. I thought it would save their lives."

"You didn't want them to commit suicide by cop," Paige said.

"I wanted them to give up, accept it was over, but they didn't want to. They'd rather be dead than go to prison."

"But not you. You ran," Xavier said.

"I didn't know what else to do. I got Katrina out, then I tried to go back for the others, but the fire was too strong, I couldn't get to them." His devastated blue eyes looked up at them. "You can ask her. She'll tell you that I got her out."

"We haven't been able to locate Katrina Finnish," Paige told him.

"She changed her name. I know where she is. We're still friends. You talk to her, and she'll tell you everything," Liam said, the first bit of confidence infused into his voice.

"Even if she confirms that you got her out before the fire got to her, that just means you had a change of heart. It doesn't mean that you weren't involved in everything your family did," Xavier said, still not convinced that Liam wasn't trying to con them. They knew the killer they were dealing with was smart. Maybe he'd concocted a plan of playing an innocent victim to get to Daisy and Thorne now that they were in police protection.

"I never wanted to be involved," Liam protested.

"But you were," he said. It was written all over the man's face. "You helped abduct the girls, right? You got them to trust you by pretending to be a runaway kid, too. Then you led them straight into a trap and captivity where your family could use them for your own sick purposes." Luring victims was supposed to be the job Daisy took on when her family brought her into the fold so it made sense that that was what all the kids did. It was why their parents told them what was going on, so they could use them.

Liam nodded slowly. "I didn't want to do it. I tried to do what Daisy did. I tried to get help. I tried to stop them. Only, I got caught. My father and uncle beat me so badly, I couldn't walk for a month."

If he was telling the truth, then Daisy was extremely lucky that she had managed to escape the same fate. "Why did you try to stop them?" Xavier asked.

"Because it was wrong. We didn't have any right to take those girls and make them have babies just so we could sell them."

Could Liam be telling the truth? He looked sincere. But he was the only member of Daisy's family to make it out of that house alive, and someone was killing off everyone involved in their deaths, so if it wasn't Liam, then who was it?

"I wanted to stop them, but after the beating, I was too scared. I was a coward. I went along with it, did what they wanted, let them bring my sister Xaria into it, and my cousins Ridge and Forrest. I stood by and did nothing. I would have let them destroy Daisy and Thorne, too. But then Daisy did it; she stopped them. I had to do something. I got Katrina out, but it wasn't enough. I've spent the last twenty-five years trying to make up for what I did, for all the pain I caused, and all the people I hurt. I didn't do this, I swear. I may have tricked those girls, but I've never laid a hand on anyone in my life, let alone killed someone," Liam said earnestly.

Believe him or not? That was the question. And right now, Xavier didn't have an answer.

* * * * *

10:46 A.M.

"Do you believe Liam Hayden is telling the truth?" Ryan asked.

"I'm not sure," Paige replied, rubbing tiredly at her head. She'd had a headache since the fire. It kept switching between a dull ache to a viciously pounding throbbing that felt like a bomb was about to go off inside her skull. Because she hadn't slept last night, right now her head felt like it was about to explode. She tried to blink away the pain and focus. "He sounded pretty convincing, but I don't know. This killer is smart; it could be this is just a ploy to try and get to his remaining victims. Once we track down Katrina, maybe we'll get some answers."

"Here, for your headache." Ryan set down two white pills and a glass of water on the table in front of her.

"Thanks." She didn't bother denying the headache. Her partner knew her well enough to know when she was lying, and there was no way she could convincingly pretend her head wasn't killing her.

"You want to go home, get some rest?"

"No, I'll be fine once these kick in. Let's get to the interviews. If Liam is telling the truth and he's not the killer, then we need to find out who is. Who's up first, Fawkner Miller or Wade Jeebes?"

"Fawkner. He wasn't pleased to be brought in."

"Let's go get started." The pills were already starting to take effect, and she just wanted to get this case wrapped up. She didn't want to walk into a crime scene to find her friend's mutilated and dead body. Daisy had been there for her so many times in their long friendship, and she wanted to make sure her friend stayed safe.

"You sure you're up to it?" Ryan checked as they headed for the interview room.

"Positive."

"All right then, let's do it."

When they opened the door to the room where Fawkner Miller was waiting for them, his head snapped in their direction. He was sitting at the table, coffee cup in his hand, angry scowl on his face.

"I didn't kill them. I hated that family enough to slaughter every last one of them, but I wouldn't have killed those cops. They didn't have anything to do with messing up my life," Fawkner announced unapologetically.

"Who would you have killed, Fawkner?" Ryan asked.

"Any Hayden or Allen I found. I researched everything on the case that I could once I was old enough to understand what had happened to me. Liam Hayden escaped that day. He's out there somewhere. And Daisy Allen was the one who started this mess. If she'd kept her mouth shut, I would have been able to stay with the only parents I'd ever known, in the only home I've ever had. There was another one, too, a younger brother. They all deserve death."

Paige frowned at the man who was being unusually forthcoming about his hatred of a family someone wanted to kill. "Daisy and Thorne Allen were only children."

Fawkner shrugged. "They would have turned in time. You come from a family that evil, it's in your genes."

"How many other young girls like your mother would have suffered the same fate if Daisy hadn't come forward?" Ryan demanded.

Fawkner shrugged again. "They wouldn't have been my concern. Thanks to Daisy Allen 'coming forward,'" he made air quotes as he said that, "I was ripped away from my home and my parents, who went to prison just because they couldn't conceive a child naturally and yet wanted to be parents. Does that sound fair to you?"

"There are legal ways of having children even if you can't have them biologically," Paige reminded him. Both her daughters were adopted, and she couldn't have loved them more if she'd given birth to them. She was their mother in every way that counted.

"Why should it be illegal to buy a baby that no one wants?" Fawkner glowered at them. "They didn't know how I'd been conceived. They were good people. They worked hard, they donated to charities, they helped their friends. They loved me, they gave me a beautiful, warm, loving home. They were great parents. I was happy. And then it just ended. I was taken, put in a group home. I wasn't allowed to talk to my parents, then I was sent off to live with strangers. Do you know what happened to me there?" he asked, then continued without waiting for an answer. "I was shoved in a closet for hours on end every time I cried. I was hit with a belt for everything they decided I did wrong. The older I got, the worse it got. Broken bones, scars I'll bear for the rest of my life. Does that sound fair? I didn't do anything wrong, and yet I was punished. So forgive me if I'm not a big fan of Daisy Allen and her big mouth."

She felt sorry for the man and everything that had happened to him, but he was placing the blame at the feet of the wrong person. Daisy wasn't responsible for what had happened to him, but the anger he had toward her certainly made him a viable suspect if it turned out that Liam was telling the truth.

"My mother killed herself," Fawkner said. His voice dropped to just above a whisper. "She didn't want to live without me. Maybe they shouldn't have paid money for a baby that they didn't know where it was coming from, but they didn't have a choice. They'd tried getting pregnant. They'd tried surrogacy … they'd tried adoption … none of it worked out. I hate the Hayden and Allen families for what they did to us. I hate them, but I didn't kill them. If it was just me, I might, but I would never do that to my wife. I love her. She's more than I deserve, I wouldn't do anything that would hurt her, and getting revenge on those despicable people would hurt her."

That was quite a confession. His hate for Daisy's family was rolling off him in waves, and she believed him when he said that he would kill them all if he could. But had he? He'd said that if he'd wanted revenge, he wouldn't have killed Belinda and Devon, and that made sense. It was why they'd initially been hesitant to believe that one of the families of the victims—or Fawkner or Wade—was the man they were looking for.

"Don't leave town, Mr. Miller," Ryan told him.

"I can go?" Fawkner looked at them suspiciously like they might be trying to trick him.

"For now," she nodded. "Think it could be him?" she asked

her partner when Fawkner had left the room.

"From the level of anger he displayed, yes."

"He said if he had he wouldn't have killed anyone other than the family."

"Or he thought that was a good line to feed us and decided to kill Belinda and Devon and Caden and Maddie to throw us off, try to convince us it wasn't him."

Ryan was right. Fawkner could be playing them just like Liam could be playing them. They needed something concrete to tie one of the two of them to the murders. Or one of the *three* of them.

As if on cue, Wade Jeebes appeared at the interview room door. "Detective Hood and Detective Xander?" he asked.

"Take a seat, Mr. Jeebes." She indicated the seat Fawkner Miller had just vacated.

"This is about my past, about how I was brought into the world, someone has been killing people involved in the case," Wade said softly as he sat down.

His demeanor was much calmer than Fawkner's had been, and if either of the black-market babies was the killer, Paige thought Fawkner was a much more likely suspect. Wade had been just an infant when he'd been returned to his family. He had never known the couple who had intended to raise him as their own, so theoretically he hadn't lost as much as Fawkner had and, therefore, shouldn't be as angry.

"It is," she confirmed. "How do you feel about the Hayden and Allen families after what they did to you and your mother?"

"What they did was wrong. But they're dead, and I've moved on. I'll never know how my life could have turned out if I'd stayed with the family who bought me, but I have a family of my own now—a wife and a daughter—and they are the most important things in my life. For the first time, I feel like part of a real family."

"Your life with your mother's family wasn't good?" Ryan

asked.

"My mother ran away for a reason," Wade said quietly. His quietness was almost more menacing than Fawkner's rage.

It seemed like both Fawkner and Wade might have been better off if they'd stayed with the couples who had wanted a child badly enough that they had been willing to pay for one. Both had suffered in the situations they had been raised in; both had reasons to hold a grudge against all involved in the black-market baby ring and the ending of it.

Instead of getting answers from talking to the only known babies that the Hayden and Allen families had sold, all they'd gotten was more questions.

* * * * *

12:34 P.M.

One minute she was asleep, the next she was awake.

Awake and panicked.

Liam.

Had Paige and Xavier found him?

Had he gotten away?

Daisy bolted upright, ignoring the pain that zinged through her still bruised body. She had to know if Liam was in custody.

"Daisy?"

"Mark." Relief flooded through her. Her cousin hadn't hurt her husband, but what about her kids? Panic made her movements frantic as she tried to scramble out of bed and find answers to the questions that swarmed inside her. "Liam? Where's Liam?"

"It's okay, Daisy. It's okay, calm down." Mark tried to grab hold of her flailing form.

"I need to know where he is." She couldn't think of anything else other than the threats her cousin had made to hurt her family if she talked to the cops. Well, she had talked to the cops, told them everything she knew, and Liam had turned up here at the safe house. She didn't even know how he'd found her, but he had to have been here to follow through on the threats.

"Daisy, stop."

The commanding tone of her husband's voice snapped her out of her panic-induced haze. She drew in a ragged breath. She'd held it together this far. She could keep it up until this case was closed. Daisy nodded to Mark to let him know she was okay. "Did Xavier and Paige get Liam?"

"Yes."

The word hung in the air. It should have brought her comfort and relief to know that her cousin was in custody and couldn't hurt her or her family or anyone else ever again, but there was something in Mark's face that told her the news wasn't as good as it sounded. "But?"

Mark hesitated for a moment, then said in a rush, "He's denying involvement. He said he came here to warn you that it's not him, so you'd be prepared when the real killer came after you."

Her mind reeled.

Liam was claiming he was innocent?

If he was innocent, then who wanted her dead?

"He wants to talk to you." Mark sat beside her on the edge of the bed and took her hands. "He's here, downstairs, in the kitchen."

"Liam is here?" Her fingers curled around her husband's as the panic that had receded came flooding back.

Her cousin was here.

In what was supposed to be a safe house.

Here in the same building as her children.

Liam might have claimed he was innocent, but he'd been involved in their family's business. She'd seen him in the basement. He'd helped kidnap the girls. No matter what he said, she knew he wasn't a good person. He was dangerous, and she wanted him as far away from her kids as possible.

"He's in handcuffs, and a cop is with him at all times," Mark assured her. "He can't hurt you or anyone else."

"Where are the kids?" No number of cops or restraints could make her comfortable with her cousin being this close to her family.

"School."

"School?" It had been the middle of the night when she'd found Liam climbing over the fence. A glance at the window showed that watery winter sunlight was streaming in. How long had she been asleep?

"You collapsed," Mark explained, apparently reading the questions on her face. "You've barely slept the last six months. You haven't been taking care of yourself. You were attacked and nearly raped and murdered; you needed rest. I gave you a sedative. You've been asleep for about ten hours."

He sounded like he was trying to defend his decisions, but there was no need to. Mark was right. She hadn't been taking care of herself these last six months, and her body was running on empty. She *did* need the rest. She just hated that Liam had been here in the house while she'd been alone and completely vulnerable in sleep.

Or maybe she hadn't been alone.

There was a blanket in an armchair, which had been pulled up beside the bed. Mark had stayed with her. That's why he'd been here when she woke up.

She had really lucked out when she'd met him.

She didn't deserve him, and yet here he was anyway. He knew everything about her and her family, and yet he hadn't taken their kids and run.

"I love you." She leaned over and pressed a kiss to his cheek.

Hooking an arm around her waist, Mark dragged her closer. "I love you, too. And stop thinking that because of who your family was it makes you unworthy. You are the sweetest, most caring, compassionate, thoughtful, brave woman I know."

He kissed her, his hand threading through her hair, holding her to him. Daisy felt herself melt into the kiss. It was so easy to let go of the stress and worries and pain and fears when she was in her husband's arms. In this safe place, she could let go of everything except being with the man she loved, with his mouth crushed against hers. She wished she could stay like this forever, forget about everything but her husband.

But she couldn't.

They were all still at risk as long as the killer was out there.

Reluctantly, she broke away. "I need to talk to him."

"You don't have to talk to Liam if you don't want to. It's up to you. No one is going to force you to do it."

"I know, but I have to. I have to know if it's him or not. I need this to be over, Mark."

"But not so badly you're going to do something stupid," Mark said as he followed her out into the hall.

She couldn't promise him she wouldn't do whatever it took to end this. Her number-one priority was protecting her husband and their children, not herself and her own safety. She could promise him something else, though; she just hoped it was enough. "I won't try to do this on my own anymore. I'll let Ryan, Jack, Paige, and Xavier help."

"Okay, I guess that's going to have to do for now." Mark slid his hand into hers as they headed downstairs.

Daisy tightened her grip on her husband's hand as she caught sight of Liam.

He was really here.

Seeing him tossed her back in time twenty-five years, and she was standing in the basement, staring at four girls only a little older than herself in cages. Her entire family—minus Thorne—surrounded her, and she'd felt boxed in like there was no escape. She'd been so scared. She may have only been thirteen, but she'd known that going against her family wasn't going to end well.

Liam had been there along with her parents, aunt and uncle, brothers, and cousin.

He was involved.

He was dangerous.

He was sitting at the kitchen table staring at her.

"Daisy." Liam tried to stand, but Jack shoved him back into his seat. "I didn't kill anyone, Dais," he implored.

She stared back at him, trying to read in his eyes if he was telling the truth. Even if he had never physically killed anyone, he had led those teenage girls into their family's trap knowing what was ultimately going to happen to them. That was as good as killing them as far as she was concerned.

Daisy knew that Liam could never be called innocent, but was he innocent of these murders?

She had to know.

"Can you give us a moment alone?" she asked Jack.

"No," Mark protested immediately, his glowering gaze still fixed firmly on Liam.

Ignoring her husband for the moment, she continued to speak to Jack. "Please, just a couple of minutes. He's handcuffed, and you can stand just outside the door."

"Call out if you need me," Jack reluctantly agreed.

"Daisy, no, he's dangerous," Mark protested.

"I'll be fine." She gave his cheek a quick peck.

Jack took Mark's elbow and pulled his younger brother out of the room along with him, leaving her alone with the cousin who terrified her.

Doing her best to remain calm and collected, she asked, "Why should I believe you?"

"Because I'm telling the truth."

"I know what you did to those girls. Why would it be so hard to believe that you would take the next step to murder?"

"I wasn't like them, Daisy. You know that. I wasn't like the rest of our family."

Liam looked so sincere, and her heart ached to believe him, but she couldn't risk her family's lives on the fact that she wanted to believe there was some good in her family. "You were there in the basement. You helped kidnap those poor runaways. That makes you like the rest of them."

"No." A spark of anger ignited in his blue eyes. "I was a coward, but I wasn't like them. I tried to get help, but I got caught. Dad and Uncle Burt beat me within an inch of my life. After that, I was scared … I kept my mouth shut … I did as I was told. That didn't mean I agreed with it. I didn't. And I did what I could to help you end it."

She gasped.

Could it be true?

"You gave me the photo. The one I gave to the police. I never remembered how I got it, but it was you."

Liam nodded. "I knew you would do the right thing. And you did. You got help, you stopped them, you did what I couldn't."

"Then why did you run?" If Liam really hadn't been involved by choice, then he hadn't needed to run. If he'd been beaten and threatened into complying, then he wasn't guilty of doing anything wrong.

"Because I was ashamed." His gaze dropped to his cuffed hands.

"You didn't have anything to be ashamed of." Daisy moved to the table and sat down opposite her cousin, no longer worried that he was a threat to her safety.

"Regardless of the reasons, I was responsible for what happened to those girls. I felt guilty. I still feel guilty. Saving Katrina wasn't enough; I should have done more. I should have done whatever it took to stop them."

"Wait. What? You got Katrina out before the house burned down?" Liam was full of surprises tonight.

"Yes," her cousin replied quietly.

"It really isn't you." All of her doubts wiped away, Daisy reached out and grasped Liam's hands. "Do you know who it is?"

"No. I wish I did, but I don't know. It could be anyone. A family member of one of the girls ... a family that missed out on a baby ... one of the now grown up babies. I heard that the two who were identified didn't end up with the best of lives."

There were too many possible suspects.

She wasn't the only one at risk. Thorne, Liam, Mark, and her kids were also in danger as long as this man was still out there.

How could they stop someone when they didn't even know who they were trying to stop?

Liam had found her.

This was supposed to be a safe place, and yet he hadn't had any trouble tracking her here.

That meant the killer could, too.

"How did you find me?" she asked Liam.

Liam blushed. "I, uh, I've been watching you all these years, making sure you were safe. I know your friends, I know your family. I hacked your kids' phones and put trackers in them. I'm sorry, Daisy. I only did it because I wanted to know I could keep you safe if someone ever came after us."

That easy.

It would be that easy for the real killer to find her, too.

This had to end.

As soon as possible.

And she would do whatever it took to make that happen.

* * * * *

2:29 P.M.

Katrina didn't want to be here.

She didn't want to be doing this.

She wanted to be back in the safety of her house, distracting herself with work, and pretending that the mess her life had been twenty-five years ago was done and finished with.

Instead, she was being escorted into a safe house where her past was about to come careening into her present, and she could only hope not her future.

She was here only because of Liam. She owed him, big time, and she would do whatever she could to help him.

"In here, Ms. Weaver," a detective whose name she couldn't for the life of her remember, placed his hand on her elbow and guided her into a living room.

Katrina shrank away from his touch. She didn't like people touching her. Moving to the farthest seat in the room, she sat down, holding herself stiffly and trying to mentally prepare for the questions she would be asked.

"We need to ask you some questions about what happened to you when you were a teenager," the detective began gently.

But she didn't want gentle.

Gentle didn't help her.

It only reminded her of just how stupid she'd been.

"Just ask your questions and get it over with," she said. "You said this was about Liam. Is he in trouble?"

"What is the nature of your relationship with Liam Hayden?"

What a question. It was one she had asked herself more times than she could count since the two of them had met. "We're friends." She decided vague was the best response until she knew exactly what was going on. "Why?"

"Someone murdered the two cops who were there the day of the fire, and the teacher Daisy Allen confessed to, as well as the social worker who took charge of Daisy and Thorne Allen."

"I know. I saw it on the news. You think Liam did it because he was the only member of the family to walk away alive." That made sense.

"Do you think he did it?" the cop asked.

"No," she answered simply.

"How can you be sure?"

"Because Liam wasn't like them. He saved my life more than once."

"So, he did save you from the fire," the detective looked relieved to have verification.

"He did."

"How else did he save you?"

From the look on the cop's face, she had already done what they'd brought her here to do—convince them Liam wasn't the killer they were looking for. So she could go. Leave and return to her quiet, safe little world.

Only her world wasn't so safe anymore.

The killer had been inside her home. He wanted her dead. He would come back—of that, she had no doubt. Sooner or later, he would come for her.

"I told you what you wanted to know. I cleared Liam. He wouldn't kill anyone, especially not the people who saved him. So I think I'd like to leave now."

The cop stood as she did. "Ms. Weaver, we're concerned that he may come after you. If you stay here, we can protect you."

He was right.

She didn't want him to be, but he was.

It was hard to admit that she needed protection outside of what she could and had set up for herself. She had spent so many years being strong, being independent, taking care of herself. Katrina didn't let anyone take care of her.

Except Liam.

"Is he here? Liam."

"Yes, he is. So are Daisy and Thorne and their families. This killer is tying up loose ends, so we're keeping everyone here until this case is closed."

She was a loose end.

She could accept their help and stay safe, or she could be stubborn—again—and possibly wind up dead.

Slowly, she sank back down onto the sofa. "I didn't run away from a bad situation. My parents were great. They took good care of my siblings and me, but I felt smothered. They were *too* good, *too* involved. I wanted to be independent. So, I ran. I was stupid. I ran from a loving home straight into hell."

"Was Liam the one who tricked you?"

"Yes. He pretended to be a homeless kid, too. Then, as soon as we were alone, another person appeared. A man. I knew as soon as I saw him that I was in trouble." The shame over being so unbelievably stupid and ungrateful still haunted her to this day.

"You were only fifteen, just a kid, you shouldn't be so hard on yourself." The cop's blue eyes were clear and sincere, as was his voice. He didn't sound like he was patronizing her. "How many babies did they make you have?"

"I had three, but one died a couple of hours after she was born." The familiar tightening in her chest came as she thought of the children she had borne.

Her little girl had died in her arms; her little boys had been ripped from her arms. It was odd to love something that came to her in such a horrific way, but those babies were as much hers as they were that horrible family's. There hadn't been a day gone by where she hadn't thought about her sons. Where were they? Were they safe? Were they happy? Did they have good lives? She prayed they did.

"I wanted to die," she said softly, embarrassed to look up and see what was in the detective's face now. Those days had been so dark she had longed for death.

"Liam changed that."

"He would sneak down to the basement and just sit and talk with us. It was my fault, he almost died. I begged him to help us, and he agreed, but it didn't work out, and they nearly killed him." Liam may have been the one responsible for her abduction, but it hadn't taken her long to realize he wasn't like the rest of them, and he had quickly become her lifeline.

"Who scared you the most?"

"Liam's uncle," she answered without hesitation. The man had utterly terrified her. Unlike the rest of them, he was violent. He *wanted* to hurt her and the other girls, not just use them to make money.

"Did he ever hit you, or touch you inappropriately, aside from the artificial insemination procedures?"

"He … uh … he … not really … he tried … one day … but Liam … he tried … it didn't …" Katrina stammered, she didn't think about that. Not ever.

"How did Liam get you out?" The detective changed the subject.

"I don't really remember," she replied, shoving the unwanted memories his questions were stirring up safely back down. "Smoke started to fill the basement. We could hear gunshots, but there was no way for us to find out what was going on. I thought they were shooting at each other. Liam's dad and uncle didn't like each other. They fought all the time. The smoke was getting so thick, and I couldn't breathe. I must have passed out because the next thing I knew Liam was carrying me out of the house. He left me in a neighbor's yard where someone would be sure to find me, and he ran."

"But he didn't really run, did he?" the cop asked. He was way too perceptive and seemed to be able to keep her talking when she wanted to keep her mouth shut.

"He tried, but he couldn't stay away." Something had connected the two of them together in those three years she had spent in that basement. Something that kept drawing them into each other's orbit.

Did she love Liam?

Katrina wasn't sure.

A legal adult by the time she was freed, she hadn't wanted to return home to her family. How could she look them in the face after what she'd done? They had loved her. They had given her everything she needed and a lot of what she wanted, and yet she had been so ungrateful. She had thrown that love back in their faces and run.

So she found her own place, got a job, got herself into night school and worked hard to build a life. It hadn't been long after the fire that Liam came back the first time.

Things between them had been explosive and passionate and they'd fallen into bed.

But then he'd left.

And so the pattern began.

Every few years, Liam would turn up on her doorstep. She'd let him in because he had saved her life and she owed him and possibly loved him. Things would start going really well; she'd start to believe that this time things would be different and Liam would stay and they would be so happy.

Then one morning, she would wake up, and he'd be gone again.

Until next time.

Liam was punishing himself. She got it, she *really* did. In her own way, she was doing the same thing to herself. Punishing herself for running from a family who adored her to end up trapped in a basement forced to bear children against her will. But how many times was she going to let him break her heart before she did something to stop it?

"Are you and Liam a couple, Ms. Weaver?"

Katrina shrugged. How could she answer that when she didn't even know?

The cop nodded understandingly. "Did you see anyone else while you were there?"

"Just Liam and his parents, Drew and Kerryn; his aunt, Violet, and uncle, Burt; his sister, Xaria, and cousins, Ridge and Forrest. I only saw Daisy that last day. Other than them, it was just us girls."

"If it's not Liam, do you know of anyone else who might want to kill you?"

"No one." Her mind wandered back to the other night. To who she'd thought had been in her room.

She had been wrong.

She knew that.

It hadn't been Kurt Allen.

He was dead. He couldn't hurt her ever again.

But this killer could.

"Is me telling you I don't think it's Liam enough to truly convince you it's not?" She didn't like the thought of anyone accusing Liam of something so heinous, but how could her word convince the cops when there was logical reasoning behind suspecting him?

The detective gave her a half smile. "Enough to make us doubt that it was him. But what cinched it was that CSU found blood at one of the victim's houses that didn't belong to the victim. Belinda Jersey shot her attacker, the blood was destroyed in the fire and they couldn't get DNA, but Liam doesn't have a bullet wound. He's not the man we're looking for."

Katrina let out a sigh of relief. "He's going to be staying here as well?"

"Yes. You'll stay, too? If you don't, we can't guarantee your safety. We don't know exactly who's on the killer's list, he might come after you."

"He already has."

The man's eyes grew wide. "He came after you and you survived?"

"I have a good security system. It alerted me to the intruder. I was waiting for him, I had him, but . . ." She trailed off, ashamed she had let her fears allow a violent killer to walk free. "But when I saw him, for a moment, I thought it was Burt Allen. I let my fears get the best of me, and when we heard the sirens approaching, he ran. I'm sorry."

"It's not your fault." The cop leaned over and patted her knee. For some reason, the gesture actually comforted her rather than gave her the usual rush of fear she felt when someone laid a hand on her.

"Can I see Liam?"

She needed him.

He was her anchor.

No, he was more than that. He was her savior, her friend, her lover. He was the only man she had ever loved. He was the only man she ever *wanted* to love. And it was time to make sure he knew it.

They both deserved a fresh start, and maybe it was time for them to have it.

* * * * *

3:47 P.M.

Thirteen-year-old Elise Xander hurried into the changing rooms.

She was running late. With everything that had been going on with her family the last few days, having to leave home to stay in the safe house, learning the truth about her mom's family, her schoolwork had definitely suffered. She'd forgotten all about a history paper she was supposed to have done for today, and her history teacher hadn't been impressed.

He'd made her stay after class and given her a lecture on the necessity of turning assignments in on time, being organized, and managing her time. Elise didn't care about history. She hated the subject. She didn't care about stuff that had happened hundreds of years ago. She liked math and English and science, but most of all, she cared about swimming.

Which was where she was supposed to be fifteen minutes ago.

Quickly, she tossed her clothes into her bag and put on her swimsuit. Wrangling her long blonde hair into a bun, she put on a swim cap, then tossed her bag in a locker, grabbed her goggles, and headed for the pool, hoping she hadn't missed too much of the training.

Her coach hated when they were late, so she was going to get in trouble. Just what she needed in her life right now, *more* trouble. At least things were looking up at home. Her mom and dad seemed to have made up. That would make her sister happy. Eve had been a mess worrying about their parents these last six months.

Elise wasn't quite ready to completely forgive her mom yet. She'd just walked out on them without a word. Okay, so she thought she was keeping them safe, but how would they have felt if she'd been killed. She should have told them. Uncle Jack and Uncle Ryan would have kept her safe. She should have trusted them. How could she ever trust her mother now knowing that her mom didn't trust them?

She sighed. The older she got, the more complicated life got. Families seemed to be the most complicated things of all.

As she threw open the door, Elise almost walked straight into a man.

"Are you Elise Xander?" he asked.

"Yes," she answered without thinking. A sense of unease settled over her.

Who was he?

Why was he here?

Was he a substitute?

Had something happened to her sister?

Was he a cop that had been assigned the task of babysitting her and Eve?

He was tall and blond. Was this the man Tony had seen?

Was he here to hurt her?

Instinct told her to run, but she couldn't get past him. He was big, and he blocked the doorway. That only left going backward. But then she'd be trapped in the changing rooms.

Still, it seemed like her only option. She didn't like the vibe she was getting from this man, and she'd always been taught to trust her gut.

Releasing the door, she retreated into the changing rooms, darting into a toilet stall and slamming and locking the door.

"Don't waste my time, kid," a voice growled.

He was coming for her.

What should she do?

Her grandfather and uncles had lectured her numerous times in what to do if she ever found herself in trouble, but right now she couldn't remember a single thing they'd said.

"Hey, where are you?" the man yelled, hammering on doors.

He was going to find her.

She knew that.

And now she was trapped. She should have tried to run past him. She should have screamed for help. Why had she allowed herself to get trapped?

"Come on, kid, I don't have all day."

His voice was getting closer; he was going to find her any second now.

Her heart was thumping in her chest so loudly she was surprised he couldn't hear it.

Elise cowered at the back of the stall, she'd never been this scared in her life.

Black shoes appeared underneath the door.

He hammered on it, and when he found it didn't open, he drawled, "Found you."

This was it.

He was going to kill her.

There was no escape.

It wouldn't take him long to break down the door.

His feet disappeared, and a moment later the door wobbled as he obviously kicked it.

She had to do something.

She couldn't just sit here and wait for him to get her.

Her eyes dropped to the wall between the stall she was stuck in and the one beside it. Could she wiggle underneath the wall and get into it? If she could, she could move down the row of toilets until she put a bit of distance between herself and the man, and then make a run for it.

It wasn't a very good plan, but it was the best she had.

Holding back a cry of terror as the man kicked the door again, Elise dropped to the floor and shimmied underneath the wall and into the neighboring stall. There were another three before she'd hit the wall, so she stayed low and kept moving.

Elise had just reached the final one when she heard the splinter of wood.

He'd kicked down the door.

He'd see she was no longer in there.

It was now or never.

She threw open the door and ran.

He followed.

She could hear his footsteps pounding behind her.

Resisting the urge to turn and see how close he was to catching her, she kept moving.

She made it out the change room door and headed for the pool at the end of the long corridor. Her coach and teammates were in there. Surely, he wouldn't follow her. He'd said her name; it was her that he wanted. He wouldn't follow her in there where there were so many other people.

He wouldn't.

Only, he did.

His footsteps continued to chase her, getting closer by the second.

She burst through the door at the end of the hall. The other kids on the swim team were in the pool. Her coach was yelling out instructions from the side.

"Help!" she screamed. "Help!"

Elise headed for her coach. A grown-up would know what to

do.

She saw the coach's eyes grow wide.

The woman said something, but fear had stolen her hearing.

She was almost there when something slammed into her from behind and sent her sprawling painfully onto the tiled floor.

Something heavy settled on her back, pinning her down.

The man.

Something cold was pressed against the back of her head.

A gun.

He had a gun.

And he held it to her head.

* * * * *

4:03 P.M.

Eve Xander pricked her finger and waited to see what her blood sugar levels were. She had to check several times a day. Mornings, lunchtime, dinnertime, bedtime, and before she did anything physical, which included before she went to her swimming training.

At first, she'd hated doing it, but now it was more a bother than anything else. It wasn't that she liked having diabetes, but there were some upsides. She liked the added attention she got, with three siblings, four cousins, plus Paige's two kids who were almost like cousins, there were a lot of kids in the family, and that often meant that individual time and attention were scarce.

Although it had been a little scary when she was first diagnosed, the doctors and nurses at the hospital, and her parents, particularly her mom, had been amazing. Her mom had been there with her every step of the way. From when she started having really bad mood swings, getting really tired, and becoming unbelievable thirsty, to the diagnosis, she had driven her to every appointment, helped her to learn how to check her levels, helped her learn how to give herself her insulin shots, helped her get into a routine to help manage her diabetes.

Her mom had been her rock. That was why it had hurt so much when she left, and why she'd wanted so badly for her to come home.

And now she was.

She smiled as she repacked her bag, and it had nothing to do with her sugar levels. Her family was finally back together again. Her parents were working things out, and as soon as whoever wanted to hurt her mom was caught, they could all go home.

Together.

Eve didn't care that her mom had lied to them or moved out or about who her parents were. All she cared about was getting her family back. She'd missed her mom every single day for the last six months. Her school work had suffered, her swimming had suffered, and her relationships with her siblings had suffered because she had been the only one who wanted Mom back while everyone else had been so angry.

Brian had been the angriest of all. She hoped he told one of their parents what was going on with him soon. The longer he kept it to himself, the worse it was, and the worse he was.

Maybe she should tell someone.

Her big brother would be mad, but at least then Mom and Dad would know.

She'd talk to their parents tonight after dinner and just hope that Brian understood.

Eve closed her locker and headed for the pool. She would check in with her swim coach and let her know that she was fine, then go and change. She picked up her pace as she crossed the empty schoolyard. It had never creeped her out before, but now knowing that someone might want to hurt her because of who her mom's family was made her feel jumpy. It was weird being escorted to school by a cop who wasn't one of her relatives. At least Uncle Jack was supposed to pick them up after their swim training and take her and Elise back to the safe house. She hoped he came early to watch. She would feel much safer with him around.

She opened the door to the pool and froze.

Her sister was on the ground.

A man sat on her back.

He held something in his hand.

Something shiny.

A gun.

The rest of the kids were in the pool.

The coach stood at the side.

The man with the gun was yelling something, but for some reason, she couldn't seem to make out the words.

Her coach's eyes met hers.

They said run.

Get help.

The man hadn't seen her yet.

She wanted to go. To find help. But she couldn't seem to move.

Then she heard her sister cry out.

He'd hurt Elise.

Eve felt the pain as though it were her own.

Part of her wanted to run to the man, hurt him for hurting her twin, but she knew she couldn't.

She had to get help.

Quietly, she stepped backward, reaching out behind her for the door handle, not wanting to take her eyes off the man.

She was shaking, badly; she was so scared he was going to see her.

He could turn at any second.

If he saw her, he could shoot her.

This had to be the man who wanted to hurt her mom.

He'd found them.

They were supposed to be safe here at school. The cops had

said that they didn't think he would come for them here with so many people around.

Obviously, they were wrong.

The seconds it took her to open the door and step through it seemed excruciatingly long.

With a last helpless look at her sister, she let the door fall closed.

And then she was running.

She didn't really know where. She just had to find someone.

Tears were streaming down her face, blurring her vision, and she didn't see anyone in front of her until she ran headlong into them.

Hands curled around her arms, holding her tightly.

Eve fought against them with every bit of strength she possessed. "Let me go!" she screamed. "Let me go!"

"Eve. Eve. It's me."

It took a moment for the voice to penetrate the terrified haze that possessed her.

"Uncle Jack," she sobbed, throwing herself against him.

"What's wrong?" He kept his grip on her arms and leaned down, so they were eye to eye.

"There's a man," she cried. Her uncle could fix this. He fixed everything. Other than her parents, there was no one she trusted more than Jack.

"What man, honey? Where is he?"

"I don't know who he is, but he has Elise and my coach and my friends," she babbled, hoping she was making sense. "He has a gun."

Uncle Jack pulled her against him and held her tightly. She heard him talking to someone. Since they were alone, she assumed he was on his phone calling for help. Eve relaxed a little. Help was coming. They would fix this. Save her sister.

"Honey, listen to me." Uncle Jack leaned back down so he could look her in the eye again. "I want you to go into the bathroom and hide. I don't want you to come out until Uncle Ryan comes to get you. You hear me?"

Eve nodded.

"Promise me," Uncle Jack demanded.

"I promise."

He leaned forward and kissed her forehead. "Go."

Without looking back, she did as her uncle commanded and ran to the bathroom.

Elise's bag lay on the floor by the door.

One of the toilet doors was broken.

The man had been in here. He'd tried to take her sister. Elise must have tried to run, but the man had followed her. And now he held her twin, her coach, and swim team hostage.

Crawling under the rows of sinks, down in the far corner, she curled herself into a ball, as tight as she could, and pressed her face into her knees.

Tears streamed down her cheeks, and she shook uncontrollably.

How would she survive if he killed her twin sister?

* * * * *

4:22 P.M.

This was not how he had envisioned this going.

He didn't want to be holding a group of kids hostage. There had to be a dozen of them. What was he going to do with them?

There was no way he could walk out of here with twelve girls and their teacher and have no one notice.

This was a nightmare.

He had to fix it.

He just had no idea how.

All he'd wanted was Elise Xander. That was it—nothing more, nothing less. He'd intended to grab her in the bathroom, take her with him, and leave. He wanted to take Daisy's daughter to teach her a lesson. He didn't want to try abducting a dozen kids at one time. That was a recipe for disaster, and he liked to play things safe.

Maybe he should just kill them all and be done with it. Sure, a pool full of dead kids was going to draw the cops' attention, but they wouldn't have any reason to link it to him. He could still get Elise, who was all he wanted anyway and maybe seeing him shoot her friends would work out to be a good thing. She would know just how serious defying him could be.

Movement caught his attention.

The kids had swum down to the far end of the pool. The woman was down there, too. She was trying to get them out. When he'd chased Elise in here, he'd told everyone not to move. How dare they disobey his orders.

"Hey!" He stood and dragged Elise to her feet with him, shoving the gun against her head. Keeping the kids in the pool helped him keep things under control, and he wanted to keep it that way. He needed to maintain the upper hand if he was going to walk out of this with the girl. "I said everyone stayed where they were."

"Please." The woman walked tentatively toward him. "They're just kids, let them go. They're scared, and they haven't done anything wrong. Let them go, please."

Too bad for her he had long since lost his heart.

"You can take me if you want; just let the kids go."

He was impressed by her bravery, and he felt no compulsion to kill her, nor would he feel any pleasure when he did it. He just wouldn't feel any regret or guilt either.

The woman took another step forward. "Please. Let them go. Don't hurt them. Take me instead."

He was unsure how much time he would have before people started showing up. He didn't know when the swimming training ended and the parents would arrive to collect their kids, so he may as well get started. Quickly, he moved the gun from Elise's head and fired off a single shot at the woman.

He got her in the heart.

Her eyes grew wide with shock, and her hands raised to the wound.

Then she fell and landed with a splash in the pool.

The kids started screaming.

Elise slumped. Caught off guard, he lost his grip on her, and the teenager rolled sideways and into the pool with the others.

That was annoying. Now he was going to have to try and get her out of there when he was finished killing her friends. He hated getting wet, so he didn't want to have to jump in and physically pull her out, especially since the pool was already filling with the blood of his first victim, and by the time he was done, there'd be a dozen more.

"Fawkner!"

He froze when he heard his name.

"Don't do it."

He spun around and found Detective Jack Xander standing a few yards away with a gun trained at his chest.

"Put your weapon down and get down on the ground," the detective ordered.

Fawkner had no intention of complying. He wanted his revenge, and he wasn't above shooting the cop to get it.

"This isn't the way." Jack Xander inched his way closer. "I know you're angry, and you have every right to be, but killing people—hurting Daisy's daughter—isn't the way to get your revenge."

He respectfully disagreed with that statement.

Revenge was all that mattered.

"Daisy ruined my life. She deserves to suffer."

"She didn't do anything wrong. She tried to do the right thing. She *did* do the right thing. If it weren't for her coming forward and getting help, then her family would likely still be abducting teenage runaways and selling their babies on the black market."

Fawkner honestly didn't care about the girls that had been spared because the Hayden and Allen families had been mostly decimated. All he cared about was what had happened to him.

He still remembered that awful day with perfect clarity.

He'd come home from school excited because he'd read his very first book all on his own and been able to read every single word. For a first grader, that was something pretty exciting. Telling his parents was all he'd wanted to do. He'd been hoping they might have had ice cream sundaes for dessert. His mom always made something special for after dinner when she was proud of one of his accomplishments.

Instead, he'd gotten off the bus and walked in his front door to find his mom on the couch in tears. His dad stood stiffly in the corner, and a dozen cops were swarming all over his house.

At first, he had been a little excited. He'd wanted to be a cop when he grew up and dressed as one for Halloween the previous three years.

But then the cops had sat him down and told him that his mommy and daddy weren't his real mommy and daddy and were going to prison. A man with a bald head and body odor had come for him, but not before he'd seen his parents handcuffed and put in the back of a police car.

The group home he'd been taken to had been okay. He'd been confused and scared, but still thought that he could go back home. He hadn't really understood what was going on.

That hope that things would all go back to normal was squashed that first night he'd spent in his new foster home, and he had lived every day since mostly dead inside.

Fawkner met the detective's gaze squarely. "Do you know what they did to me in foster care?"

"They raped you," Detective Xander said quietly. "That's why you were going to rape Daisy at the hotel."

He nodded. "I was six years old. *Six.*" Horrific memories of that night replayed in his head.

Life was so unfair.

He hadn't done anything wrong and yet he'd lost his home, his parents, his friends, been raped and beaten and had more bones broken than he could even remember.

"I'm so sorry that happened to you." The detective looked and sounded sincere. "I know what that does to a person. My wife was raped, and if I'd been able to get my hands on the men who hurt her, I would have ripped them to shreds. I understand wanting revenge, but it has to be the right person. And the person who hurt you isn't Daisy. It's your foster parents who raped and beat you. It's Daisy's family who abducted your mother and forced her to have you. They're the ones responsible for you being hurt, and they're all dead. I looked into the family who fostered you. Both your foster parents are also dead. I understand why you've fixated on Daisy because it seems like she's all that's left, but you know she didn't do anything to you."

"When she opened her mouth, she set in motion the chain of events." Daisy had destroyed his life. It was only fair he returned the favor. "I wasn't going to kill her kid. I was going to take her. I was going to make her see what it was like to have your child taken from you. I was going to do to her what her family did to my mother and so many other innocent girls. You think Daisy is innocent, but she was one of them. She lived in that house while teenagers were being held in cages in her basement."

"What should she have done then, Fawkner? If you don't think she should have been involved in her family's business, and you don't think she should have told the police what was going on, then what should she have done?"

"I don't care what she should have done. All I care about is making sure she suffers."

"Don't do this, Fawkner. Think about your wife. Don't hurt her by doing this."

He loved his wife, but not more than he hated Daisy Xander.

Nothing was more important to him than destroying her. If he couldn't kill her, then he could at least do the next best thing.

Part of him had always known that it was going to end this way. When he'd started down this path, what other ending could there be?

Pointing his gun at the pool, Fawkner began to fire.

* * * * *

4:51 P.M.

She was frantic.

She wanted to go running inside the school.

In fact, Daisy had tried to when they'd first arrived. Xavier had to physically restrain her to stop her. She'd fought to get out of his arms. Her daughter was in danger. How could he ask her to do nothing?

She was the one the killer wanted. Not Elise. Not those other kids. If she could just get in there, then she was sure she could convince him to let her daughter and the other children go and take her instead. Daisy would gladly lay down her life if it meant ensuring her daughter's safety.

It had only been Mark's threats that if she didn't calm down and stay out here with him, then he would sedate her, that had her waiting here.

She had no doubt he would follow through on the threat if he thought she was going to put herself in danger, which was the *only* reason she was still standing here.

Well, standing was a bit misleading.

Daisy was pacing frantically. Ignoring her protesting body that still ached from the attack in the hotel room a couple of days ago, she kept moving. If she didn't, she feared she would lose her mind and go running into the school regardless of the consequences.

Both Mark and Xavier seemed to sense that and were watching

her like a hawk.

Mark was sitting in the back of an ambulance with Eve huddled on his lap. When Daisy looked at her trembling daughter, she realized it could very easily be both her girls being held at gunpoint.

By some fluke, Eve had been late to training and wasn't in the pool along with the other girls. She didn't know what had held her daughter up, and she didn't care. She was just beyond grateful that Eve was safe.

Ryan had already brought her out and left her with Xavier by the time she and Mark had arrived. And the first thing she'd done when she'd jumped out of the car and seen her daughter sitting in the back of an ambulance was run to her and fling her arms around her child and squeeze her so hard Eve had eventually cried out.

Her world had stopped spinning when Paige had called to tell her what was going on, and if Elise didn't walk out of that building alive, then it would never start up again.

The drive from the safe house to the school, a mere five minutes, had felt like an eternity.

It was the worst kind of hell to know her child was in danger and she couldn't stop it.

Well, she could, but no one would let her.

Xavier hovered no more than a couple of steps from her side, ready to stop her if she tried to get inside the school again.

There were cops everywhere. Even if she could make it past Xavier, one of them would surely stop her. She should feel reassured by the police presence. A hostage negotiation team were on their way, and Jack and Ryan and Paige were in there. She trusted all three of them implicitly, but this was her baby, and she knew how to get those kids out of there alive.

How was she going to face all of those parents if their children were murdered because of her?

How was she going to face her husband if their daughter was

murdered because of her?

How was she going to face Eve if her twin was murdered because of her?

How was she going to face herself if her little girl was murdered because of her?

She couldn't think about Elise, and yet she couldn't stop.

What was her daughter thinking right now?

Did she think she was going to die in there?

Did she blame her?

She couldn't do this any longer. She had to go in there. She had to stop him before anyone got hurt.

"Don't, Daisy." Mark suddenly materialized before her.

"Where's Eve?" Her gaze darted about. She didn't want her daughter alone.

"She's right there." Her husband pointed behind them where Eve still sat in the back of the ambulance.

"Go stay with her." Daisy wanted to be with her daughter, but her guilt was crushing her. Every couple of minutes she stopped her manic pacing to go and hug her girl, but whenever she held Eve in her arms, she saw Elise and the need to do whatever it took to save her daughter was almost more overwhelming than she could cope with.

"You know you can't go in there," Mark said instead. His face was worried. He knew her well enough to know that she would eventually crumble under pressure. "Please." He lifted a hand and brushed his knuckles across her cheek. "Don't do something stupid."

She wouldn't do anything stupid.

But, unfortunately for her husband, she thought they both had completely different opinions on what stupid was. Mark thought it was stupid for her to go running in there and sacrifice herself to save their daughter and a dozen other innocent kids.

That was easy for him to think. He wasn't the one responsible.

"Daisy." Mark threaded his fingers through her hair and gently pulled her face closer and rested his forehead on hers. "I don't want to lose you."

Too.

He didn't say the word, but he didn't have to. He had already accepted the possibility that Elise wouldn't walk out of the pool alive.

"Mark," she whimpered. If Elise died because of her, she would lose everything. Her husband, her children, her family, none of them would want to be around her anymore. They would blame her, and that would wind up decaying their love for her until it was gone.

"Don't think that," he said softly. His lips hovered just a hairsbreadth for hers, but he didn't kiss her.

"I didn't say anything."

"I can hear you thinking. I am always going to love you. I hate that you lied to me and didn't trust me with the truth about your family, but I understand. We still have a lot of things we need to discuss and sort out before we can get back to where we were before. We can't do that if you get yourself killed."

She wanted so badly to get her relationship with her husband back to where it had been before she left. She wished she could take back all the lies she'd told and the destruction they had caused, but she couldn't, and now her daughter's life might be the price she had to pay.

"I love you, Daisy. Are you hearing me?"

She was hearing that she had caused him pain and that her lies and decision not to go to the cops with what was going on might cost them both their daughter.

"I love you." He touched his lips to hers. "When you think about risking your life, try to remember that. I don't want to lose you."

She didn't want to lose him, either—or her daughter or herself—to the guilt that would kill her if this man murdered Elise. Daisy made herself look into Mark's bright blue eyes. Fear lurked in them—and hurt—but what she saw most was love.

Despite everything she'd done, he still loved her.

How could she hurt him more by putting herself in danger?

"I love you, too, Mark. I won't—" She stopped short when a loud bang rang out.

Was that what she thought it was?

Before she even knew what she was doing, she was running toward what she was positive was a gunshot.

Gunshot*s*.

She had counted at least seven.

Arms snapped around her waist pulling her back, and she was pinned against a rock-solid chest.

She struggled wildly.

Panic was brewing inside her, bubbling up and out, consuming her.

Daisy screamed and thrashed.

She had to get inside.

That man was shooting innocent people.

He could have shot her daughter.

It was her he wanted, and he could have her.

If only she could get free, she would give herself to him.

Anything to make him stop shooting.

Anything to spare her daughter.

It should be her.

"Let me go," she screeched. Panic continued to swell inside her. She wanted to rip off her skin, pull out her hair, anything to let it out before it reduced her to nothing.

"Daisy."

She heard Mark's voice, but it seemed so far away. Like he was miles away and not struggling to keep her in his arms.

"It should have been me," she sobbed. Whoever had been shot didn't deserve to die. She did. For everything that her family had done, for keeping secrets and lying to her husband their entire relationship, for placing her children in danger.

"Daisy." Mark jostled her, attempting to get her attention, but all she could think of was getting inside and stopping the killer before he hurt anyone else.

"It should have been me." She was shaking so badly her teeth were chattering, floods of tears stole her vision, and her drumming pulse robbed her of her hearing. "I deserve to die. Let me go, please, so I can stop him."

"Daisy, stop it, listen to me!" Mark's hands clamped around her biceps and roughly spun her around, shaking her until he managed to clear away some of the fear clawing its way around her body. "She's okay. Elise is okay."

What?

Had she heard him right or had her mind finally snapped and thrown her headlong into hallucinating insanity?

"Are you hearing me? Elise is okay. Look." He gestured his head behind her, then forcibly turned her around, so she was facing that direction.

It took a moment for her watery eyes to clear enough for her to see, but when they did, she gasped.

Jack was walking toward her.

In his arms was Elise.

Her daughter was wet and wrapped in a towel, but she appeared to be unhurt.

Mark's arm hooked around her waist, keeping her upright as her knees buckled.

Elise's head had been on Jack's shoulder, but she lifted it, and their eyes met.

"Mom," Elise sobbed, struggling to get out of her uncle's arms.

The next thing Daisy knew, Elise was in her arms, and both of them were in Mark's.

And then Eve was there, and the four of them were just holding each other and crying.

Her daughter was alive.

Daisy couldn't believe it.

She kept expecting to wake up at any minute and learn that she had passed out upon being informed of her daughter's death and this was nothing more than a dream.

"You're not dreaming," Mark's voice whispered against her hair, and a moment later she felt a sharp jab on her arm as he pinched her. "See?" he grinned down at her. "You're not dreaming."

Elise was alive.

They were all alive.

And safe now.

The killer was caught.

It was over, and somehow she and her family had survived.

* * * * *

10:19 P.M.

"Are you sure you're all right?" Mark asked as he sat on the edge of Elise's bed.

"I'm fine, Dad." She gave him a tired smile.

His daughter amazed him. He was so proud of her. She was every bit as strong as her mother, who also amazed him. Elise had been a trooper. She'd given her statement, and after being cleared by the paramedics, they'd finally been able to take her home.

Home.

With Fawkner Miller dead—killed by Jack, Ryan, and Paige, who had opened fire on him when he began to shoot at the kids—there was no longer a death threat hanging over their heads, and they could return home and go back to their lives.

Tonight they'd enjoyed some family time. He had been worried it would feel odd having Daisy back in the house after her being gone for so many months, but it hadn't. Everything had felt just right. Perfect, in fact.

Mark was under no illusions. He knew his family had a lot of healing to do. Elise needed to see a therapist after what she'd witnessed—the death of her coach, several of her friends being shot, the death of Fawkner Miller—she would need help processing all of that. His daughter had asked about speaking with Laura, his brother Jack's wife who was a psychiatrist. He was a little hesitant about her speaking to a relative, but if that was what would help her, then he wouldn't say no.

Tony and Eve should probably speak to someone, as well. And maybe if Brian spoke with someone, he could find out what was going on with his oldest son.

Then there was Daisy. She definitely needed help letting go of this guilt she felt about what her family had done. She was blaming herself for what had happened to Elise, as well. She had been quiet and distant all night.

When the cops were done with them, they'd bought pizza on the way home and eaten together as a family, sitting around the dining room table just like they used to do. The kids had asked for ice cream sundaes, and Daisy had made them with a smile on her face, but there was something wrong with her smile. It didn't make it to her eyes.

As soon as they were alone, Mark intended to talk to her about it. But first, he needed to make sure his kids were settled for the night.

"If you need us, for anything at all—you get scared, you have a bad dream, anything—you come get us, okay?" he said.

"Okay," Elise agreed.

"You too." He turned to Eve, who was having a harder time dealing with things than her sister.

"Okay, Daddy."

"Goodnight, honey." He kissed Elise's forehead.

"Night, Dad." She threw her arms around his neck and hugged him hard.

Although he wanted to hold her in his arms all night and keep her nightmares at bay, the girls had said they were fine to sleep in their own room, and he had to respect that. Besides, his room was right down the hall. The girls could come and get him if they needed to.

"Goodnight, sweetie." He went and kissed Eve.

"Night, Daddy." She, too, gave him a hard hug.

Daisy was standing awkwardly in the middle of the room like she wasn't sure what she should do or say. Her growing dissociation was starting to worry him. "Dais," he said quietly as he stepped toward her, nudging her.

She blinked slowly, then pasted on a smile. "Goodnight, girls." She walked stiffly to each bed and gave both the girls a hug and a kiss.

The vacant look in her eyes, and her flat tone told him just how much she was struggling. He and the kids had only been thrown into this nightmare a couple of days ago, but Daisy had been living it for months, and the toll it had taken was evident. She'd reconciled herself with the idea of dying rather than getting help and risking their safety, and then when she'd finally taken that leap of faith and told them everything, her worst nightmare had very nearly come true. Mark didn't know how to convince her that none of what had happened—now or in the past—was her fault.

The girls didn't seem to notice their mother's odd behavior. They returned her hugs, kissed her, and echoed her goodnights. They looked so young with their blonde hair fanned out on their pillows, framing their pale faces. He hated that his babies had lived through something so traumatic and hoped that it wouldn't leave lifelong scars.

Taking Daisy's arm, he led her to the door. "Call out if you need us," he reminded his daughters, then flicked off the light, and stepped into the hall, bringing Daisy with him, and closed the door.

They'd already put Tony to bed, and Brian had said his

goodnights and shut himself up in his room, so Mark guided Daisy to their room. As soon as he let go of her, she just stood there, right where he'd left her, looking lost. His heart ached; he didn't know how to help her.

"Daisy, don't ... please," he begged. He couldn't stand to see her shutting down. Shutting him out. Again. She'd shut him out of her past and how much it still affected her the entire time they'd known each other. She couldn't do it again. He was afraid if she did, this time the damage to their relationship would be permanent.

"What?" Her unfocused eyes turned in his direction but stared straight through him.

"Don't try to do this on your own. I'm here. I'm not going anywhere. Let me help you." He took her hands, found them freezing. Her whole body was ice cold. Standing so close to her was like standing with the refrigerator door open, and she was trembling. He was concerned she was slowly going into shock.

"You hate me," she intoned dully. "I lied to you. You don't trust me. You don't know if we can fix things because I ruined everything we had. Because of me you almost lost your daughter."

She had taken what he'd said to her back at the school and twisted it because her mind couldn't process everything that had happened. She was in emotion overload right now, so she was blocking everything out, refusing to allow herself to feel anything at all. It was a defense mechanism he understood, but it wasn't going to help her right now. She was safe; they were all safe; now it was time to heal.

Mark didn't think words were enough for Daisy right now. She needed to *feel* his love for her. Placing her cold hands over his heart, he dipped his head and kissed her, willing her to understand that he could hate something she had done, but he could never hate her.

"I love you, Daisy. Please try to remember that," he whispered against her lips.

"How could you love me? The girls' swim coach was killed because of me. Caden, Belinda, Mrs. Pickle, Devon Paddy—they're all dead because of me. Elise was almost killed because of me."

As he looked at her, he could virtually see her walls come crumbling down. Tears filled her eyes, collected on her long lashes for a moment, then flooded down her pale cheeks as she began to sob. Her knees buckled, and she collapsed into him. Her fingers curled into his T-shirt, and she pressed her forehead against his chest.

"Shh," he soothed, holding her tightly with one arm and rubbing circles on her back with his other hand. "Let it out, honey. Don't try to hold it in; you've been doing that for too long. You're not alone. I want to share your pain."

"You shouldn't have to," she mumbled against his chest, her tears already soaked through the thin material of his T-shirt.

"Why? I love you. When you hurt, I hurt."

Her arms moved to wrap tightly around his waist. "I don't deserve you."

"It makes me so angry when I hear you say something like that," he muttered. He felt her start to withdraw, again misinterpreting his words. "Don't pull away," he said quickly. "I'm not angry *at* you, I'm angry that you don't see yourself as I do. As I always thought you did. You always seemed so strong, so confident. I never knew that you doubted yourself and your worthiness. That makes me mad and sad. I thought you knew how much I loved you, but maybe I didn't make it clear enough."

"No." She quickly pulled back so she could look up at him. "It's not your fault. I was ashamed and scared. I didn't want to turn out like my parents."

"Sweetheart, you're nothing like them." He kept her secured against him, afraid she would run if he let her go. "How could you think you were? You got help, you stopped them, even though you loved them, you did the right thing."

"I didn't do the right thing." She dropped her gaze and went stiff in his arms. "I should have told Jack and Ryan and Xavier and Paige what I knew before so many people were killed."

"You were in an impossible situation," he reminded her. He'd already told her he understood the choices she'd made, but it seemed he was going to have to tell her many more times before it finally sunk in.

"I'm so sorry I lied to you, Mark. I'm so sorry I hurt you and the kids by moving out. I thought I was doing the right thing, but I don't know anymore. I'm sorry," she murmured, her blue eyes imploring.

"I know you are," he assured her.

"How do I fix things between us?" she asked anxiously.

"There's nothing to fix. I can't pretend I'm not hurt by you not telling me the truth, but I really do understand. I just want you to promise me that you won't do it again. We're a couple—a team. You can't try to do it on your own. I want you to trust me." He let the vulnerability he felt seep into his voice because he thought she needed to hear it.

"You're right. We are a team. I'm sorry that I didn't trust you with my past."

Mark pressed a kiss to her forehead. "I love you, Dais. I want you to always remember that. There isn't anything you can't tell me. Now let's get you into bed, you're ice cold and you need rest."

"Oh," she said, looking disappointed.

"What?"

"I thought maybe there was something else we could do in bed other than sleep." She raised a suggestive eyebrow.

His body responded instantly.

It had been six long months since he and Daisy had had sex, and he'd missed the feeling of being inside her, of seeing her face when she tipped over the edge into ecstasy.

Mark swung her up into his arms. "I guess sleep can wait a

little longer."

He laid her down on the bed, and for a moment he just stared at her. Her eyes were still haunted, but he saw his Daisy lurking in their depths. She was still in there. It would just take time for her to find her way back out.

JANUARY 30TH

2:12 A.M.

One second she was asleep; the next, she was yanked awake as pain sliced through her scalp.

Automatically, her hands flew to the site of the pain and found a hand tangled in her hair. The hand was pulling her out of bed.

What was going on?

She was at home with her family ... in bed with Mark ... it was over ... Fawkner had been killed.

It was supposed to be over.

She struggled to keep her balance as her feet thumped painfully to the floor.

"Daisy?" Mark asked sleepily as the jostled bed woke him.

"Move a muscle, and I'll blow her brains out," a voice snarled into the darkness.

Mark's form froze under the covers.

She froze, too.

The voice.

Daisy recognized it.

It was Thorne.

Why was her little brother in her house, in her bedroom, in the middle of the night, with his hand roughly holding her hair, and a gun shoved against her ribs?

"What are you doing?" she asked, sure this must be some kind of joke. Thorne had always loved practical jokes. She couldn't count the number of times he'd driven her crazy when they were kids with his stupid stunts. Fake spiders in her bed, Jell-O in her shoes, hiding in her closet and jumping out to scare her. She'd hated all of them and complained so many times to their parents and begged them to make him stop. It didn't matter how many times he was punished, Thorne just couldn't stop with the pranks.

That had to be what this was.

Some crazy prank.

"I'm here to finish what I started," he whispered in her ear.

What he'd started?

Her brain refused to comprehend her brother's answer. "What did you start?"

"The teacher you told, the social worker who took us to foster care, the cops who killed our parents, next comes cousin Liam and his girlfriend the survivor. That just leaves you, sister dear."

"Liam is dead?" she gasped.

"Not yet," Thorne drawled in her ear. "I thought you might like to watch that one."

So he didn't intend to kill her here and now. He was going to abduct her, make her watch him kill Liam and Katrina, and then kill her in some no-doubt-horrific way. Did that mean Mark and her children were safe? If he was the one who'd done all of this, then he'd promised not to hurt her family, that she was the one he wanted.

But then she'd done the one thing he told her not to.

She'd talked.

Did that mean he was going to follow through on his threats?

"I don't care about your husband," her brother answered, seemingly reading her mind. "As long as you do as you're told, I won't hurt him."

Daisy sighed inwardly in relief. Mark was safe, but what about the kids? What if one of them came in here? They'd told them that if they needed anything during the night to let them know, but if one of them wandered in here, Thorne might kill them.

"You'll leave Mark and the kids alone if I go with you?" She would sacrifice herself in a heartbeat if it meant saving her family.

"Daisy, no!" Mark cried out.

She ignored him. It might make him angry if she allowed Thorne to take her and kill her, but at least he'd be alive to be angry.

"I said I'd leave your husband alone." She could hear the smile in his voice. Thorne was loving every second of this. "I never said I'd leave your kids alone."

"You said you would," she protested desperately. "You said you didn't care about them, that you wouldn't touch them."

"Ifff ..." He drew out the word. "... you didn't go to the cops, but you did, didn't you?"

Thorne's hand was still in her hair, and he yanked her head back so harshly she cried out, causing Mark to bolt upright on the bed. "Daisy?"

"I told you not to move," Thorne told Mark, then slammed the butt of the gun into her stomach, making her gag as pain shot out around her body. He did it again, just because he could, and he obviously enjoyed hurting her. "Next time, I shoot her in the foot," he warned.

Gasping, trying to still the nausea and pain so she could think, Daisy said, "Please leave my children alone."

"I can't. They're Allens. It's time they learn the family business."

Daisy almost threw up.

Tears were streaming down her face, and with her head pulled back so far, she almost choked on them.

Her brother had obviously restarted what their parents had done.

Thorne wanted to take her children and teach them to abduct girls and impregnate them and find couples who were so desperate for children they would pay to get a baby.

The very thought of it made her sick.

She didn't want her precious children anywhere near her brother.

"Please, Thorne ... you can take me ... you can kill me ... you can torture me … I don't care. Just leave my kids alone," she cried.

"No, Daisy." Mark moved in the bed, no doubt wanting to grab her and never let her go, physically preventing her from going with her brother.

Thorne didn't hesitate.

He fired the gun.

Pain bloomed in her left foot.

Her brother released her, and she crumpled to the ground, clutching at her foot.

"Daisy?" Mark's panicked voice asked.

"I-I'm o-okay," she answered quickly. She didn't want to risk him trying to get to her and getting himself shot in the process. She could feel the crushing impotence rolling off him, and if she didn't put him at ease, then he was going to get himself killed.

Blood slicked her hands as she tried to ignore the pain enough to put pressure on the wound. She had no idea how bad it was, but it was certainly going to make it harder for her to fight her brother.

She had no intention of going with him.

It was one thing to sacrifice herself to save her family, but she would not, under any circumstances, allow him to hurt her children.

She would do whatever she could to stop him or die trying.

"I warned you," Thorne singsonged to Mark.

Her brother was insane.

For the first time, it really hit her just how different she was from the rest of her family. If she hadn't been her mother's mini me she would have thought she was adopted.

"How could you do this, Thorne?" Daisy needed answers. She needed to understand how her little brother, who had been spared being indoctrinated into their family's insanity, had ended up restarting the black-market baby business and getting revenge on everyone who was responsible for their parents' and brothers' deaths. "You sent Fawkner Miller to rape me." That her own brother could do that to her hurt her worse than anything else.

"I had nothing to do with that lunatic. He's just some nut job with a grudge against you who managed to track you down and get his revenge."

Took one to know one, it seemed, since her brother had done the same thing. He'd come back to kill everyone he blamed for what had happened that day. He'd threatened her and made her leave her family. He'd let their cousin take the fall for the murders. He'd broken in here tonight to kidnap her and her children. He wanted to destroy her.

She knew what he'd done and what he planned to do, but she didn't understand why.

He couldn't have been brainwashed by their parents into thinking that what they did was okay. He hadn't even known about it until after they were dead.

So why was he doing this?

Daisy could understand that he blamed her. She *had* been the one who had set the chain of events in motion that led to their family's deaths. But this all seemed so extreme for someone who had only been ten when it had all gone down.

"Why? Why are you doing this? You didn't even know what was going on in the basement until after they died, so why are you so bent on getting revenge?"

"Stupid sister. You know nothing."

* * * * *

2:33 A.M.

Daisy was so stupid.

Thorne sincerely hoped that her kids had inherited more of the Allen and Hayden family genes. Daisy was some fluke in their family, something he hoped would never be repeated.

It was time for the next generation to take their rightful places in the business. Once they were properly initiated, he would put the older boy and the girls to work bringing in new girls. The younger boy was still a little young, but it wouldn't hurt him to start learning the ropes now—in preparation of his thirteenth birthday. Once the kids were settled into their new home, he might even teach the older boy how to snap someone's neck. It was such a quick, easy method of killing someone and one that he would use many times once he joined the family business.

He looked down at his sister, huddled on the floor, clutching at her bloody foot. Thorne wanted to grab hold of her and beat her until she was nothing but a bloody, unrecognizable mess. He wanted her to hurt. He wanted her to be as hurt as he had been when she single-handedly destroyed their family.

She deserved death.

A long, slow, painful death.

And she would have it.

He would take her away, make her watch Liam and Katrina's deaths, maybe even make her watch as he trained her children to become true members of the Allen family. Then he would torture her mercilessly until the anger inside him was abated. Then, maybe, he could find some relief from the ball of pain that had been planted inside him the day his parents died and grown every day since.

He had waited.

He had been patient.

Now it was time to get what he wanted.

Unable to resist, Thorne stooped and slammed his fist into Daisy's face. She groaned in pain, and he heard movement in the bed behind him. Her husband was having trouble following orders. He didn't want to kill the man—he had no grudge with him—but he certainly would kill his brother-in-law if the man gave him no other choice.

"Uh-uh-uh," he warned. "Unless you want me to shoot your

wife again, you stay where you are."

Mark growled but stilled.

He took another shot at Daisy's face for good measure and got a huge sense of satisfaction seeing the blood that marred her pale skin. Her blood had splattered over his shirt. He was obsessed with cleanliness, and he hated to soil his clothing. If one of the girls required a lesson, he usually stripped off his clothing first, but today he would wear his sister's blood with pride. It was a symbol of his victory, of justice for his family.

"I knew before Ridge," he told her and was rewarded with a sharp gasp.

"B-but you would have only been five," Daisy said.

"I was."

"How? How did you find out?"

"I went down there one day," he told her. They were forbidden to go in the basement, but even as a little boy he'd always been one to push the boundaries and break the rules. It was Daisy who had been the Goody Two-shoes. "I found the girls in their cages. They begged me to help them, but I didn't. I didn't know why they were there, but I was intrigued. It was kind of like having a pet. A pet that was better than our dog because they could talk back."

"They weren't pets; they were people," Daisy said, sounding so sanctimonious and self-righteous that his fist had connected with her face before he even realized it.

"They were nothing," he hissed. "They threw their lives away. They lived on the street. They were never going to become anything anyway. No one wanted them, and no one cared about them. We gave them a purpose."

"You used them to make money," his sister corrected. She thought she was so much better than the rest of them. What gave her the right to play God with their lives? "They didn't deserve what you did to them."

Thorne kicked her in the ribs, then again in the stomach,

taking comfort in the fact that she curled into the fetal position, clutching her middle. Pain painted her face, but it wasn't enough. She deserved so much more. "They deserved whatever we decided they deserved. They were nothing. Just like *you* are nothing. You think you're so perfect. You turned on your *family*—your own flesh and blood. How could you do that?"

"I had to do the right thing."

"Who were you to decide what that was?"

"It wasn't me deciding it was wrong; it just was. You can't take someone against their will, and rape them—"

She broke off as he delivered another swift kick to her stomach. How dare she accuse him and her family of being rapists. "We never raped those girls," he spat out.

"You artificially inseminated them without their permission. That's sexual assault," she wheezed.

"Didn't you care about what happened to our family?" he demanded. All these years later and Thorne still couldn't comprehend how his sister could tell the police what their parents were doing knowing that the authorities wouldn't understand and their family would be punished.

"I never really thought about it. I just did what had to be done."

"They died because of you. You sent the cops to our house. You may as well have shot Mom and Dad yourself. Don't you feel guilty?"

"Yes," came the soft reply, so quiet he almost didn't hear her.

"You blame yourself?" he asked, confused. Did Daisy regret what she'd done? If she did, would that change things?

Growing up, he'd idolized his father, wanted to be just like him when he grew up. He'd been jealous when Ridge had turned thirteen and their father had introduced him to the family business. That jealousy had grown on Forrest's thirteenth birthday when he, too, became initiated into the family. He had dreaded his sister's birthday. He didn't want her to come and steal more of their father's time.

Then, in an instant, his world had changed.

If he had known what Daisy was planning on doing, he would have killed her. Thorne didn't have one single iota of doubt about that. He had made his first kill at the age of seven. It was the day he knew who he really was. It had taken him several tries to snap the girl's neck. Her cries of pain hadn't repulsed him; they hadn't sickened him. Instead, they had made him feel alive. After that, it became his job to kill the girls when they were no longer useful, and by ten he had been quite proficient at it.

But he hadn't known, and she had told. Daisy's teacher should have told her to keep her stupid mouth shut. He shouldn't have believed her. He shouldn't have brought the cops in.

His family would never submit, never give up, never let some cop tell them what they could and couldn't do in their own home.

His family had fought with honor and died with honor. All except his cousin.

Liam was a traitor.

He was weak and pathetic. He hadn't deserved to be the oldest, the one who would inherit the business.

And he hadn't.

His stupid cousin had been a coward. He hadn't stayed to fight with the family against the intruders. Instead, he'd grabbed one of their girls, freed her, and then run.

He was a pathetic excuse for a man.

Thorne had stepped up. With his family gone, he had always known that one day he would rebuild their empire. As soon as he turned eighteen, he moved out on his own and kidnapped his first woman. He had grown his business carefully, just like his father had taught him. Never keep too many girls at once. Always carefully dispose of the bodies. Never get emotionally attached. Never get too close to the girls. They were a tool—nothing more.

He had only ever faltered once.

One girl had gotten to him in a way no one else could.

She had called to his soul. She was like him; he could tell just by looking at her. He had become obsessed with her. She had scarred his body and in doing so, his heart, as well. He knew he would never be free of her. He'd had to have her. And he had.

That was an exception.

There would be no others. He kept his cool, remained calm, only losing his temper a handful of times that had left those in his sights a broken and bloody shell of a human being.

And that's what would happen to Daisy.

It didn't matter if she was repentant. It wouldn't change anything. Their parents would still be dead, and she still would have betrayed the family. It was too late for guilt. Too late for sorries.

Now was the time for revenge.

Thorne looked down at his feet and saw that Daisy had crawled across the floor to the other side of the room.

Stupid woman. Where did she think she was going?

He stalked over to her, reached down and grabbed her by the hair, yanking her to her feet. She cried out in agony, her battered body trying to fold in on itself in an attempt to minimize the pain and discomfort.

"Please, Thorne," she begged, tears mixing with the blood on her face and making pink trails down her cheeks. "Just go. Leave us alone. We won't tell anyone you were here. We won't tell anyone that you were the killer. You can just go and live your life, and we can live ours."

As if that was going to happen. Twenty-five years was long enough. He wasn't waiting any longer. He was going to get what he had always wanted.

To kill his sister.

* * * * *

3:02 A.M.

Daisy hoped this worked.

If it didn't, she was going to die.

Facing death this closely terrified her. The thought of her children growing up without her left her feeling like her heart had been ripped out.

She felt like she was breaking inside.

The physical pain that possessed her body was nothing compared to the pain of knowing what Thorne planned to do with her children once he'd killed her. Nothing could destroy her so completely than her brother turning her own children into the very people she had given up everything to stop. Daisy didn't think that he could do it; she didn't think he could turn her children into monsters. Her children were strong, but they were just kids, and he was going to kidnap them. They would have lost their father, their mother would be murdered or in the process of being murdered, and they'd be vulnerable and possibly susceptible to Thorne's brainwashing.

Thorne wanted to kill her. He wanted to make her suffer. She knew she couldn't convince him otherwise, but she had to try. She couldn't just give up. "Please, Thorne. I'm your sister. How can you do this to me and my children?"

"We are *not* family. I'm going to beat you so badly you're going to wish you were dead, and then I'm going to nurse you back to health and do it all over again. I'm going to make you pay for every bit of pain you caused me. I hate you." His words were accompanied by his fist, which connected with the side of her head.

Pain exploded inside her skull. She panted through it, trying to keep her focus. She and Mark needed to work together if they were going to get out of this alive. She had done her part by keeping Thorne's attention on her, allowing her husband to quietly cross the room.

On cue, Mark growled like an animal and then pounced.

He was a split second too slow.

Thorne spun around.

The gun fired.

The room fell silent.

Where was Mark? It was dark, and she had blood all over her face, dripping into her eyes. Along with her tears, it blurred her vision. Had Thorne shot her husband?

"M-Mark?"

He didn't answer.

"I didn't want to do that," Thorne muttered. "He should have done as he was told. Let's go. We should get out of here."

Her brother reached for her, but she shrank away. She had to get to Mark. He could be bleeding to death. She had to help him. Daisy curled her fingers into the carpet and tried to drag herself toward her husband.

She didn't get far.

Thorne stomped a boot down onto her outstretched hand.

The pain was so sudden and so intense on top of the agony that already wracked her body, that she almost passed out.

Daisy didn't need an x-ray to know it was broken.

Hope left her.

Mark was going to die, if he wasn't already dead. Thorne was going to take her and her children, murder her, brainwash them, and, if he couldn't, kill them, too.

Then a thought occurred to her.

Where were the kids?

Thorne had fired two shots; it should have been enough to wake them. Hopefully, they were hiding someplace or had managed to get out of the house, but what if her brother had hurt them?

They needed her.

She couldn't give up.

But what could she do? She was injured, and Thorne had a gun.

There was only one thing she could think of that might work.

It was risky, but she didn't have any other options. She was already teetering on the brink of unconsciousness. If she passed out, she and her children were as good as dead.

Before she could second-guess herself, Daisy gathered all her strength and flung herself at her brother.

Not expecting that, he stumbled as her weight crashed into him, sending them both tumbling to the floor. Pain flared through her body as they landed with a thump, but she had no time to think about it before a barrage of blows rained down on her.

Her world was nothing but agony, but she tried to compartmentalize the pain and keep her mind focused. While Thorne unleashed his rage on her, with her good hand, she felt around for the gun he had dropped.

She came up empty.

Summoning strength she didn't know she had, she moved her injured hand about.

Her fingers brushed against something cold.

The gun.

Daisy had to force her broken hand to curl around the weapon.

She didn't want to do this, but Thorne had given her no choice.

She lifted the weapon and fired.

Her mother had loved shooting, and had taught all of them how to handle a gun and hit your target by the time they started school.

And this time, she hit her target perfectly.

The bullet pierced Thorne's temple, entered his brain, and killed him instantly.

Her brother dropped. His big body landed on top of her, crushing her.

Somehow she managed to get out from underneath him, and shoving aside her own pain, she scrambled to where Mark lay, unmoving.

Her knees got wet as soon as she got close.

Blood.

Mark's blood was pooled around his body.

She was sure he was already dead, and when she felt his pulse fluttering beneath her fingertips, she nearly fainted in relief.

It was still dark in the bedroom, Thorne had never turned on a light, so she couldn't see where Mark was hurt. Instead, she ran her hands over his body, stopping when she felt the slick wetness of blood on his chest.

She needed something to stem the flow of blood; she needed to find her phone to call for help; and she needed to check on her children. Most of all, her battered body was screaming at her to lie down, close her eyes, and rest.

Daisy was just working up the energy to push herself to her feet when arms suddenly wrapped around her.

It was just like in a horror movie when you thought the bad guy was dead, only for him to come back to life one more time.

She thrashed.

She screamed.

The arms tightened around her.

Then she heard the voice.

"Daisy, it's okay. It's Jack. It's Jack."

Had she heard right? At the moment, she didn't really trust herself. She knew she was in bad shape, barely hanging on. "J-Jack?"

"I'm here."

"Thorne shot Mark," she sobbed. "It wasn't Fawkner. He just attacked me in the hotel, but he's not the killer."

"We know. That's why we're here. Belinda shot her attacker. Fawkner didn't have any partially-healed gunshot wounds. As soon as we learned Fawkner wasn't the killer, we came straight here. I'm sorry we didn't arriver sooner."

A moment later, the light flickered on, and she let out a sob when she saw her husband. He looked dead. He was completely still, his face was a horrible pasty gray color, and he was drenched in blood.

She tried to get to him, but Jack swung her up into his arms as Ryan and Xavier ran to Mark.

Jack set her down on the bed, then whispered, "Oh, Dais." From the look on his face, she assumed she looked as bad as she felt.

But right now, she didn't care about herself. All she cared about was her husband.

"Stay put. I mean it," he added. "Ryan and Xavier are taking care of Mark, and an ambulance is coming. You need to let me take care of you right now."

She gave a half nod, her gaze fixed firmly on Mark as though she could will him to keep breathing. Jack returned and cleaned away some of the blood from her face so he could see how badly she was hurt. Then wrapped her injured foot and broken hand.

"Where else are you hurt?" he asked.

"My chest and stomach," she replied, and winced when he eased up the T-shirt she slept in to examine her abdomen. "The kids?"

"They're fine. Paige is with them. It looks like your brother drugged them. They're stable, but they'll be coming to the hospital with you and Mark."

Relief had her falling into a hazy sort of dream state. She continued to stare at Mark as she let Jack tend to her. She tried to avoid looking at Thorne's body. That she had killed her brother hadn't sunk in yet. She was sure it would hit her later, but right now the only thing that consumed her was fear for her husband.

Medics suddenly bundled into the room—a pair went to Mark, a pair came to her. Daisy did her best to answer their questions while trying to listen in to what the EMTs tending to Mark were saying.

When they brought in two stretchers, she flatly refused one. If she let them put her in it, that meant that they were taking her to the hospital in a different ambulance than the one that would transport her husband. She couldn't do that. She had to stay with Mark. He was hurt because of her. It was *her* brother that had broken into their room tonight. And he was trying to save *her* when he'd been shot. She wasn't leaving his side under any circumstances.

A wheelchair was produced instead, and she allowed Jack and a medic to help her into it and take her to the ambulance. The entire ride to the hospital she watched Mark's face. She needed to see it to convince herself he was still alive. Daisy refused any treatment that might hamper her ability to stay close to her husband. It felt like if she left him, she might lose him. As long as they were together, she still had him.

At the emergency room, she again fought off any attempts at treatment. Her compulsion to stay close to Mark was all-consuming, and the doctors and nurses seemed to sense that and didn't press her to let them check her out.

Mark was rushed through the ER and up to surgery.

It wasn't until she was sitting in the surgical waiting room with Jack and Ryan, and their wives Laura and Sofia, and Mark's parents, that it all hit her.

Thorne, the little brother she'd thought she was protecting when she went to the cops and turned in her family was perhaps the evilest of them all. He had killed so many people. He had threatened her family; he had drugged her children, and he had shot her husband.

The tears came in a flood.

Doctors and nurses came at her, wanting to drug her into calming down.

Her family came to her wanting to soothe her fears.

Daisy shrank away from all of them.

She didn't want their false comfort right now.

None of them could give her what she wanted. They couldn't

guarantee that her husband would live.

Her pain was increasing; she wouldn't be able to hold it back much longer.

It was Jack's hands on her knees as he crouched in front of her chair. "You need to go and let the doctors look you over. You're hurt, and when Mark wakes up and sees you looking like this, it's going to freak him out."

"When?" she repeated feebly. Did Jack really believe that Mark would make it through this, or was he just trying to placate her?

Jack nodded. "*When*. He's going to be mad at me if I haven't looked out for you. So I asked one of his friends to come and examine you here. Is that a fair deal?"

She wanted to say no. She wanted to say that she deserved to be in pain until she knew that Mark would be okay because this was all her fault. She wanted to protest for reasons her exhausted brain couldn't even fathom right now, but in the end, she didn't have enough energy to argue.

When she nodded her assent, a woman she recognized but couldn't for the life of her recall her name, approached. The woman stitched a gash on her left cheekbone, another along her jaw on her right side, and another on her right temple. A cast was put on her broken hand. The bullet wound in her foot wasn't bad. Whether intentional or not, Thorne had shot the edge of her foot leaving a nasty gash but no other damage. Without x-rays, the doctor couldn't discount broken ribs, but after examining her, it was determined they were likely only cracked.

Patched up, she huddled in her chair and waited.

The longest wait of her life.

Daisy didn't know how many hours had passed when a surgeon finally entered the room and asked for Mark Xander's family.

This man had the power to destroy her world with a single word.

She stood. She owed her husband that, and with Jack's help,

hobbled over to hear the news.

Would it be good or bad?

"Is he dead?" she asked, her voice sounding nothing like her.

"No."

The surgeon said more, but she didn't hear it. Her body and mind finally hit a brick wall and she fainted.

* * * * *

8:57 A.M.

She was so cold.

That's all Heather thought about now. Not the gnawing knot of hunger in her belly, not the dull aching throbbing in her head, not the ache between her legs.

Cold.

It seemed to come alive as she lay on the concrete floor of her cage. It lived, it breathed, it crawled its way inside her and claimed her. It lived inside her, growing while she shrank and slowly faded away.

Her body shivered, every movement sending little spikes of pain running through her skin.

She couldn't take much more of this.

Heather had always known that she would die in here. She'd thought she was ready, but she wasn't. She didn't want to die. She wanted to be free. She wanted to track down her stolen children. She wanted to go to school, and then college, and get a job and her own house, and have a life like everyone else.

Yes, what had happened to her was unfair, but she didn't want to dwell on what she'd been through, she just wanted to move on.

But moving on wasn't in her future.

Death was her future.

And with how she felt right now, her future was quickly bearing down on her.

It had been days since she'd last seen anyone.

They'd had a huge argument. The Scar Man, whose name she'd learned was Thorne, the woman, and the younger guy who had tricked her and brought her here. They'd disagreed on something. She wasn't sure about what, but she'd heard them screaming at each other all the way from down here.

Then the younger guy had come down. He'd opened the door to her cage, and Heather had been convinced he was about to murder her. Instead, he had ordered her to strip, then made her lie on her mattress, positioned himself between her legs and raped her so roughly, he'd left her bleeding and so sore she couldn't stand up.

She didn't understand why he'd done it. He'd never sexually touched her before, other than the night he had kidnapped her. The Scar Man—Thorne—didn't like for him to touch any of the girls here. What had changed?

After raping her, he'd taken Colette and left.

Now she was alone down here. There was no one to bring her food or water. There was no one to talk to. There was no one to offer comfort—even if it was false comfort.

He had left her here to die.

For whatever reason, he no longer wanted her.

That shouldn't hurt, but for some reason, it did. For the last three years, this was all she'd known. This cage, these people, this was her life, as pathetic as it was, and to be left behind like some unwanted piece of garbage cut at her heart.

There was something wrong with her.

There had to be.

Maybe she'd developed that thing where captive victims fall for their captors.

Whatever. She had little strength left to worry about it. Little strength to do much of anything but lie here and wait for dehydration or hypothermia to claim her.

Heather was just drifting off to sleep, or possibly to

unconsciousness when she heard a sound.

Footsteps.

Someone was here.

Had they come back for her?

Part of her hoped they had and part of her feared they had.

The door to the basement opened. Heather tried to lift her head to see who was there, but she didn't have the strength. Instead, she turned it so her face was in the direction of the stairs.

She saw shoes.

And then a moment later, people.

Strangers.

It wasn't the Scar Man ... it wasn't the younger guy ... it wasn't the woman. It was strangers. A tall man with brown hair, and a lady with a head of brown curls surveyed the room, guns drawn.

Guns.

Cops?

Had someone found her?

Heather could tell the moment their gaze fell on her because the woman put her gun away and hurried over. "Xavier, there's someone in here. Honey, can you hear me?"

"Yes," she croaked.

The woman fiddled with the door. "It's locked. Honey, my name is Paige. Do you know if there are any keys here?"

"I think he took them with him." Talking had suddenly become very difficult. She felt drained and empty. Was she dying? She couldn't die now. Not when she'd just been found. She should be rejoicing, she should be jumping up and down with relief and happiness. Instead, it was all she could do to keep her eyes open.

"Thorne?" Paige asked.

"Who? Oh, the Scar Man. No, I think it was the other guy."

"Other guy? Do you know who he is?"

"No. I don't know his name. I only just learned Thorne's."

"Xavier, we need something to cut through the metal bars,"

Paige told the man, who had joined her at the cage's door. "And we need blankets and water. Honey, can you tell me your name?"

"It's Heather. Heather Blight. Did you come for me? Did my mom send you?"

"We came because of Thorne."

"Oh," was all she could say to that. Had her mother given up on her? Decided she was long since dead and stopped looking? Or maybe she'd never cared enough to look in the first place.

Sensing her distress, Paige pulled out a phone. "Hold on, honey, let me look." She fiddled with her phone for a moment and then turned it around so she could see it. "Your mom was looking for you. She filed a missing person's report when you first disappeared three years ago."

It felt like a weight had been lifted off her chest.

Her mom cared.

Tears began to trickle down her cheeks. "What about my babies? They took them and sold them."

"How many?" Paige asked gently.

"Three."

"How long ago?"

"My little boy isn't even two weeks old. Please, can you get him back?"

"I can't promise you that I can," Paige answered truthfully. "But I can promise I'll do everything in my power to find him."

Footsteps sounded on the steps again, and her head flew in that direction. Were Thorne and the other guy back? Were they going to kill her and Paige?

But it wasn't Thorne, and it wasn't his partner.

It was the man Paige had called Xavier and a couple of firefighters. Xavier handed Paige blankets and a bottle of water, and the woman moved around to the back side of the cage.

"Can you move over here, Heather? The firefighters are going to cut through the metal bars, and we'll have you out of there as soon as we can."

Heather wasn't sure how, but somehow she managed to drag herself over to where Paige was kneeling. The woman handed her the blankets, and she wrapped them over her shivering body. They were so soft, so warm. She'd had nothing but scratchy woolen blankets since she'd been brought here, but these were like being wrapped up in heaven.

"Try to drink a little water." Paige handed her a bottle.

She took a tiny sip, but her stomach protested. After so long without food or water, it couldn't handle anything. She forced herself to take another sip and then another, and then she set the bottle down.

"Xavier's calling your mom. We'll have her meet us at the hospital," Paige told her with a smile.

A shiver of nervous anticipation settled in her already queasy stomach. She wanted to see her mom, and yet, so much time had passed, and so much had happened.

"We'll take things as slow as you need to." Paige reached through between the metal bars and took her hand, squeezing it lightly. "If you need more time before you see her, that's fine."

She nodded, not sure what her decision would be yet. "Did you find Colette?"

"Colette?"

"She was here with me, in that cage." She pointed to the one next to hers. "They brought her here a couple of weeks ago, but the man took her with him when he left."

"Thorne?"

"No, the other one, the younger one."

"There's no one else here, honey. Do you know her last name?"

"White. Colette White."

"Let me see if she's been reported missing." Paige withdrew her hand, and Heather shivered at the loss of human contact that she had missed so much these last three years. A moment later, Paige put her phone away again. "I'm sorry, Heather, I don't see any missing persons reports for a Colette White."

Pain stabbed at her heart. Her mom had been looking for her, but no one cared that Colette had disappeared. "No one was looking for her?"

"It doesn't look like it," Paige answered softly.

That was awful. No one deserved to be so unloved and uncared about that they could be snatched away and imprisoned and no one even noticed.

"We'll look for her," Paige promised, reclaiming her grip on Heather's hand. "Just rest now. You're safe, it's over, you're going home."

Home.

The word sounded surreal, and she feared that this all may be just some elaborate hallucination.

Could she really be this lucky?

Could this really all be over?

Could she really be saved?

Could she really be reunited with her family and go home?

As hard as it was to believe, it seemed like it was really true. The firefighters cut through the metal bars of her cage. Paige came around to hover beside her. Paramedics came bustling in, treating her with kid gloves as they examined her and carefully lifted her onto a stretcher.

This was it.

She was about to leave the cage that had been her prison for three long years.

She was about to face the outside world that she hadn't even seen since she was brought here.

She was about to see people—lots of people—after so long with no one but the other captive girls and her captors for company.

Overwhelmed, Heather reached for Paige's hand. "Will you stay with me?"

"Of course, I will." Paige smiled, and some of her fear melted away.

Home.

She was going home.

* * * * *

4:40 P.M.

It had been a wild goose chase kind of day.

After going to Thorne's house, expecting to find it empty but hopefully with some evidence that might lead them to some of the black-market babies, he and Paige had been shocked to find one of the girls barely alive in the basement.

Xavier had been concerned that she might not last until they got her help, but as Paige talked to her, the girl seemed to grow stronger as she realized that she was safe and soon to be free. Paige had accompanied Heather to the hospital while he had remained behind to search the house, finding nothing of value. Thorne had obviously had the presence of mind to clear it out before he went to deal with Daisy. That meant that he had intended to move somewhere else, no doubt wherever this mystery man had taken Colette White.

With nothing to learn at the house, he'd gone to the hospital to check on Mark, who was stable and settled in ICU, and Daisy, who looked like a walking zombie as she sat at Mark's bedside refusing to leave him. Then he'd collected Paige, and leaving a sleeping Heather with her mother, they'd gone to Thorne's workplace.

Daisy's brother worked at an IVF clinic. It was probably the perfect place to find vulnerable couples who were willing to pay big money for a black-market baby.

They'd managed to find a receptionist who was scared enough about being charged with being an accessory in the false imprisonment, sexual assault, and murder of those girls, and the selling of the babies, to give them the name of a lawyer.

The lawyer had been less willing to talk.

Until his wife found out what he'd been doing.

There was nothing more terrifying than an angry wife, and the man had given them everything he had, starting with the names of the people who had taken Heather Blight's baby boy.

Now he and Paige had pulled up outside the house of Walter and Becky Gruber.

"Is it wrong I feel a little bad for them?" Paige asked quietly.

Given her history, Xavier thought it made perfect sense. Paige had been beaten almost to death and her resulting injuries required her to undergo a hysterectomy. It had taken her several years before she was at a place where she was ready to adopt, and he was so glad she had. She was a fantastic mother and he loved her girls as if they were his own.

"I know what it's like to want a child so badly and not be able to have one."

He reached over and took her hands. "But you didn't do anything wrong. You got your children the right way. The Grubers could have adopted. They could have fostered, even. They could have done things the right way; no one forced them to buy a baby."

"They must have been so desperate to resort to the black market."

"I'm sure they were. But that doesn't mean they get to buy a baby. You were desperate, and you never even considered doing something like this. They made their choices, and now they have to live with the consequences."

Paige looked up at him, her large brown eyes watery. "I know you're right, but I still ..." She trailed off.

"You still empathize with their situation. There's nothing wrong with that," he assured her. "As far as we know, they weren't aware of what Thorne was doing. They didn't know that the mothers were prisoners."

"Let's go get this over with. Taking the baby back to Heather is going to be a lot better than ripping it away from these people who already love it like their own."

Paige got out of the car, and he followed. Xavier understood loving a child before you even got to meet them. He already loved his and Annabelle's twins, and it was still three months before they would enter the world. He loved to curl up on the couch with Annabelle in his lap, his hand resting on her stomach feeling his children kick their tiny feet inside her. He couldn't wait to be able to hold them in his arms, to kiss their tiny little heads, to have their tiny fingers curl around his own. He couldn't imagine what Heather had felt when her baby had been ripped from her arms. Paige was right. Bringing him back to her was going to be much better than taking the infant from the Grubers.

The house was huge. According to the lawyer, the Grubers had paid Thorne Allen over half a million dollars for Heather's baby. He couldn't comprehend having that much money to throw around to get what you wanted. Why hadn't the couple taken in one of the thousands of children in the foster care system?

As they waited for one of the Grubers to answer the door, Paige fiddled with the locket she always wore around her neck that he knew contained a picture of her husband on one side and her girls on the other.

When the door finally opened, Mr. Gruber took one look at them and his face drained of color.

He knew what they were there to do.

Xavier wondered if the couple had lived in constant fear of the cops turning up on their doorstep to take away their baby.

"Mr. Gruber, I'm Detective Montague; this is Detective Hood. We're here for Heather Blight's son."

The man's eyes darted from him and Paige to the six cops behind them. They hadn't known how the Grubers would react or if they'd do anything reckless, so they'd come prepared for the worst.

"He's our son," Mr. Gruber said, trying to sound firm and confident, but instead sounding petrified.

"He's not. We know you bought him; we spoke to the lawyer who drew up the papers. The baby belongs to a seventeen-year-old girl who was abducted and impregnated against her will."

"She's so young, and if she was raped, how can she love him?" a voice spoke from inside the house, as Mrs. Gruber came up behind her husband, the baby cradled in her arms.

"That's not up to you or me to decide that for her," he reprimanded the woman. "We have a court order for temporary custody of the child to be turned over to Heather Blight. Once a DNA test is done to confirm maternity, she'll be given permanent custody of her child."

"His name is Harrison," Mrs. Gruber said, holding the crying baby closer.

Mr. Gruber gave them another look, then the officers behind them, before finally turning his gaze to his wife and the baby. "Give him to them," he said, defeated.

"No!" Mrs. Gruber screamed. "He's ours."

"He wants his mother."

"I *am* his mother," the woman protested.

"He knows you're not. He hasn't stopped crying since he got here. It's like he knew he didn't belong with us," Mr. Gruber said sadly.

"How can you say that?" his wife demanded.

"Because there's no way they're walking away without him. Don't make this harder than it already is." Mr. Gruber went to his wife and gently pulled the baby from her arms, handing him to Paige.

"No!" the woman shrieked, running after Paige as she headed for the car. "Give him back; he's mine! I'm his mother, he needs me. No, come back. No!" she wailed.

Mr. Gruber grabbed hold of her and held her as she struggled to get free. Leaving the officers to place the couple under arrest,

Xavier followed Paige to the car, blocking out Mrs. Gruber's wails.

"Can you hold him while I make sure the car seat is in properly?" Paige asked, already holding the crying infant out to him.

Xavier took him, and immediately the baby calmed. His little red face relaxed and he blinked open his eyes. He stared down at the baby. Soon it would be his own child he was cradling in his arms.

"You're a natural." Paige grinned at him. "He likes you."

"The poor little thing has already gone through so much in his short little life."

"He'll be back with his mother soon, and Heather's mother will make sure that she gets the help she needs so she can be a good mother to her son," Paige assured him. "Want to sit in the back with him, keep him calm?"

"Sure." He put the baby in its car seat, then went around the other side to get in the back.

"I always used to play this for Arianna when she was teething and crying her little heart out," Paige said starting some music as they headed for the hospital. It seemed to help. Within minutes, the baby had fallen asleep.

It was only a ten-minute drive to the hospital, and the farther they got from the Grubers' pain, the closer they got to Heather's joy. She was going to be so pleased when they gave her back her baby. She deserved some happiness after everything she'd been through.

When Paige had parked the car, he scooped up the baby, and they headed for Heather's room. Xavier thought the girl might be asleep. She'd certainly looked like she needed rest when she'd been brought here earlier today. But when they entered her room, she was wide awake and staring out the window like she couldn't get enough of looking at the outdoors. After three years locked in a cage in a basement, Xavier couldn't blame her.

Heather turned instantaneously as she heard the door open. Her eyes grew wide and filled with tears when she saw what was in his arms. "Is that him?"

"It is." He carried the child to her and laid him in her outstretched arms. Remembering her, the baby immediately nuzzled into her, seeking her breast for a feed.

"How can I ever thank you?" Heather's mother cried. "You saved my baby and her baby."

"You don't need to thank us," he told the woman. He was just grateful things had worked out for Heather when they hadn't for all of Thorne's other victims. They still had to identify the partner who had taken Colette White and fled, and try to find out how many other girls had been victims of the pair so they could give their families closure.

"Thank you." Heather smiled at them through her tears. "You kept your promise and gave me my son back. Thank you."

One happy ending out of all the pain the Allen and Hayden families had caused was better than nothing.

* * * * *

11:13 P.M.

Daisy hadn't moved from Mark's bedside since she'd regained consciousness in a bed in the emergency room shortly after she'd fainted. It had taken a bit of convincing to be allowed to come here and not be confined to some bed by a doctor who meant well but didn't understand that the only thing that could help her right now was being able to see her husband. If she was kept away from him, she feared she'd lose her mind.

She was already hanging pretty precariously by a thread.

One little push and she would lose it.

While she'd been out of it, someone had removed her clothes, which had been stained with her blood, Mark's blood, and her brother's blood. They had also wiped away most of the blood from her skin.

Now she felt cleaner on the outside, but no cleaner on the inside.

Inside, she felt so dark and dirty with guilt.

Her husband and her children had almost been killed because of her.

Brian, Eve, Elise, and Tony had been sedated by Thorne. He'd injected them while they slept, and they hadn't known what had happened until they had awakened in the hospital. Before she'd come up to Mark's room, she'd spent a bit of time with them, calming them down, explaining what her brother had done and reassuring them that their father would be okay.

Only she wasn't sure she believed that.

She *wanted* to.

Desperately.

But she was so afraid that all the lies she'd told, and all the secrets that she'd kept had ended up costing her her husband.

"Daisy, why don't you go home, get some rest," Jack said for what had to be the hundredth time.

Her brother-in-law had outright refused to leave her side, and he had made one of the nurses come and check on her every hour on the hour. Daisy appreciated that he was looking out for her, and she knew that she was lucky to have family who cared about her so much, but she just wanted to be alone right now.

"I don't need to rest," she said. "I slept for a couple of hours earlier."

"You didn't *sleep*, you *passed out*," Jack corrected. "I'll stay with Mark. I'll call you the second he wakes up. You need rest. You have more injuries than I can count. You should be in a hospital bed yourself, but since you refused, you should at least get some sleep."

She didn't care about her injuries. She was doped up on painkillers, so the pain wasn't so bad. She just felt empty.

Completely empty. Like there was nothing left. She was so tired. She'd never felt this exhausted in her life.

But no matter how tired she was, she wasn't leaving her husband.

She was going to sit right here until Mark woke up.

Because he *would* wake up.

He had to.

He couldn't leave her.

More tears streamed down her cheeks. She'd cried so many the last six months, she was surprised she had any left inside her. She might have been embarrassed to cry in front of Jack, but it was Jack, and she'd known him most of her life. He was like the big brother she wished her own big brothers had been.

"I can't leave, Jack," she said quietly, hoping he understood. She physically couldn't leave this room. If she did, she would completely break down, and Daisy was very afraid that if that happened, she would never be able to rebuild herself.

There were too many thoughts in her head. Too much fear, too much guilt, too many worries and anxieties and doubts. The only thing keeping them at bay was feeling Mark's warm hand in hers, watching his chest rise and fall with each breath he took, listening to the reassuring beep of the machines that insisted he was still alive.

"Why don't you close your eyes here, then? That way you can get some rest, and you'll still be here when Mark wakes up."

Daisy shook her head. Her eyes wouldn't close. She'd tried, but every time she forced her lids down, they just popped back up like they were on springs.

She didn't want to sleep.

She wanted Mark to wake up.

She needed so desperately to hear his voice.

It had been hours now since he'd been out of surgery. Long enough for him to have woken up. Was there a problem? Maybe there was a reason that Mark wasn't waking up. What if something was wrong and no one wanted to tell her because they were too concerned about her?

Her pulse began to skyrocket. Everyone could be lying to her. Mark could be dying. Or maybe the damage the bullet had caused was so severe he was going to spend whatever time he had left in a coma.

"What's wrong?" Jack noticed her growing panic and materialized at her side.

She tried to tell him, to beg him to be honest with her, but her throat had closed up.

He snatched up her wrist and checked her pulse. "I knew this was a bad idea. You can't handle this right now. I'm getting a doctor."

No.

She tried to say the word aloud but thought she only said it inside her own head.

If Jack got a doctor, she would be admitted and sedated, and she wouldn't be allowed back here.

She stood to grab Jack's arm and beg him for a little more time, but she didn't get very far.

"Daisy."

Both she and Jack froze.

"Daisy."

They both turned toward the bed. Her husband's eyes were open, and he was looking straight at her.

Relief had her knees buckling, and if Jack hadn't wrapped an arm around her waist, she would have collapsed.

"Daisy," Mark said again, only this time more panicked and he tried to move.

Her tears were back with a vengeance, but they couldn't outweigh her concern for her husband. "Mark, I'm all right," she assured him, gently pushing away Jack's supporting arm and stumbling toward the bed.

His eyes roved her body, taking in the cast on her arm, the

stitched cuts on her face, the bruises and her swollen eye, and the way she hunched over protecting her cracked ribs. Daisy knew she looked the opposite of all right, but she really was, knowing that Mark was awake and okay made everything else fade away.

Tentatively, she reached out a hand and touched his pale cheek. "Are-are you okay?" She wanted to believe this was real but she was afraid to.

He smiled at her. It was a weak smile, and he was clearly in pain, but it was a smile, nonetheless, and it did wonders to ease her nerves. "Yes," he croaked, "but you're not."

"A little battered, but I'll be all right. Jack made sure someone checked me out."

Relief washed over Mark's features, and he shot his brother a grateful smile.

"I'll go get a doctor," Jack said, leaving the room.

"Are you sure you're okay?" she asked once they were alone.

"A little battered, but I'll be all right." He repeated what she'd said, a small grin on his face.

Daisy tried to laugh, but it came out as a sob. They had both come so close to dying, and seeing her big, strong husband, lying in a hospital bed, made reality hit hard.

"Hey." Mark lifted a hand and brushed the back of his knuckles across her cheek, catching her rapidly falling tears. "Don't cry."

"I almost lost you. I'm sorry, Mark, I'm so sorry. Thorne shot you because you were trying to save me. I'm so sorry," she wept. The logical part of her mind told her she shouldn't be sobbing and blubbering and burdening Mark with this when he'd just woken up, but she couldn't seem to stop.

Mark's fingertips brushed gently around the neat rows of stitches marring her face. "I let him hurt you," he murmured, distressed.

"To try and stop him from hurting me more," she reminded him.

"He's dead?"

"Yes. I shot him."

Mark relaxed. "It's over now, we'll heal." Then his eyes fluttered closed as he passed out.

Daisy sank into a chair. He made it sound so simple.

In time, their physical injuries would heal, but what about their psychological ones? Could those ever heal? Could their children heal? What scars would they all be left with? Would their family recover?

Or was Mark right, and they would all heal?

JANUARY 31ST

12:22 A.M.

"Okay, this time it's not up for debate. This time you are going to let Ryan drive you home, and you are going to climb into bed and close your eyes and go to sleep."

Daisy blinked and looked up at Jack who was standing over the chair she'd been sitting slumped in ever since Mark had drifted back off to sleep. A doctor had come in and examined him, assuring her several times that her husband was doing well and should be fit to go home in a couple of days. The doctor had then checked her out, told her what she already knew—that her body needed sleep—and offered her more painkillers and some sleeping pills. She accepted the painkillers, and thankfully, after the doctor had left, Jack had left her alone to her thoughts for a while.

She'd been pondering what Mark had said. She thought he might be right. Maybe in time, they would all heal, maybe even come out of it stronger than they had been before.

At least, she thought he might be right, but her brain was so tired that thinking was a little bit of a struggle right now. She knew she couldn't go on like this indefinitely. Sooner or later, she was going to have to sleep.

"Dais." Jack sounded exasperated. "You're dead on your feet. Mark is going to be out for hours, and I'll stay with him. Please, go home and get some rest."

She could argue. Beg and plead to stay here with Mark, but ultimately, Jack was right. Her husband would sleep for hours, and she needed to rest. Defeated, she nodded. "Yeah, okay."

"Okay?" Jack looked surprised. He'd obviously expected her to put up more of a fight. But she was done fighting. She wanted Mark to recover as quickly as he could, and if she was such a mess that he was worrying about her, then that would hamper his recovery.

Daisy shrugged. "I don't have any fight left in me."

Jack smiled down at her and placed a comforting hand on her shoulder. "Things will look better in the morning when you've had a good night's sleep."

Maybe he was right. It certainly didn't seem like they could be any worse.

She pushed to her feet, swaying a little from exhaustion and was glad for Jack's steadying hand on her elbow. She stepped closer to the bed, and leaned over to kiss Mark on the forehead. Her fingers lingered on his face, unwilling to leave in case something happened and he wasn't here when she returned.

"He'll be fine," Jack said softly, his hands falling onto her shoulders, kneading gently.

"I know, it's just …" She trailed off.

"Hard to leave," he finished for her. "I know it is. But you're doing the right thing. You need to take care of yourself, let your body and your mind heal. It's only for a few hours, and then you'll be back here with him."

Daisy allowed him to guide her to the door, and then out through it and into the hall. If Jack hadn't still had hold of her, she doubted she could have made it out the door.

Ryan was sitting on the floor, his head resting back against the wall, and he jumped to his feet when he saw them. "Everything okay?"

"Fine," Jack assured him. "Can you take Daisy home so she can get some rest?"

"Sure." Ryan gave her a comforting smile and pulled her into a hug. She leaned wearily against him, letting him hold her up. She was ready for sleep.

Her brother-in-law kept an arm around her as he led her through the hospital and out to his car. They didn't speak on the short journey to her house, and she was thankful for the quiet time to pull herself together. Walking back into the home that Thorne had violated by breaking in and drugging the kids, then trying to kill her and Mark, wasn't going to be easy. She wished she didn't have to do it alone. She wished that Mark was here to do it with her. It would have made it so much easier.

But wishes were just that.

Wishes.

Mark wasn't here, and she was strong enough to do this herself.

"Want me to come in with you?" Ryan asked when he pulled up into her driveway.

"Thanks, but I'll be fine. I'm just going to go straight to bed."

"All right. I'll come by in the morning to pick you up and take you back to the hospital." Ryan kissed her cheek.

As she climbed out of the car, her aching body began to protest. It wasn't happy with her pushing it so far, and the beating her brother had given her was brutal. Not an inch of her body had been spared from his vicious assault.

She did her best not to hobble because she knew Ryan would be watching until she was safely inside the house. If he knew how much pain she was in and how badly she was feeling, he was likely to bundle her back into the car and take her straight back to the hospital.

Somehow she made it to the door, and after giving Ryan a wave, she stepped inside.

Her house was quiet.

Too quiet.

With four kids, there was always something going on, and she wasn't used to this level of silence. It felt heavy, almost crushing.

Bed was starting to look really appealing. Lying down on the soft mattress, her head on her feather pillows, her thick quilt covering her. Although her and Mark's bedroom was forever tainted by Thorne's actions, right now all she cared about was sleep.

She was so glad that her family had organized for someone to come in and clean up the bloody mess in her bedroom as soon as CSU had finished up in there. She really didn't think she could have faced doing it herself.

Daisy hadn't even made it to the stairs when a shadowy figure appeared in front of her.

She froze.

Closed her good eye and rubbed it.

Her mind must be playing tricks on her.

There couldn't be anyone inside her house. Who would it be? The kids were with Mark's parents at their house. Jack was at the hospital. Ryan was heading back there. Laura and Sofia were home with their kids. No doubt Paige and Xavier were home with their families too. There wasn't anyone who should be standing in her kitchen at one in the morning.

She opened her eyes, expecting to see the room empty.

It wasn't.

"At last, we meet." The figure took a step toward her, flicking on a light.

The figure was a woman. A few years younger than herself maybe, with shoulder-length red hair and amber eyes that were so bright they practically glowed.

"Who are you?" Daisy tried to keep her voice calm but failed miserably.

"Desiree, Thorne's wife."

She didn't need to ask to know what the woman was doing here.

"You killed him." The woman's face aimed pure hatred at her. It was clear why she was here. Revenge, plain and simple. Desiree wanted to kill her because she had killed Thorne.

"You knew what he was doing," she accused. Maybe it wasn't

the smartest thing to do to antagonize the woman, but she couldn't understand how a woman could do this to other women.

As angry as Daisy was with her father for what he had done, it was her mother's behavior that sickened her the most. Her mother who had sat with her on nights when she was sick or had bad dreams and stroked her hair and sang to her. It was her mother who listened to her problems when she was worried or scared or upset, and who helped her find a way to fix them. It was her mom who hugged her good morning each day and kissed her each night before bed. Her mother's betrayal was what hurt the most.

"I was one of them," Desiree admitted.

"One of them?" she repeated, confused.

"I was one of Thorne's first girls. I ran away from hell and straight into your brother's arms. He kept me in a cage in the basement. He wanted to use me, but I recognized something in him. Something that called out to the broken part of me. We were the same. We'd both lost a lot. We'd both been betrayed by people who were supposed to love us, who we were supposed to be able to count on. One day I pretended to have passed out. When he came into my cage, I pounced, cut him from here," Desiree touched her right collarbone. "Down to here." She touched low on her abdomen.

"Did you run?" Daisy asked. Had Thorne managed to catch her, brainwash her somehow?

Desiree looked shocked. "No. I tended to his wounds. I showed him my scars. I told him I understood. I told him I loved him. After that, we were together."

This woman had developed some sort of Stockholm Syndrome type love for Thorne. Nothing else made sense. She'd been abducted. She knew what Thorne had intended to do to her, and yet, she hadn't run when she had the chance. Instead, she'd stayed and helped him do it.

"How involved were you?" she asked.

"I helped screen the adoptive parents. I performed the insemination procedures on the girls. I cleaned their bodies once they'd been terminated so that if they were ever found no one could trace it back to us."

The look on Desiree's face was demented. The woman had lost her mind somewhere along the way. Possibly long before she even wound up in Thorne's basement. She wanted love so badly she would even take it from a monster, then become his perfect puppet.

"I'm not like my husband." Desiree began to advance on her. "He wanted you to suffer. He wanted to kill you slowly, drag out every bit of revenge he could. I don't care about making you hurt. I just want you dead."

Daisy slowly backed away, but between her injured foot and beaten and broken body, she stumbled and tripped.

Then Desiree was on her.

A rope was wrapped around her neck.

Tightening slowly.

Cutting off her air supply.

She clawed at it, trying desperately to pull it far enough away from her neck that she could draw a breath. But she couldn't. It was too tight, the fibers already cutting into her skin.

She couldn't believe she had survived everything else just to die anyway.

Frantically, she tried to claw at Desiree, her movements already growing sluggish.

White spots began to dance about in front of her eyes, and her pulse thumped loudly in her ears.

Her arms dropped limply down at her sides.

Daisy closed her eyes. She didn't want to see Desiree's face as the woman took her life.

Blackness began to trickle into her mind.

Growing quickly.

Claiming her.

When it consumed her, it would take it with her back to where it had come from.

The world had mostly faded when she heard a loud bang, followed by the loosening of the rope around her neck, then wetness flooded over her, and she was crushed by something heavy.

"Mom."

Someone called out to her. Brian, maybe?

Then the pressure on her body was gone, and someone was grabbing hold of her, lifting her torso off the floor.

"Mom, I'm sorry. I'm so sorry I was so mean to you. I was just scared. I thought my cancer had come back and then you left. And I was so angry. The doctor said I was fine, but I blamed you. I'm sorry. I'm sorry, Mom."

She only half heard what Brian was babbling as she struggled to suck in air.

"Daisy."

The house suddenly filled with the cops who had been surrounding it.

They'd suspected that Thorne's wife might come back here looking for her. Although her brother had never mentioned being married, when Xavier and Paige had gone to the IVF clinic where he worked, they'd found out he was. So they'd asked Daisy to play bait, try to draw out Desiree, so they could catch her before she disappeared and started up the black-market baby business someplace else.

They had wanted Thorne's wife alive so they could get information from her. Find out who Thorne's partner was. Find out where Colette White had been taken. Find out where the bodies were buried so the girls' families could get closure. Find as many of the black-market babies as they could. But despite all of that, Daisy was glad Desiree was dead.

"Brian? What are you doing here?" Xavier asked as he knelt beside them. Obviously, she'd been wrong. He hadn't gone home to his wife, he'd stayed here to help watch her house.

"I came back to spend the night. I had to. I don't know why. I was upstairs when I heard something. I grabbed Dad's gun, and when I saw someone attacking Mom, I shot her. I didn't know you were all here," Brian rambled.

"All right, it's okay," Xavier soothed, as he gently pried her from her son's arms so he could see how badly she was hurt. "Daisy, can you hear me?"

She wanted to answer.

She really did, but she was still struggling just to remain conscious and suck in enough air to remain living.

It didn't matter anymore. She was safe, and this time it was really over.

She could let go and fell into the blackness.

* * * * *

9:34 A.M.

It was a bright and beautiful new day.

Wade Jeebes was feeling on top of the world. Thorne Allen was dead, and the business was all his. He still had Colette White, who could already be pregnant with the very first baby of what would soon become an empire. And with his boss out of the way, he was free to run things his way.

He had packed his family up, and they were on the road. Traveling where he wasn't sure yet. Somewhere a safe distance from the cops who no doubt knew that Thorne had a partner. He'd left behind Heather Blight. It was too risky to be traveling with two kidnap victims, and since she'd already had three babies, she seemed like the better option to leave behind. Since the cops would have Heather, they would know about Colette, so he wanted to be someplace far away where no one would ever find them.

Growing up in the abusive home his mother had fled from had made him cold and hard. Taking any emotions he may have once possessed and squashing them down until they were nothing. He didn't have time to feel. He was sick of being poor and living in poverty, and he relished the idea of one day being a millionaire, free to do and buy whatever pleased him.

It was that desire to become rich that had helped him survive his childhood. The knowledge that one day he could fly away and never have to return to that despicable place.

Now, he had flown.

The world was his for the taking.

He would find a city where he could settle down. He would buy a funeral parlor so he could acquire free and easily accessible sperm. He would make sure his wife got another job at an adoption agency so they would have access to couples who were never given a baby. He would buy a house with a huge basement that he could fill with tiny cages to keep his girls. He would find another lawyer that could be blackmailed into making the adoptions look legal. And then he could begin.

There was nowhere to go from here but up.

Unlike Thorne, he wasn't interested in revenge. Daisy had made the choices she'd made to do what she thought was best. He held no grudge. He felt nothing for the woman at all.

He felt nothing for anyone.

Even his wife and daughter served a purpose. He had physical needs that must be attended to and a wife who took care of that. She cooked and cleaned, and once they had their business up and running, she would learn to perform the artificial insemination procedure. His daughter would also work in the family business once she was old enough. She would bring him in as many girls as he could possibly house, and then once she was too old to believably play a runaway teenager, he would find another role for her to serve. Maybe even the same one the girls she had helped to bring him served.

One day, he would be rich. Richer than he could imagine. Tracking down Thorne Allen to see if he had continued on his family's trade had been the best decision he ever made. In time, the tiny twinge of guilt that pricked at him every time he'd lured a young girl into a trap had faded. Thoughts of his mother, young and scared, always came to mind, and he often wondered how people could walk past a clearly homeless kid on the street and do nothing. It was the only time he ever felt something even resembling an emotion.

Now it was time to throw off that guilt.

His mother had made her choices, just as all the other girls had. And he had made his. Money, enough to buy himself peace and happiness. That was his only goal, and he would achieve it by any means necessary.

"Come along, Holly," he called to his wife. "It's time to get moving. Get the baby in the car."

Leaving his wife to collect their daughter, he rolled the last suitcase out of the motel room and over to the car. Hoisting it into the back of the SUV, he paused and unzipped it a little.

Colette White's dirty, tear-streaked face peeped out at him. The bruise on her face had darkened, and she was no doubt still very sore between her legs. Now that Thorne was gone, he no longer had to abide by the never touch the merchandise rule. He'd made use of Heather before leaving her behind, and now he could get his fill of Colette whenever he wanted. Wade had quite enjoyed the spark of jealousy in his wife's dark eyes as he pounded into his new toy until the girl had been sobbing through her gag.

"Ready for another day of traveling?" He smirked at Colette.

She whimpered through her gag. At night, he had to bring her into the motel room with them. He couldn't risk her making a noise and being discovered. During the day, he packed her into a suitcase, unconcerned with how uncomfortable and pain-inducing the cramped conditions must be for her.

He stroked her hair and smiled when she tried to recoil from his touch. "You're anxious to stop again for the night?" he mocked, sliding a hand down to roughly squeeze her breast. "So am I." Colette whimpered again and he laughed. "I am never letting you go. No more four babies and then a quick death. You will be mine until you die or you can no longer get pregnant."

With a last vicious tug on her nipple, he zipped the suitcase closed. His family was already sitting in the car, ready and waiting to obey his every command.

Power and money; they were a heady combination.

He had the power, and soon he'd have the money.

Life was good.

* * * * *

1:28 P.M.

The first thought to cross Mark's mind when he woke up was his wife. She hadn't looked like she was in very good shape when he'd woken up earlier. Her face was a mess of bruises. One eye had been swollen closed. He'd counted three new stitched cuts. Her arm had been in a cast, and he knew she'd been shot in the foot, although since she'd been standing, he guessed the wound wasn't serious.

He had to see her.

His eyes snapped open and he sat up. "Daisy?"

"She's okay," a voice answered. His oldest brother's voice, not his wife's.

Mark didn't believe that. If she was okay, she'd be here. "What happened?"

"Don't freak out." Jack stepped closer to the bed.

Of course, the only reaction when someone said that to you *was* to panic. "What. Happened?"

His brother sighed. Clearly, he didn't want to answer, and for a moment, Mark thought he wouldn't, but then Jack spoke. "We found out Thorne had a wife. We thought there was a possibility that she might come after Daisy, and if we could get her, we might be able to get answers, find some of the babies, and the missing girl Thorne's partner still had."

He stared at his brother in shock—unable to comprehend what he'd just said. "You used my wife—my traumatized and injured wife—as bait?"

"Not bait," Jack corrected. "We didn't know for sure that Desiree Allen would go after her. We were watching the house just in case. She agreed, Mark. We didn't do anything behind her back. We asked her about it, and she agreed because she was tired of living in fear."

He was fuming. If he hadn't just been shot and had surgery, he probably would have hit his brother. "She was in no condition to agree to anything like that, and you know it. You manipulated her. You used her—"

"They didn't," Daisy croaked.

His head whipped sideways, and he saw her sitting up in the bed beside his. Angry red marks circled her neck. They hadn't been there before. Daisy hadn't just played bait, she'd been hurt.

Now Mark saw red. "How bad?" he demanded.

"How bad what?" Jack asked.

"How badly was she hurt?"

"I'm okay." Daisy winced as she spoke.

It was clear she wasn't okay. "How … badly … was … she … hurt?" he repeated, over-enunciating each word.

"Desiree wrapped a rope around her neck. She was barely breathing by the time Xavier got to her," Jack replied.

"I wanted to do it," Daisy said. "I couldn't live like that anymore. I'm sorry."

Her apology put a little dent in his anger. He didn't want her to apologize, and he didn't like the worry in her eyes like she was afraid he'd be angry with her. Mark knew what she was thinking, that he was going to walk away from her because she wasn't good enough for him. Although he hated knowing those thoughts ran through her mind, he was going to have to accept that it would take time for them to fade.

"I'll give you two some time alone," Jack announced. "Fifteen minutes, then I'll be back. You both need rest." He left before either of them could argue.

"How are you feeling?" Daisy asked tentatively.

"I don't know; I'm too angry," he muttered.

"I'm sorry," Daisy said immediately.

Mark sighed and ran his hands through his hair, ignoring the sting as it pulled on the IV in the back of his hand. His chest was starting to ache, and a headache pounded at his temples. "Don't be sorry. I'm not angry with you, just my brothers."

"Jack was being misleading. They didn't want me to do it; I insisted. I didn't want to think that Desiree could come back at some point. And I didn't want her to run and keep doing this. And I'm really okay," she rambled even though each word she forced through her raw throat no doubt caused her pain.

"Is she dead? Thorne's wife?"

"Yes. Brian killed her."

"Brian?" What had his son been doing there?

"I didn't know he was there," Daisy said quickly. "If I had, I wouldn't have gone back there. I wouldn't have risked Desiree hurting anyone."

"Anyone but you," he said softly.

Daisy fell silent. Her head rested back against the pillows. She looked so worn out. Not just physically, but mentally. The toll of the last six months was showing. If he could have, he would've gone to her, but he didn't think he was strong enough to make it out of bed.

"Can you stand up?" he asked.

She turned her head and looked at him, nodding.

"Come here."

Daisy threw back her covers, and staggered to her feet. For a moment she teetered unsteadily, but somehow she managed to keep her balance and make it to his bed. Carefully, he moved the wires and tubes attached to his body out of the way and helped her lie down beside him.

She nestled her head against his shoulder, then froze. "Am I hurting you?"

"No." At least, not enough that he was going to tell her to move. He wanted to hold her right now. He reached up a hand and gently brushed his fingers across her throat. "How badly does it hurt? And don't even think about lying to me," he warned.

"Quite a lot," she replied reluctantly. "If Brian hadn't come in when he did ..." She trailed off.

Daisy didn't have to finish her sentence. If Brian hadn't turned up when he did, he would have lost her. Mark shuddered and felt her do the same in his arms. "If you knew they were watching the house, why didn't you call for help?"

"It all happened so fast."

Running his fingers through her hair, he pressed his lips to her temple. "How are you doing? With everything?" Mark was tired, and his eyes longed to close, but he wanted to take advantage of every second he had with his wife before his brother returned.

"I don't know." She rested her broken hand on his stomach. "I feel odd. Lost. Thorne was the only family I had left, and then I learned the truth about him, and now he's dead. I have so many unanswered question and no one to give me those answers. Thorne could have told me when our parents started selling babies, and why they did it—he could have told me how many girls they kidnapped and killed, how many babies they sold. He could have told me all the things about our family that I never knew."

"Would knowing those things help?" he asked, continuing to smooth her hair He didn't think that having answers would make this any easier for Daisy to deal with.

"I don't know." She snuggled closer. "I'm glad you finally

know the truth about my family. I hated hiding it. I was just scared, maybe unwarrantedly, but that's how I felt."

"I don't want you to ever be afraid again. I love you, Daisy. Nothing is ever going to change that. We have four beautiful children together. We're going to watch them grow up, and we're going to grow old together. We all have some healing to do after everything that's happened, but we're all together, we're all strong, and we can help each other heal. Our family will be okay. *We* will be okay."

"I love you, Mark," she whispered, and he felt her relax against him as she drifted off to sleep.

"I love you, too, Daisy," he said, letting the feeling of his wife's weight at his side lull him off to sleep, too.

* * * * *

11:54 P.M.

He surveyed the park.

Surely, there would be someone wandering around here at this time of night.

He was excited. This was the first time he'd ever done this. His parents had said he wasn't quite old enough yet, that he wasn't quite ready. But he knew that he was.

Blaze Allen was ready to join the family business.

More so than ever now that his parents were both dead.

It didn't seem real yet.

His father had gone to get his aunt Daisy and his cousins, to bring them to the house. Only, he'd never come back.

Mother had told him to go with Wade and Holly and their baby, saying she would catch up to them later.

But she hadn't.

And then Wade had sat him down and told him that his mom and dad had been killed. Wade had also said that if he intended to continue to live with them, then he had to earn his keep. He had to prove that he could be of service.

So here he was, in the park at midnight, looking for a girl.

As upset as he was about his parents, it couldn't diminish the excitement inside him. He was thirteen now. He'd been begging for the last two years to be allowed to go on an abduction run.

His eyes fell on movement up ahead.

Blaze looked closer. It was a girl. She was standing under a streetlight by a park bench. She looked only a couple of years older than himself.

This was it.

He took a deep breath and walked toward her.

She noticed him as soon as it was clear he was heading in her direction. He could see her eyes darting nervously all about as she twisted her hands together.

Blaze stopped a few steps away. He fiddled with the straps on his backpack, then pulled his patched coat tighter around himself. Finally, he lifted his gaze to meet the girl's and gave her a shy smile. "Hey."

The girl smiled shyly back at him, obviously having deemed him not a threat. "Hey."

She was beautiful. Long chestnut locks that tumbled over her shoulders, large gray eyes that shone with intelligence and warmth. She was perfect. Everything he could have dreamed of.

He'd never kissed a girl before. He was homeschooled, and the only kids he ever came into contact with were the girls in the basement, and he wasn't even allowed to talk to them. He was rarely even allowed to go down there. Blaze wondered what it would be like to feel this beautiful girl's lips on his. What would she taste like? Would he like it? Would she? Would she let him touch her other places, like her breasts?

How much time would he have alone with her before Wade arrived? Hopefully enough to at least kiss a little.

"You cold?" he asked. He knew it was a stupid question, but it was hard to concentrate and think clearly when the pretty girl was looking at him.

She nodded.

"I know a place." He looked down at his shoes. "If you want."

She paused for a moment, looked around, obviously weighing up her options, but then she nodded again. "Thank you. I don't know what I would have done tonight if you hadn't been here."

He tried not to laugh aloud at that. She was thanking him, but really, she should be running from him.

This was too easy.

"It's just on the other side of the park," he told her, turning and walking in that direction, confident she would follow him.

She did.

He was going to enjoy doing this.

Wade thought that the business was his, but he was wrong. Wade wasn't family. One day, *he* would take his rightful place as the head of the Allen family and empire.

Jane has loved reading and writing since she can remember. She writes dark and disturbing crime/mystery/suspense with some romance thrown in because, well, who doesn't love romance?! She has several series including the complete Detective Parker Bell series, the Count to Ten series, the Christmas Romantic Suspense series, and the Flashes of Fate series of novelettes.

When she's not writing Jane loves to read, bake, go to the beach, ski, horse ride, and watch Disney movies. She has a black belt in Taekwondo, a 200+ collection of teddy bears, and her favorite color is pink. She has the world's two most sweet and pretty Dalmatians, Ivory and Pearl. Oh, and she also enjoys spending time with family and friends!

For more information please visit any of the following –

Amazon – http://www.amazon.com/author/janeblythe
BookBub – https://www.bookbub.com/authors/jane-blythe
Email – mailto:janeblytheauthor@gmail.com
Facebook – http://www.facebook.com/janeblytheauthor
Goodreads – http://www.goodreads.com/author/show/6574160.Jane_Blythe
Instagram – http://www.instagram.com/jane_blythe_author
Reader Group – http://www.facebook.com/groups/janeskillersweethearts
Twitter – http://www.twitter.com/jblytheauthor
Website – http://www.janeblythe.com.au

sic enim dilexit Deus mundum ut Filium suum unigenitum daret ut omnis qui credit in eum habeat vitam aeternam